Betrayed

by a Scot

A

Conor McDermott

Novel

Published by Anthony J. Harrison

Copyright© 2018 Anthony J. Harrison

License Note

ISBN: 978-1-7324081-1-1 (printed version)
ISBN: 978-0-4633624-6-4 (ebook version)

Cover design by:
Robert Gray of Channel Islands Design
http://www.channelislandsdesign.com

Editing performed by:
David Keefe, Reedsy.com

This book is dedicated to:

Those individuals who find the courage to stand up and face the injustices that plaque others, even if it means being subjected to the same injustice for their actions.

TABLE OF CONTENTS

Prologue

Two men stood in the evening shadows of the harbor facing each other; one with his gloved hand holding onto the handle of a knife, the other with the knife's blade buried completely in his thorax.

Death came rapidly to Calvin Baxter. The former customs official could feel his final breath slowly leaving his body. He stared hopelessly into the eyes of his killer. Little did he know, this was no ordinary thug dressed as a dockworker. This was Angus Dunbar, former British SAS (Special Air Services) sergeant and current hired assassin.

Dunbar had shoved the knife upward under the sternum. He could feel the dual-sided blade push past bone and cartilage, making its way through Baxter's lung and into the smaller chamber of his heart.

As he looked into Baxter's eyes, Dunbar saw the awful familiar expression of fright and confusion he'd seen repeatedly in the faces of his past victims. It was invariably the same: the look of why me? etched on their faces. Dunbar's reply, however, was unique for each casualty and corresponding offense.

"What you need to understand, Baxter," Dunbar murmured, his Scottish accent thick and guttural, "is that Mr. Higgins doesn't suffer fools gladly, and greedy attendants never." As he removed the blade, he twisted the knife's handle to prevent the wound from closing. He then set the body against a nearby heap of wooden pallets. The echoes of the harbor masked the commotion of his actions while the shadows from the fuel tanks protected the scene of the crime from the view of any passersby.

Stepping aside, Dunbar looked himself over under the glimmer of the lights bordering the harbor, making sure no blood had spilled over onto his disguise. Dunbar noticed the crimson spot in the center of Baxter's chest grow slowly larger with each passing second.

"All you had to do was keep silent," he scolded. "But no, you had to pipe up to the constable about needing more money. You're an idiot." However, as much as he despised Baxter, this was business, not personal. Killing Baxter carried a message to others associated with Dunbar's employer. There was still work to be done.

He reached into the satchel he had with him and took out several balloons filled with hashish. After placing the drugs into the inside pocket of Baxter's coat, Dunbar now began to clean his knife with a rag. It had been his father's combat knife, and he always cleaned it immediately after finishing a job. After putting it away, he crumpled up the bloodstained rag, discarded his gloves, tore off the worker's overalls, and jammed everything into the satchel at his feet. At the water's edge, Dunbar lowered the evidence into the dark water below.

As he watched it sink, he calculated that this had been the fifth time in two years he had been required to dispose of a risk to the Irishman. Payback for extended silence regarding a deed Dunbar had committed four years beforehand in Wales.

As twilight was descending on the harbor, Dunbar trekked up the road away from the waterfront, stopping beneath a flickering streetlight. He reached into his coat and got out his cell phone. Dialing a private number in Belfast, he was soon conversing with Mr. Higgins.

"Good evening, Angus," the Irishman said.

"Aye, it's a lovely evening," Dunbar replied.

"I presume you've accomplished your first task on this contract. Am I correct?"

"Aye, sir, you'll nae have to worry 'bout Mister Baxter. He won't be creating any further requests."

"I'm sure I don't need to warn you how serious it is holding to our plans, do I, Angus?" Higgins asked.

The Irishman Higgins, whose true name was Michael Connolly, had struggled for a year putting his plan into motion. Duping Nazim Aziz, the French-Algerian drug trafficker, out of twenty thousand kilos of hashish was just the first part. Bringing it through the Scottish port of Aberdeen was a risk he was willing to take to keep his affair covert.

Higgins's idea was as simple as it was ingenious. Utilizing his position as Chief Operating Officer of an up-and-coming pharmaceutical corporation, he planned to produce his own brand of PCP-laced hashish and dispense the drug amongst the Scots. Once taken effect, the market would inevitably cry out for a reciprocal drug to abate the buyers from their addiction. He would thus produce and provide the anecdote, at twice the price.

"No, sir," the Scotsman replied. "I'm fully aware of the repercussions, if you're found out." Dunbar knew other members of the executives' security team could eliminate a less-than-cordial representative of his clientele as he had just completed. I'm not the only one he can call on, I'm sure, he thought.

The two had met in Wales—Dunbar being with the SAS, and the Irishman a member of the French Foreign Legion—and he learned that no Legionnaire ever fought alone.

"Will you have any complications with the others on your register?" Mister Higgins asked, watching the flames flicker behind the glass doors of his fireplace.

"I'll nae have an issue with them," Dunbar replied. "I'll just be inventive with future tasks; that's all." Moving his palm across the handle of the combat knife, he felt confident and assured he could defend himself. Picking up a few measures from eliminating enemies of the Crown while with the SAS, he'd revisit his profession for the Irishman.

"I look forward to our next discussion," Higgins said. "Good night, Angus."

After ending the call, Higgins took up his glass of whisky and observed the sparks from the fire through the amber liquid. For a moment, he recalled the trials of his great-grandfather during the rebellion against the British in the early 1900s. Soon, he thought, the family will have its rightful place in Ireland's history.

Before putting his cell phone away, Dunbar scrolled through the notes application. Here he saw the names of people Mister Higgins wanted silenced. He closed his phone and turned to continue on his path when he was caught by surprise by the appearance of a prostitute as she stumbled out the entrance of a nearby pub.

"What's a nice lass like you doing here?" he asked, catching her before she tumbled into the road.

The woman, her hair a snarled disarray of chocolate-brown curls, looked at Dunbar and beamed. "I'm sticking around for a bloke like you to come along," she said, tugging at the sides of her skirt. "It's still early enough to share a drink, isn't it?"

Looking the woman over, it was apparent to him she was one who struggled hard to appear younger than her actual age. Under the glow of the streetlight, he could see the dark make-up and glittery aqua-blue eyeshadow adorning her eyes. Her crimson lipstick was smeared at one edge of her mouth, most likely from a failed attempt to entice a patron in the pub. Her garb included a floral summer frock, dipping at the front to display a black lace bra, which from all appearances was several sizes too small for her breasts.

He removed a few bills from his pocket and handed them to her. "Go see yourself to a proper supper and a ride home." he said. He then turned and strolled up the road towards the bus stand.

Peering at the money, the prostitute giggled and shoved one bill into her bra while holding the others in her fist. Twirling unsteadily on her heels, she made her way back towards the pub door and the free drink the stranger had just paid for.

After Dunbar cut across the thoroughfare toward the city bus stand, he looked back at the harbor and the lights of the vessels sparkling across the waters. He smiled to himself. Aye, it truly is a lovely evening, he thought.

His next appointment would be with the chief of a Glasgow syndicate. After the bus drew to the curb, he climbed aboard and found a spot in the rear. He reached into his coat and removed a weathered moleskin notebook and pencil. He leafed through the pages until he came upon the end, where he noted the date and the name of Calvin Baxter.

Chapter One

Chief Inspector Conor McDermott and Inspector Andrew Fletcher, both of Scotland Yard, sat working at their desks in the crowded office of Police Scotland's Aberdeen building. The two men poured over a year's worth of investigation reports.

McDermott glanced up to see constables constantly coming and going through the office door, scurrying amongst the dozen or more detectives and suspects, passing the odd document amongst them. *Chaos, utter chaos*, he thought. *They've nae clue*. It was apparent to McDermott that the constables of Police Scotland had good intentions but lacked uniformity. He shook his head and returned to the stacks of files in front of him. Each file contained snippets of clues into the burgeoning drug-trafficking activities of the Scottish city set along the shores of the North Sea.

"Did you get the reports on the drugs seized from the *Standard-Apollo* yet?" McDermott asked.

"Yes, over there on the right side of your desk," Fletcher said.

McDermott snatched up the folder and read the results from the hashish they had seized from the support vessel, two weeks ago. *Drugs*, McDermott thought. *They're the scourge of the poor and the working-class folk.* He stopped reading and looked at Fletcher. "These findings are like the ones from Portsmouth, aren't they?"

"I couldn't tell you; I didn't look at the report yet," Fletcher said. "Even if I did, my major was in business, not chemistry; I wouldn't know what I was looking at anyhow."

"Any reason it didn't interest you?" McDermott asked. "I mean, we are here to investigate the drug trafficking, aren't we?" He was flustered at Fletcher's apparent lack of initiative. "We need to be in sync with this investigation, or they'll be calling us back to London."

"Inspector Gordon believes they're similar," Fletcher responded.

"Are you telling me you learned that from your pillow talk with the lass, now?" McDermott asked, glaring at the young inspector.

"No, we discussed her findings and the results over lunch yesterday. It's not like they're a secret. I mean she's part of Police Scotland's forensic labs, isn't she?"

McDermott gulped down the last of his lukewarm tea before responding. "You need to be mindful of others possibly hearing what is being said, not just that young lass you're with. Some poor citizen could hear you, and then we've got a tainted pool of jurors for the trial."

"I don't think a lunchtime conversation between two police officers would be of any interest to anyone," Fletcher said. "And why should we be worried about the trial of the ship's crew at this point?"

Not wanting to engage his partner in a lengthy debate, the chief inspector turned his attention back to the forensics report. He pointed to the numbers listed on the page in front of him. "They still haven't figured out this unknown chemical?" McDermott asked, his shoulders slumping. He remembered it had taken the Navy lab months to figure out which drug had killed Seaman Kyle Smythe of the HMS *Edinburgh* in Malta.

"Since you brought it up, did we ever get confirmation on the origin of the tip-off call?" McDermott asked.

"Nothing has come through yet," Fletcher said. "All we've received from London was the normal transcripts: date, time, and number. Oh, and they confirmed it was a man calling and it was from a cell phone using Sprint-Europe as a provider. Are you still thinking it was a ploy against us?"

"Aye, I do. It was too simple and easy for us. Practically as if someone was leading us by the nose," McDermott said. "But there's something we're missing from the arrests."

"Such as, how drugs get into gas bottles in the first place?"

"Drug runners are nae stupid. They'll figure some new and keen way to move their stuff; using propane bottles is just another means," McDermott said, leaning back in his chair. He tried placing himself on the boat, being responsible for moving almost one hundred kilos of hashish from the ship to his client. "The transcripts, that's it!" he uttered, jumping to his feet.

"What are you talking about?"

"Radio calls," McDermott said. "The ship had to make them to arrange for someone to pick up the drugs. All we need to do is find calls from the ship to shore. We'll need to go over the transcripts from the Maritime office again." He strode out the door.

Dodging a handful of constables outside the briefing room, Chief Inspector McDermott stepped through the security doors leading to the evidence room. After reaching the counter, he paced back and forth looking for the civil constable on duty. His patience waning, he slammed his hand down on the courtesy bell.

The voice of an older woman came from behind a set of bookshelves. "Hold your trousers on, I'm coming!" An elderly matron came around the corner, dragging her feet, carrying several large folders in her arms. She dropped the folders onto the counter with a resounding thud and let out a sigh. "Now, what can I do for you, officer?" she asked, brushing back several stray hairs from her forehead.

"Greetings, ma'am. I'm Chief Inspector Conor McDermott," he said, showing his ID. "I was hoping to look at the transcripts on the Wallace investigation."

"The Wallace case, heh? I'll need to give the super a call before I let you have them. His orders, you know."

"Of course, ma'am," McDermott nodded approvingly, and she reached for the phone.

"Miss Sinclair, this is Constable McLeish in the evidence room. Can I speak with Mister MacCallum, please?"

McDermott looked about the room before settling into one of the chairs. He relaxed for a moment as he listened and waited for the clerk to finish her conversation. After several minutes, she motioned to him as she hung up the phone.

"You'll be needing to sign for them," the clerk said, pushing the custody log in front of McDermott. "Make sure I can read your name and office when you're done." As she shuffled off behind the shelving, McDermott noticed she was wearing light-blue house-slippers.

After several minutes, she returned holding a small file box. "Here they are, Inspector," she said, sliding it across the counter. "I hope you find what you're looking for."

"Thank you, ma'am," McDermott said, taking the box.

He strode back to the detectives' office, placed the box on Fletcher's desk, and pulled the lid off. "Here's a stack for you," he said, handing the young inspector a pile of transcripts before placing a stack onto his own desk.

"What are we looking for?"

"Any calls the sergeant made to the Maritime office or the ship," McDermott said. "I'll wager Sergeant Wallace was involved with moving the drugs off the docks."

"How much are you willing to lose?"

"I'll put up ten pounds," McDermott said, opening the first file.

"You've got a bet," Fletcher replied, opening the first of many transcripts staring him in the face.

***

The two inspectors from Scotland Yard, having lost track of time, were startled when the lights dimmed. McDermott and Fletcher were engrossed in their respective thoughts, each man keen on finding the nugget of evidence linking the constable sergeant to the drug trafficking.

"Anything unusual jump out of your stack?" McDermott asked.

"I've come across two separate calls to the Border Protection Office, a handful of calls from Victoria Station, Queen Street, Belgrave Terrace, and almost all the offices. But none to or from the Maritime office," Fletcher said, rubbing his hand across his eyes.

"You said the sergeant made two calls to the Borders office," McDermott said. "Why does a desk jockey like Wallace need to contact the Borders, I wonder?" He scratched his temple with a pen. "Does the transcript include what was said?"

"No; just the date, time, and number called."

"Set it aside so we can refer back to it," McDermott said. "Keep your eyes open for any calls to the sergeant from the Maritime office; the boat could've called him just as easily." He returned to his own stack.

Another ninety minutes passed as each inspector returned to reading handwritten notes from the constables investigating every drug-related crime in Aberdeen—from the petty use of marijuana by students at the university to the hard-core heroin users found in the city's less desirable locations. Each small morsel of information was selected as if they were trying to piece together a larger mosaic of the drug use and trafficking throughout Aberdeen.

"Anything new?" McDermott asked.

Before Fletcher could respond to the question, the desk phone rang.

"Police Scotland, Inspector Fletcher speaking. What? —Yes, constable. I'll let him know right away." He quickly hung up the receiver.

McDermott looked at the young man from London. "What are you going to let me know?"

"Central Dispatch just received a call from one of the Victoria Station patrols," Fletcher said. "Seems they've come across a corpse."

"And I'm supposed to be concerned about it for what reason?" McDermott snorted. "We're here trying to find drug traffickers associated with our Portsmouth incident, Andrew. We're not dispatched to help the locals with their murder investigations."

"They said it was drug-related, and they identified the victim as a member of the Customs Enforcement Division."

McDermott closed his eyes and took in a deep breath. *It's never a good thing when an officer is killed*, he reminded himself. After conveying a silent prayer, he looked up at his younger partner. "Go run this back to evidence," he said, tossing the transcripts back into the box.

McDermott sat recalling the death of Kyle, the seaman from his time as a lieutenant in the Royal Navy. As it turned out, he was the younger brother of his best friend, Malcolm Smythe. Like most young men, Kyle succumbed to the temptations associated with being in a foreign country. While in Malta, he allowed himself to be duped by several locals into trying hashish, which had been laced with LSD. Soon afterward, he was found dead in an alley near the docks. McDermott never forgave himself, though Malcolm and the rest of the family did, as it was Kyle's choice.

He looked up just as his partner returned from the evidence room.

"Did you know Miss McLeish was wearing slippers?" Fletcher asked.

"Aye, I did," McDermott said. He ran his hands through his hair and let out a sigh. "Come on, then, grab your coat. We'll go see if we can point these folks in the right direction."

Fletcher slid the drug report results into the top drawer of his desk and locked it. He grabbed his sport coat from the chair and put it on as he followed his senior partner down the hall.

Shortly after leaving the office, Chief Inspector McDermott and Inspector Fletcher arrived at the docks. McDermott could make out several constables trying to keep the odd citizens, dockworkers, and seamen from crowding the crime scene as well as the police vehicles. Spectators gathered behind yellow police tape, their heads bobbing back and forth straining to catch a glimpse of the police officers' actions.

McDermott and Fletcher walked past the police tape, showing their identification to the constable before entering the crime scene. As they made their way to the senior police officer, McDermott wondered why he and his partner even needed to be present. "Sergeant, what's the fuss about?"

"Oh, Chief Inspector McDermott," Sergeant Giles said pleasantly, once he found out who was speaking. "I'm glad you came. Seems we've come across another druggie from your trafficking party." He pointed toward the forensics team moving about the body.

An uncontrollable shiver coursed through Fletcher's body as he got a glimpsed of the corpse. "Who found him?" Fletcher asked his notepad at the ready. McDermott turned toward the young man, a less than pleasant look on his face at hearing this question.

"That'll be Mister Willetts," Giles said, pointing to a nearby older gentleman. Willetts stood grasping his woolen flat cap in one hand while the other held a smoldering cigarette in the other that shook. "He's a local driver," the sergeant continued, reading from his notebook. "According to the constables doing their initial questioning, he had stepped behind the pallets to relieve himself when he found the victim."

"He's your concern, not ours," McDermott said, stepping towards the body. As he passed in front of the driver, he noticed the small wet spot on the crotch of his pants. "Did he ever finish peeing?"

"I'm not sure, why?"

McDermott peered over at the driver and noticed him shuffling his feet as he stood next to one of the constables. "If you don't want a mess in your van, I'd let him go finish."

They left the sergeant and soon found Chief Inspector McIntyre and his forensics team busy gathering bits of evidence at the murder scene. The victim's body, ashen and contorted, lay against a pile of broken shipping pallets. A trail of blood had seeped from a single chest wound visible on the gray sweatshirt, one of several signs of trauma on the body.

14

"Get as many angles as possible," CI McIntyre told his photographer while wearing a surgical mask and gloves, holding up the plastic yellow drape.

"What have you got, Graham?" McDermott asked as he sauntered up to him. The forensics officer was bending over the victim.

"Ah, Chief Inspector McDermott, good afternoon to you too," McIntyre replied. He stood up as he said this, rising to his full six-foot, four-inch height. "I heard the constables were soliciting your expertise on this case." His easy smile and pleasant temperament belied the seriousness with which he took his work. "Well, I'm afraid to say, this was once Mister Calvin Baxter, just thirty-five years old, and the recipient of a sharp-edged instrument," pointing out the bloody entry wound.

"I was led to believe it was drug related," McDermott said, "but so far, no one's handed me anything. I'd hate to think Fletcher and I were called out just to prop up the police presence in the vicinity."

As he pulled the mask from his face, McIntyre turned to one of his team members. "Gavin, can you show the good inspector what the constables removed from the victim?" The technician handed the transparent evidence bag to McDermott for his inspection.

Holding it up at eye level, McDermott spied the contents—two rubber balloons, their contents held behind crude and simple knots. "They appear to be ones any drug user would have in his or her possession," he said. "But it doesn't explain why Inspector Fletcher and I need to be called out." He handed the bag back to the technician. "Was there any other drug paraphernalia found?"

"Nothing more than what the constables handed over, I'm afraid," the forensics chief said. "McDermott, you need to know Superintendent MacCallum was adamant having you and Fletcher involved in any drug-related issues, especially here on the waterfront."

"I'll have a talk with the chief, then," McDermott said. "I'm nae fond of being someone's flavor of the month." He turned his attention back to the corpse. Same ash-gray complexion as most victims of violent crimes like this, he thought. "Inspector Fletcher," he said, prompting his partner, "what would be your next step?"

Looking about the scene, Inspector Fletcher spied several CCTV cameras mounted on the buildings near the docks. "I'd try to find out if any of the cameras are working," he said, pointing them out. "With any luck, we might come across an image or two of the assault taking place."

McDermott smirked. "Good thinking," he replied. "Go on, then, see what you can come up with."

Feeling dismissed but determined, Fletcher slipped his notebook into his jacket pocket and made his way to the closest building.

"Being a little harsh on the young man, aren't you?" McIntyre asked McDermott.

"He needs to think and act on his own," McDermott said. "If I can get him to start doing that without my permission, he'll be on his way to being a fine inspector." Shifting his back to the setting sun, McDermott looked at the forensics chief. "I read your department's report from the batch of hashish we seized off the Standard-Apollo; you've still not identified the one unknown chemical?"

"No, our diagnostic machine isn't calibrated to analyze abstract combinations," McIntyre said, pulling his gloves off. "We're waiting for results to come back from the university lab and the main forensics office in Gartcosh. I'm optimistic though. Between the three, we'll have something more substantial to put our finger on regarding the drug type."

"How soon can you analyze these balloons?" He pointed his thumb at the technician behind him. "I mean, if Mister MacCallum expects me to investigate crimes involving drugs, I need to know it's linked to my case," There was a sarcastic undertone in McDermott's words.

"As soon as we're done, I'll get Inspector Gordon on it right away," McIntyre said.

Hearing her name mentioned reminded McDermott of something. "Speaking of Inspector Gordon, do you have a problem between her and Fletcher? It appears they're getting cozy."

"Why do you ask?"

"Fletcher mentioned they were discussing your toxicology report over lunch the other day," McDermott said. "Does nae sound like something to be mentioned in public, does it?"

"They're young, and they have a common ground, being police officers. However, since you look concerned, I'll have a talk with Sheila. I'll remind her to be more careful when and where she talks about work," McIntyre said. "Will that do for you?"

16

"Aye, for now," McDermott said, taking one more look at the yellow fabric covering the body before walking away and towards the edge of the dock. He inhaled deeply and felt a slight bite of the salt air in his nostrils as the ocean breeze stung his breath. As he examined the surface of the water along the edge of the dock, he spied a strap caught on a rusted bolt protruding from a piling.

"Sergeant Giles!" he shouted. "Do we have a boat in the water?"

"I can call one over from the Maritime office, why?"

"I'd like to know what is on the end of that strap," McDermott said, pointing below his feet. "I would encourage you to get your constables to canvas the area again. We don't want to overlook any potential evidence." He could see that his rebuke provided the desired effect of making the sergeant cringe.

The sensation of someone watching him caused the hair on McDermott's neck to stand on end. *If I did nae know better*, McDermott told himself, *I'd say there's a witness looking on.* He scanned the various boats tied to the docks, glancing at the windows of each one's bridge deck, noticing one with an occupant staring back at him.

"And who might you be?" he muttered to himself.

McDermott wandered along the dock until he stood alongside the service boat. Several seamen were discussing the results of a soccer match when they saw McDermott standing there. "Can we help you?" one of them asked.

"Aye, is your captain on board?" McDermott asked, pulling out his identification.

"He is. Give us a minute and we'll get him."

A trickle of sweat ran down the side of McDermott's brow as he stood under the summer sun. What breeze there was coming off the water did little to cool him under his field coat. The squeal of metal on metal sounded as a hatch swung open, announcing the arrival of the officer, and came to a stop with a resounding thud against the superstructure.

The ship's master ducked as he passed through the opening, a smoldering pipe clenched between his teeth. A robust mountain of a man, his graying hair visible from under a Greek-fisherman-style hat, he walked to the edge of the deck towards McDermott. "You wanted to see me?" he asked, removing the pipe from his mouth.

As McDermott watched the ship's master walk towards him, he got the sense he was a tough but fair taskmaster. He noted this by the way the two crew members working on the deck gathered behind him. Smoke curled upward from the briar pipe as the captain returned it to his lips.

The scent of the burning tobacco reminded McDermott of the incense burned during his father's funeral, only sweeter, more aromatic. "Aye, I did. I'm sure you've seen the circus come to your dock today," he said, waving his hand at the scene over his shoulder. "I was wondering if you happened to see anything out of the ordinary."

The captain leveled his gaze at the inspector, his eyes not wavering from their target. "And who are you to be asking the questions?"

McDermott flipped open the billfold containing his identification. "Chief Inspector McDermott, with Scotland Yard. And you are . . .?" he said, all the while keeping a watchful eye on the two seamen as they stood behind their captain.

"Captain Duncan, of the Nordic Supplier," the officer responded.

"Well then, Captain," the inspector said, "did you happen to see any unusual activity on the docks last night or earlier this morning?"

"The *Nordic* was finishing up a scheduled replenishment assignment. We've only been tied up, oh, maybe two—no—three hours," the captain said. "I just completed a three-rig run to the Erskine fields."

"I see," McDermott said, biting the inside of his lip.

"So, to answer your question, Inspector: no, I didn't see anything on the docks relating to your police activity," Captain Duncan said, taking a drag on his pipe, the lit embers hissing as air passed through the burning tobacco.

"Well, if you, or a member of your crew, happen to hear anyone mention something, give Sergeant Giles a call at the district office, will you?" McDermott said. The captain nodded.

McDermott turned away and began sauntering along the edge of the dock, when he saw Sergeant Giles pointing to something and shouting at the boat crew in the water.

McDermott watched from the edge of the dock as constables used a boat hook to pass a black knapsack onto the dock. Water

18

seeped from the canvas bag, pooling around the sergeant's feet as he leaned over to examine their find.

"Sergeant Giles, don't touch it," CI McIntyre shouted as he made his way to the edge of the dock. "How many times do I have to tell you patrolmen to keep gloves in your kit to handle evidence?" He immediately pulled out a fresh pair of gloves and put them on.

McDermott stood and chuckled to himself, realizing he had been guilty of the same thing just eight months ago during an investigation in Southampton. His eagerness had almost set a drug dealer free when the lawyer defending the case learned of McDermott's mistake, citing the evidence had been planted by the inspector.

"Inspector McDermott, we're in luck," Inspector Fletcher said as he joined his partner at the water's edge. "There are two businesses that have security cameras functioning, which should offer us with something to work on."

"Let Sergeant Giles know that it'll be his job to secure the warrants from the sheriff's office," McDermott said. "When CI McIntyre and his forensic team provide us with their analysis of the drugs they found, then we'll get involved."

McDermott kept a watchful eye on McIntyre as he witnessed him remove a bloody seawater-soaked rag and a used pair of surgical gloves from the bag. "Is it possible the killer dropped something as he left the scene of his dastardly deed?" McDermott muttered as he stood over the forensics chief.

"It would appear so," McIntyre said. "We should be able to pull some blood from the rag to see if it matches the blood of our victim." He slid the cloth into an evidence bag. "No distinguishing marks or logos on the satchel, and the gloves are available at any chemist office."

"Seems quite careless for the killer to leave evidence behind, doesn't it?" Fletcher asked. "You don't think it came from one of the boats?"

Chief Inspector McDermott looked around, examining the harbor, and could see a myriad of possibilities based on his partner's question, but attempting to do so would be foolish. "We'll know when the other detectives have finished their investigation," he said.

McDermott tapped Inspector Fletcher on the shoulder and motioned the young man to follow him. "Before we get back to our own investigation," he said, tossing the keys behind him as they strolled toward their parked car, "you can treat me to a fish supper."

Chapter Two

A gentle knocking came from the door as Michael Connelly's executive secretary stepped into his ornate office to deliver him the day's mail. Turning in his chair, he smiled at the young woman as he took the handful of envelopes from her. "Good morning, Erin. You're not by any chance giving me a pile of notices we can't pay, are you?" he said with a chuckle.

"I wouldn't know it if I were, Mister Higgins," she said, using his preferred alias.

"Has Mister Callahan returned from Vienna?" Connelly asked.

"According to his schedule, he'll be coming in from Dublin on the 10:45 train."

"Did he happen to send anything ahead from the conference? I was wondering if we'll still be in business?" he asked with a chuckle. Operations for the second most significant pharmaceutical in Ireland were his responsibility, and it was running with great efficiency. His elder partner's presence at the medical conference in Austria was more of a show than a need to drum up more business. *Once my plan gets moving*, he thought, *we'll be set for the next twenty years*. Turning his attention to the pile of mail on the desk, he looked up at Erin one last time.

"Make sure my driver Geoff is at the station in time; I don't want Mister Callaghan waiting more than a few minutes," Michael said. "Is there anything pending on my schedule?"

"If I recall, you've got a teleconference at eight o'clock with Mister Gilmore," Erin said.

Michael Connelly twisted in his chair to look at the timepiece sitting on his credenza, noting he had thirty minutes before his planned call with the lawyer. "Make sure there's a fresh pot of coffee made beforehand; I suspect I'll be in need of it after the call." He then dismissed his secretary.

Connelly opened most of the letters and read through them, digesting their contents—notices of payment, confirmation of delivery orders, and several solicitations for collaborations in the drug field. One particular envelope caught his attention; its postal stamp showed its origin to be Durbin, South Africa.

The address had been done in French handwriting, but its contents were easy to identify. It showed confirmation of shipment for five hundred units of 'product' from Johannesburg to Dublin. The items being shipped were Belgian-style FN SCAR 7.62 assault rifles Connelly had negotiated for from the former mercenary turned arms dealer, Kurt VanHoorst. His perusal of the letter was interrupted by the buzz of his intercom. "Yes, Erin, what is it?" he asked.

"Your call with Mister Gilmore is pending, and I'll be in with your coffee in a few moments," she said.

"Thank you, Erin."

He slid the letter into a folder and placed it inside his desk. He then picked up the phone and pressed the flashing button marked CALL WAITING.

"Good morning, Mister Gilmore," Connelly said. "Sorry for the delay. How are things in Aberdeen?" At this moment, Erin entered with a pot of coffee along with the accompanying condiments.

"Everything is fine, sir. It turns out—"

"Just a moment, Sean," Connelly said as Erin began serving his coffee. After she left, closing the door behind her, he turned his attention back to Gilmore. "Sorry about that; please continue."

"As I was saying, it turns out the young man Mister Hunt used as the liaison with the French will be released in the coming days," Gilmore said. "And I've secured our litigator for the trial with Sergeant Wallace."

"I needn't remind you, Sean, there can't be any connection between myself and the constable, you understand?" Connelly had been given information regarding the former officer, which he determined could expose how he secured his sample of hashish from the French earlier in the year.

"I understand," Gilmore said. "I've discussed the details with Miss El-Sayed, and she's aware her task is to keep all parties out of the crosshairs."

"And what do we know of Captain Duncan and his crew? Are we confident there will be no issues with him?"

"I've yet to meet the gentleman, but I'll be doing so in the next day or two."

"I may need his assistance in the future, so see to his well-being," Connelly said. Having the captain's services are paramount when it comes to the rifles, he thought. "If need be, Sean, you might have to use your contact in London to keep us informed of matters."

"I understand, Mister Higgins," Gilmore said. "Is there anything else?"

"Do you trust Miss El-Sayed?" Connelly asked. "I mean, will she keep her wits about her and not ask too many questions?"

"Yes, I have faith she'll do everything in her power to see things through," Gilmore said. "And she's smart enough to listen and know when not to ask questions."

"We'll see how this works in the coming weeks," Connelly said, sipping his Jamaican Blue coffee from the china service. "I need not remind you if things get out of hand, I'll be prepared to use other measures."

"And when will I know about those?"

"You won't," Connelly said. "It's something I will do of my own accord. It's better for you and your colleague. But whatever happens, it will be done to protect my business interests and me."

"Certainly, sir. I understand," Gilmore replied, trying to hide the discomfort in his voice. He had read in the news of several unexplained murders in and around Belfast that coincided with events in which his employer had taken part. News of Mr. Higgins having someone else doing his bidding added to his theory. "Will there be anything else?"

"No, not for the time being," Connelly said. "Oh, I will be taking a brief business trip in the coming weeks. It's not final, but I'll have Erin fill you in before I leave."

"If there's nothing else," Gilmore said. "I should get back to the courtroom."

"Yes, I shouldn't detain you anymore, very well. I'll be in contact when necessary." The call ended.

Connelly rotated his chair toward the windows and looked out at the view he had of the harbor below. Small crafts made their way through the waterway, passing the historic birthplace of the infamous ocean-liner Titanic, while several freighters sat along piers being loaded.

Closing his eyes, Michael Connelly envisioned his great-grandfather and his struggles to rid his birthplace of the tyrannical rule of the British. As a leader of the pro-independence movement, his great-grandfather had been singled out. Moreover, after being wounded during the Easter uprising of 1916, he was amongst the first group of rebellious members shot by a firing squad.

His thoughts ran through his head like an old cinema newsreel with crude and unfocused black-and-white images playing out on the screen. He also recalled passionate talks with older family members who dreamed of a free Ireland, a united country, instead of the troubled one in which he had grown up—the one with the Protestants and Catholics consistently fighting here in Belfast, causing their conflict to become the symbol of the nation for the world rather than their cause.

"Mister Higgins?" his secretary's voice asked from the intercom.

Jolted back to his office, Michael Connelly turned his attention back to present-day issues. "Yes, Erin, what is it?"

"I'm sorry, sir. But you've got a call from a Mister Dunbar," she said. "He's rather persistent in needing to talk with you."

"That's all right, Erin; I'll take his call."

After leaving his unit with the French Foreign Legion, Connelly asked the Scotsman Dunbar to complete several criminal feats over time. As the rumors spread throughout the criminal syndicates of what the Northern Irishman was accomplishing, and who protected him, Michael (aka Mr. Higgins) rose in stature throughout the European underworld.

"Mister Dunbar," he said once he picked up, "this is an unexpected surprise."

"Good morning, sir," the Scotsman said. "I apologize for the early call, but I wanted to let you know I was in Glasgow preparing to visit my next client."

"I see. And what means do you plan on using against this individual?" Connelly asked.

"Hunt is well versed in blackmail and coercion, so I was considering turning the table on him," Dunbar said. "I was told he was trying to protect himself and the young runner by hiring some local muscle. It turns out they've been pinched, along with the young lad." Dunbar chuckled. I'd never allow the police to catch me, he thought.

Connelly looked out his window. The early morning sun was glistening off the water below the downtown buildings. Having Dunbar applying the pressure helped his cause, but he knew the Scot could take (and had taken) things into his own hands in the past. "Angus, mind you don't overstep your bounds with him," he said.

"Aye, I'll keep to the plan," Dunbar said.

"Good, then. I've still a need for Mister Hunt's services, which he must keep his focus on till it's completed," Connelly said. He planned to still use the members of the Glasgow crime syndicate to provide security for the weapons shipment.

"I'll see he's kept from harm," the Scotsman sneered. "If you'll excuse me, I've got an appointment to keep."

"I look forward to hearing from you soon," Michael Connelly said, and hung up. Pausing at the window facing the coast, his concern about the hired assassin grew. "Do I need to keep a firm hand on you, Angus?" he said aloud watching a pair of pleasure craft racing up out of the harbor towards the Irish Sea.

***

One hundred and forty miles away, rain pelted the windows as a summer shower passed over the city center of Glasgow. Alistair Hunt spun away from the window in his chair, looking at the cup of tea on his desk.

With eyes closed, he recalled the events of the last few weeks affecting his criminal activities. *First, there's the arrest of Gordon's cousin. Logan was providing valuable information on police activities in Aberdeen, including the assault on the drug handler, Ewan. Now there's the demand to transport a shipping container by 'Mr. Higgins.' In addition, the arrest and trial of the crewmember from the support vessel used to carry the drugs.* Each event was making it more tenuous in maintaining his anonymity.

The shrill buzzing of the intercom broke into his thoughts. He stabbed the flashing button, answering the call. "Yes, Janice, what is it?"

"There's a Mister Angus Dunbar here to meet you," Janice spoke, clearly reading from the gentleman's business card. The guest stood before her, his bowler in hand while several rivulets of water trickled from his coat.

"Please show him in," he said, still completing his thoughts about the trial. Hunt straightened the files on his desk, removing one, which noted his arrangement with Mr. Higgins. As the door opened, he rose and walked around his desk, offering his hand.

"Good morning, Mr. Dunbar," Hunt said, shaking the hand of Glasgow's notorious criminal-for-hire.

"Good morn' to you, Mr. Hunt," Dunbar replied, shaking his hand.

"Please have a seat." Hunt offered him the chair in front of his desk.

"Would you like some coffee, tea, or something a wee bit stronger?"

"No. Thank you, though," Dunbar answered, resting the bowler on his lap.

"What brings you to my office this morning?" he asked. He knew of Dunbar's reputation as a killer-for-hire amongst the criminals in Glasgow but had only needed his unique service once before today. Hunt kept is gaze on Dunbar as he settled into the leather-bound chair before beginning the discussion.

"I felt it was important to meet, given your current position with Mister Gordon Wallace," Dunbar said.

The mention of his friend's name took Hunt by surprise, though he fought to keep his face neutral. The tone his guest used when making the statement made him leery of the conversation's outcome. "So, what is it about Mister Wallace we need to discuss?" Hunt asked, ready to deny whatever accusations Dunbar might be preparing.

Dunbar stared at Hunt before speaking. "It turns out the police in Aberdeen are focusing their investigation on the calls made by his cousin, the former Sergeant Wallace," he said. "It's my understanding these include many calls made to his cousin, Gordon." Dunbar leaned back in the chair, a smug grin on his face. "You realize these calls could lead to you."

Hunt's brow became moist with nervous sweat. "And you have this information on good authority, I take it?" He held his hands together on top of his desk, trying to avoid showing any outward emotion.

"Yes, my sources said they were submitting information to the district office," Dunbar replied. "Turns out the police are establishing a pattern of calls, with the dates on which they took place," he added. "It's just a matter of time before they make the connections, so to speak." He chuckled at his own joke.

Hunt leaned back in his leather chair, hands clasped across his torso, thinking of times he had asked Gordon for information over the phone. *I've had hundreds of calls asking for his help in the past*, he thought. "And what sort of help can you offer me?" he asked.

"I'm proposing that I be allowed to apply some external pressure to the police and their investigation," Dunbar said. "I've already begun preparations to carry out a plan to bribe the chief superintendent of the police," he said. Dunbar knew this part of his plan would protect his employer, Mr. Higgins.

"And this ploy to bribe the chief will protect me?" Hunt asked.

"I plan to show a pattern of improper use of power," Dunbar answered.

"And what will this cost me?" Hunt demanded, knowing Dunbar didn't offer his services without a price attached.

"Let's say it'd be negotiable. Commencing at, oh, let's say twenty-five thousand pounds."

Hunt drew on every ounce of restraint he possessed in order to keep his face neutral. "As you say, it's a negotiable fee. And I'll consider your proposal after you've provided some tangible proof." He rose from behind his desk. "Mister Dunbar, I recommend you get whatever evidence together, as expeditiously as possible, if you want to see one gold farthing coming from me." This was his attempt to end their discussion.

"I'll see you get your evidence of my actions soon enough," Dunbar said, rising from his seat. "Please let your secretary know to expect a package in the coming week." He held out his hand.

"Aye, I'll let her know," Hunt said as he shook Dunbar's hand with reluctance. "Good day to you, sir." He gestured toward the door for Dunbar to leave.

After leaving the meeting with Alistair Hunt, Dunbar soon found himself sitting in a small pub near the city center. Having a sip of his drink, he looked at the text message on his mobile phone. It read; SY HOLDING EVIDENCE AGAINST ES, NEED INFO AGAINST THE INSPECTOR. Satisfied his inquiry was correct he pushed the SEND button.

It was three weeks earlier when Mister Higgins of Belfast, a former acquaintance from his service days, had contacted Dunbar. The Irishman had asked if Dunbar had the means to discredit the police's attempt at prosecuting the former constable, Logan Wallace.

The former sergeant with Britain's Twenty-Second SAS Regiment gave Higgins several ideas, one being to taint the evidence used against the former constable sergeant. *To get one hundred thousand shillings added to my account will go a long way toward early retirement*, he thought. Ever since his ouster from the special-forces unit, Dunbar worked hard to set up and keep his own anonymity. Only a select group of people knew of what he'd done while in uniform. Higgins was one of those individuals who'd learned of Dunbar's sordid past and paid him well to handle clandestine jobs.

After Dunbar was unceremoniously drummed out of the SAS, he plied his skills to the highest bidder amongst the various criminal syndicates operating within the United Kingdom. He used his expertise as a sniper to significant effect, usually to the highest bidder. After several narrow escapes with the Metropolitan Police in London, Dunbar used several specific and private actions, ensuring his anonymity would be kept from law enforcement.

"Another pint, sir?" the ginger-haired server asked standing next to the table.

"No, but thank you," Dunbar said kindly to the young lass.

Looking at his watch, he thought, *I'll need to begin planning my return trip to Aberdeen.* Dunbar recalled his earlier conversation with Sergeant Wallace before the officer had been arrested. He remembered learning the chief superintendent was allowing the inspector from Scotland Yard to see a constable working in the forensics lab. *Nothing like a scandalous affair to shake things up*, he concluded. After consuming the last of his ale, he placed the glass on the table. He pulled out a stylish leather billfold, picked up the empty glass, and set five shillings under it as payment.

Dunbar stepped out of the pub into the bright afternoon sunlight. He walked to the curb and hailed a passing taxi. "Errol Gardens," he announced as he got in and planted himself in the back seat. As the driver navigated his way to the south side of the town, Dunbar made several mental notes for his upcoming trip to Aberdeen.

Chapter Three

Sunlight glistened off buildings bordering the highway as Chief Inspector McDermott and his partner drove to their third stop. Another business supplying service boats with welding equipment and gases to the oilrigs. After pulling into a vacant parking spot, McDermott sat back, absorbed in thought.

"Do you recall which lorry we need to follow?" McDermott asked as he sipped his coffee. Staring through the window of their unmarked car, he spotted three lorries, each sporting the same green and white symbols of the gas service provider. Since their confiscation of the hashish on the PSV (platform support vessel) Standard-Apollo, this was the most promising lead he and his partner had.

His partner, Inspector Fletcher flipped through his notebook and read off the numbers for the lorry in question. "The numbers should be on the cab and the rear lift gate," he replied.

McDermott only half listened to the answer as he thought of the incidents from two weeks ago. After receiving an anonymous phone tip, their investigation revealed almost ninety kilos of refined hashish concealed inside a gas cylinder used by welders. After they examined the ship's log and supply manifests, they determined the business delivering the cylinders to the ships and oil-derricks.

"So, Andrew," McDermott said, "put yourself in the drug traffickers' place. How would you move the narcotics from here?"

Fletcher sat and reflected on the query. "Well, it's like the theory we have on the boats. Someone on the inside knows what is being turned over or picked up," he stated. "It's a question of whether they extract the drugs here. And with all the movement, that seems improbable." He pointed to the trucks driving in and out of the fenced-in yard.

"Which means someone working for the gas business has possible connections to the Glasgow syndicate," McDermott replied. "The trouble is the reports filed by the detective constables here in Aberdeen never established the relationship until we showed up with

29

our case." He drained the last of his coffee. "Make a note to have Sergeant McKee obtain a register of the employees, and examine the phone listing from Wallace, as well. He might have called here once or twice."

After several minutes, McDermott spotted smoke belching from beneath one lorry. "We've got one pulling out," he said, starting the car. "Take a picture of the driver as he moves past us, will yeh?" McDermott shifted the police car into gear and pulled out of the parking spot, accompanying the delivery truck as it headed out.

"Do you suspect any of those bottles have drugs in them now?" Fletcher asked as he pointed at the many cylinders chained in the back of the truck.

"I'm nae sure at this point," McDermott said, keeping an eye on the truck ahead of them. Glancing about, he noticed they were pulling onto Ellon Road, which would lead to downtown and the harbor. "If the driver does nae change his direction, we'll be on King Street soon."

After thirty minutes, McDermott watched the delivery truck pull into the Waterloo Quay dock area near the Euro-line Shipping facilities. He briefly lost sight of the truck when he had to slow down to dodge a small tractor pulling a container trailer. Just as he got around a corner, McDermott slammed on the brakes to avoid a speeding red car that had entered the docks from a surface street. "Bloody hell, he nearly took out our bonnet!" he shouted.

"I've got his number and make," Fletcher said, jotting down the information in his notebook.

"We'll let the other constables handle that twit," McDermott replied. He returned his attention to their surveillance of the gas company truck and their drug investigation. "Can you make out any vessel names?"

Fletcher twisted in his seat and examined the harbor. "There are a few 'Grampian' boats," he answered. "I can't see Captain Kinkaid's anywhere from this vantage point. In addition, two of the Chevron-Europe boats, *Hercules* and *Poseidon*, are secured across the way."

"And there's our delivery truck," McDermott said, parking alongside one of the fenced-in lots. The driver was already outside walking towards a group of men standing about the building's entrance. "Can you take any pictures of them?"

Fletcher raised the camera and clicked away, getting a dozen photos of the driver and the dockworkers. "The lab should be capable of enlarging these without a problem," he said, setting the camera aside.

A dozen multi-colored service boats filled the harbor, each one swaying as the tide rolled down the River Dee and toward open waters. Shouts from the dockworkers could be picked up over clanging chains and roaring motors of lorries moving along the dock. Every few minutes, a bundle of pipe or other goods would be swinging from the cable of a crane's derrick mast onto the deck of an awaiting craft.

A gleaming red Ford Focus rounded the corner of the lane before coming to a halt near the junction. A young man exited the car attired in a tattered army-coat and dirty jeans. Skirting past the entrance near the Euro-line Shipping service, he sauntered towards some freight containers where a group of workers stood as if he was wandering into a pub. Spying the unwanted visitor, Allen Doyle broke away from his crew and addressed the man.

"What do you think you're doing here?" Doyle asked.

"I was sent by Sutherland," the young man said.

"He advised you to show up here? Now?"

"Yes. I need five more balloons," the young man said. "He didn't have any more and told me you did. I've got cash." He pulled a bundle of bills from his pocket.

"Put that aside, you fool," Doyle said, clutching the man's arm and leading him behind a stack of pipes. "What in the hell made you think of seeking to make a purchase in broad daylight, anyway?"

The young man shook his arm loose from Doyle's grasp, rubbing where he had clutched his arm. "I've got people standing by. Sutherland promised me a regular supply of hashish, and since he's nae got any, he suggested you might."

"Find me by the Asco House after eight o'clock," Doyle said. "And if you come up any sooner than that, I'll feed you to the gulls." He turned the youth around and forced him towards the road.

McDermott saw the exchange between the delivery driver and a dockworker when the driver of the red sports car reached them. He opened the driver's-side door and stepped out. "Come on," he said. "Let's see if we can ruffle a few feathers."

As Fletcher got out of the car, he realized he was already several yards behind the briskly walking inspector and had to trot to

31

catch up with him. "What do you think they're chatting about?" he asked, struggling to catch his breath.

McDermott walked through the gate of the freight business, keeping an eye on the men who were gathering about a stack of shipping cages. The driver of the truck was easy to locate as he wore the lime-green shirt, which matched the company colours. As Fletcher and he drew closer, he noticed one of the men step aside and soon drive off in the red sports car from earlier.

Allen Doyle glanced at the officers approaching and stepped aside from the group to address them. "Can I help you gents?" he asked, standing between McDermott and his workers.

"Aye, you can," McDermott said, offering his ID. "I'd like to see the supervisor in charge of the yard." He was looking past the dockworker at the driver.

"That'd be me," the burly Scot announced.

"And your name is . . .?"

"Doyle. Allen Doyle."

McDermott exchanged a glance with Fletcher before he proceeded with his questioning. "Well, Mister Doyle, what's the routine when you have a delivery? Like those gas bottles on the truck there?" he asked, pointing to the lorry.

"First off, I make certain they're part of a delivery order," Doyle said. "Then," he continued, "If we're not loading them right away on a ship, we'll store the bottles. When needed, we'll group them together in one cage and get them to the appropriate ship for loading when needed

McDermott scanned the yard, noting where numerous cages sat, some with bottles painted in various colors secured inside them. "You din nae mind if we take a look at one of the cages, do you?" he asked, pointing to several that were lining the dock.

"Be my guest," Doyle said and began walking them towards the waiting load.

"How do you know if you're accepting a full bottle?" Fletcher asked.

Doyle looked at the young inspector. "They're tagged and sealed from the supplier." He spun off a cover to show the metal tab wired to the valve.

"And what do you do with the empty ones coming back?" McDermott asked, knowing there would be a prepared answer to his question. "Seems they'd get mixed with new ones relatively easy in a yard when it was busy."

Before he could answer, the radio on Doyle's hip squelched as a call from the central office came through. He put the radio to his ear. "You'll have to excuse me . . .," he said, stepping away to take the call. The two inspectors nodded and stood aside.

"So, all the bottles are tagged as ready from the supplier," Fletcher said.

"Aye," McDermott said. "And the used ones aren't." He looked at the rows of multi-colored cylinders lining the fence. "So, if the drug traffickers on the boats hand off the bottles, and they come here . . ." His thoughts trailed off.

"Someone here in the holding yard is part of the trafficking ring," Fletcher said, finishing McDermott's statement.

McDermott didn't hear Fletcher's full response. He stepped away and towards the driver of the truck who was leaving the office, papers in hand. McDermott waved at him. "Excuse me," he said, "do you mind if I ask you a question?"

"I've another stop in East Tullos," the driver said as he continued walking to his truck.

McDermott stepped in front of the driver and pulled out his ID. "Give us a wee break," he said. "I just need to ask you a question. We can do it here, or down at the district office, it's your choice." He stood with his arms folded across his chest.

"All right, then. Ask away."

McDermott backed up a step and pointed to the truck. "Is this a regular run for you? Coming to the dock that is?"

"One of several," the driver answered. "I'll do a drop here, a shop in East Tullos, one in Altens, and then my last for today is at Maersk Training in the Badentoy Industrial Park."

"And you're only dropping off?"

"No, I'll be picking up any empty cylinders for servicing if the shop has any," the driver said with a hint of nervousness in his voice.

"Are you picking up any empty cylinders here?" McDermott asked.

"No. I only make drop-off's here since this is my first stop of the day," the driver said. "We've another driver making pick-ups here later in the week."

"Aye, then; what type of gases were you dropping off?" he asked.

"Four cylinders of argon and one of helium," the driver said.

McDermott considered what the driver was telling him and felt it was the truth. If the routine was as he described, the drugs weren't moved to the docks from the gas suppliers. Watching his partner pacing nervously near the dockworkers, he dismissed the driver after getting his name.

"Inspector Fletcher, I believe we're done," McDermott said, waving him towards the car. As he walked away from the yard, McDermott considered his next step. *If the drugs came off the boat and were picked up by another truck, they'll need to stake out the harbor*, he thought. To do that, we'd need to know when the drugs are being delivered and we're no closer to learning that than before. As he looked over the harbor, McDermott felt overwhelmed at his task.

"You all right, Conor?" Fletcher asked, seeing his partner's facial expression change.

"Aye, lad, I am," he said, sliding behind the wheel. "We're going to need to have a chat with Superintendent MacCallum so the constables know to look for unusual activities when they patrol the docks. If we consider the empty cylinders being used for the drugs, we need to follow them off the boats."

As they made their way along Regents Quay and the main thoroughfare, McDermott turned to Fletcher. "Do you still have the name of the fella we pinched for beating on Sutherland?"

Fletcher opened his notebook and thumbed through the pages of scribbled wording. "Dunnigan. He claimed to be restraining Sutherland because he heard a deckhand shouting he'd stolen something from off the dock."

McDermott glanced over his shoulder as he pulled the car into traffic along the A95. "We'll need to see if he's still in the sheriff's office or if they moved him to the holding cells. In addition, we'll need to have Sergeant Ames look into this fella Doyle. I'm nae fond of his temperament," he said.

After driving past the granite and glass buildings of downtown, McDermott pulled into the police car park. "You go and see the sergeant about our longshoremen," he said.

"And where are you going?" Fletcher asked.

"I've got some wee business to discuss," he said. "Go and make sure we can meet with the chief."

"How long should I wait?" Fletcher asked.

"I'll nae be but a few minutes; go on, now."

"Twenty minutes. Afterwards, I'll see the chief without you," Fletcher said as he walked away.

Waving Fletcher off, McDermott walked a block down the street, entering the bank building and headed straight for the information desk.

"Can I help you?" the young clerk asked.

"Aye, hen, you can. Is Mr. Gallagher available?"

"One moment," she said. "I'll check to see if he's available."

Standing patiently, he looked at the gentleman occupying the manager's office, listening to her conversation on the phone. "Mr. Gallagher will see you, sir," the young woman said, pointing to the office where the manager sat.

McDermott made his way across the bank lobby, walked up to the office's open door, and stepped in. "Hello, Uncle Duncan."

Glancing up from the stack of paperwork on his desk, the senior bank executive looked at his young nephew standing in the doorway. "Well, well, look what the cat drug through the door; what brings you back to Aberdeen?" He then turned his attention back to his computer.

McDermott looked down at his shoes, which were scuffed at the toe and in need some polish. "I've been assigned to the case involving Edna," he said in a voice filled with remorse.

Peering up from the screen again, Duncan Gallagher slid the glasses off his face. "Well, now. You couldn't find time to come to her services, but you've taken an interest in who did the killing?"

"You know full well I've never been kin to family gatherings," McDermott said.

"No, of course not. You're too 'high and mighty' for those, aren't you?" Gallagher said. "I mean, you couldn't even make time for your mother's service, either."

Hearing his uncle remind him about missing his mother's funeral was like a sharp knife plunging deep into his soul. McDermott felt the pain being reminded of the broken promise to her of being there for her after his father passed away. "That's nae fair, you know full well I was on board the Edinburgh and was nae able to leave," McDermott said. "And I did nae come to argue, I wanted you to know I'll be giving my best effort to find out who's responsible for causing Edna's death."

"Best effort is it, huh?" Gallagher asked. He set his glasses on the desk and pulled a neckerchief from his waistcoat, wiping the corners of his eyes before looking at McDermott. "You'd better, young man, it's the least you can do for your poor cousin. She thought the world of you, you know. You used to be her knight in shining armor when she was a wee lass. But you don't actually care, do you, Mister Big-Time Inspector with the Yard? Now, if you'll excuse me, I've work to finish." He began looking over the ledgers sitting on his desk computer.

Realizing their discussion was over, McDermott turned away from his uncle and walked solemnly out of the bank. Removing the photo from his jacket, he looked at the face of the young girl standing next to the naval officer. The teenager wore a floral dress, her hair draped over one shoulder. But her smile, it radiated with pride for her older cousin. The young woman also had an uncanny resemblance to McDermott's mother when she was in her teens. *I'll find the ones responsible for causing your death, Edna. I promise.*

Chapter Four

The train's whistle reverberated off the sides of the terminal as morning service from Glasgow arrived in Aberdeen just before twelve o'clock. Sporting a navy-blue Brooks Brother's suit, Dunbar looked like most businesspersons—leather satchel over his shoulder, travel bag in hand, and raincoat folded over his arm. Walking toward the exit of the train depot, he glanced at several constables scanning the throng for any altercations.

Drifting past them with a smug grin, his attempts to remain anonymous amongst fellow-criminals was worth it. In a well-rehearsed performance, Dunbar rubbed against another patron who slipped a key into his cupped hand. Wandering towards the section where long-term lockers were, he discovered the one associated with his key and extracted its contents. With the bag in hand, he made his way to the waiting group of taxis outside the station depot.

Going up into the first available taxi he said, "City Centre Hotel, please." Having a seat in the back, he considered his plan to place the police chief on notice. He even considered the prospect of slandering the detectives from Scotland Yard. *My first piece of business is to meet with this Mr. Burns*, he told himself. The hearing of the seamen from the *Standard-Apollo* wasn't associated to Mr. Higgins yet, but he was being rewarded to make certain it went on as such.

Minutes later, the taxi drew up to the hotel. "Here you are, sir," the driver said. "It'll be five quid, six-pence."

Dunbar pulled a ten-pound note from his wallet and handed it to the driver. "Keep the rest," he said.

As he strolled through the front vestibule of the hotel, he made his way to the reception counter.

"Good day, sir," the receptionist said.

"Good day," Dunbar said. "I've got a reservation under Walker. Andrew Walker."

Most residents of Scotland wouldn't recall the name he chose for his alias, but for those with a flair for pursuing historical cases, it might have summoned up reminders of the mass-murderer.

The clerk typed his name into the computer and identified the information. "Yes, we've got you staying a fortnight," the clerk said. "If you'll just sign the electronic notepad, I'll prepare your keys."

Dunbar signed, and the clerk handed over the data card for unlocking the suite.

"The lift is to your right; you're in room 415."

"Thank you," Dunbar said, accepting the cards. He picked up his bags and made his way to the lift.

Dunbar strode out of the lift, discovered the room almost immediately, and entered. After setting his bags, case, and coat on the bed, he stepped over to the window. Here he saw the harbor in the distance, the masts of the vessels cresting the rooftops. Smoke trailed a ferryboat as it entered the breakwater in the distance.

As he pulled open the drawer of the nightstand, he noticed the city directory which furnished him with the listing for the sheriff's office and printed the address. Getting out the map he purchased back in Glasgow, he soon established the area of the courthouse and the direction he would go later that evening.

Next, as he set out the map, he took the case from the bed, removed the padlock, and opened the lid, exposing the weapon of his trade. The sniper rifle was broken down into its three major pieces. *Hello, Clementine*, he said to himself, picking up the stock and carriage assembly like a newborn baby. He began assembling the rifle together. He set these onto the desk before he picked up the Leupold 9 × 40 scope from the case.

Dunbar stood at the window and put the telescope to his eye. He twisted the knob to focus on his subject as he caught sight of the car ferry entering the harbor. With the twist of the knob, he caught sight of an officer giving directions to the crew. *This will do*, he thought, putting the scope back in the case. Having a seat at the desk, he spread out a cloth and toolkit in order to clean the rifle for the proposed use to come.

The alarm on the nightstand chimed as it reached three o'clock in the morning, building its intensity every five seconds. Rolling over, Dunbar silenced it before getting up. Already dressed in grey slacks, he pulled on a woolen sweater and made his way out of the hotel and towards the Sheriff's Court.

With the same prudent and attentive skill, one he learned in the SAS, he stepped with purpose until he found himself a block from the courthouse. Dunbar stood in front of a boutique window to focus on the entrance to the court and its surroundings. Two constables stood outside shuffling their feet, attempting to keep awake in the early morning twilight.

He glanced up the length of the thoroughfare, spying a position that would serve as a shooter's nest. Walking out of the shadows, he strolled passed the lit front of Police Scotland's Aberdeen station. Here he discovered half-dozen constables making their way to patrol cars, as they prepared their early morning patrols of the slumbering city.

"Pardon me, sir, are you lost?" one police officer asked him.

"Oh—what? No, I'm sorry, officer, no, I'm just a bit of an insomniac when I travel," Dunbar replied, feigning surprise.

"And where did you travel from, if you don't mind me asking?"

"America. Houston, Texas, to be exact. I'm here to check up on several of the Chevron rigs," he said, trying hard to suppress his highland accent.

"Well, then, mind yourself. We've got a few criminal-types making a name for themselves, especially addicts," the policeman informed him, getting into his patrol car.

"I'll be careful, and thank you," Dunbar said as he proceeded to stroll along the avenue.

Turning to speak to the police officer allowed him to examine the surveillance cameras on the building. He noted two on each corner and one over the central entrance. He was also able to identify each camera's position. From this point, he likewise could see the back entrance to the sheriff's office where prisoners transited between the jail and courts. *A bit of a risk trying to eliminate the seaman here*, he thought, turning the corner before heading back to the hotel.

After his encounter with the police officer, Dunbar made his way back to his room. He noted the hair he'd put across the gap was still there. This told him no one had entered while he was out. Dunbar slid the handgun from behind his back and returned it to the strongbox before locking it.

He took the map and spread it across the desk where he could indicate the position of the surveillance cameras he saw earlier. To create the diversions would take a day or two and then a day to place, he thought regarding the number of improvised explosives he would need. Having the police officers' attention directed elsewhere would be the risky part, he told himself. Now, to plan my escape routes, he thought, finishing his plan to assassinate the suspect arrested by the police. Propping the pillows on the bed, he settled down, realizing his tasks for the day were just starting.

The commotion of a family walking down the corridor woke Dunbar from an exhausted slumber. Rolling over and peeking at the alarm, it showed it was half past nine in the morning. Sitting up, he stripped off his slacks and sweater, and put on the overalls from the local service company. Dunbar left the hotel again, this time through the maintenance entrance. Making his way along a back alley, he paused at the freight entrance of a local business fronting Union Street.

Trying the door, he discovered it open and soon made his way to the building's rooftop.

Sheltered behind the façade, he gingerly removed the riflescope from its protected pouch. Glancing over the lip and setting the scope to his eye, he focused in on the constables walking the street. From here, he was judging the distance and angles to the front of the Sheriff's Court on Union Street. "The police are making matters easy for this opportunity," he murmured looking at the barricades creating the clear space into the bus lane. Pairs of constables walked along the street, peering into parked cars or lorries for anyone or anything of a suspicious nature.

Dunbar noted the sun's position and the whipping, swirling wind. The three- and four-story buildings lining the boulevard created a natural wind tunnel. Dunbar jotted down the information just as his cell phone chirped with a text message. Glancing down, he saw it was from the office of Callaghan & Higgins in Belfast. The text read: CALL WHEN ABLE. HAVE MORE ASSETS TO MANAGE. After reading the message, he shrugged.

He pushed the buttons across the phone's keypad. DOES MISTER SUTHERLAND STILL NEED HIS CLEANING SERVICE? He typed with his thumbs and pressed SEND. In moments, his phone chirped again with a text. A simple YES, MORE SERVICES ARE IDENTIFIED FOR IMMEDIATE ACTION was all it read. With this information, Dunbar now knew full well he would need to exercise more caution, as the risk had just become greater.

Returning to his room, the former Army sergeant took the time to make himself presentable for his next excursion. With the hot water cascading off his shoulders, Dunbar rinsed off the grime of his early morning reconnaissance. With the water turned off, he grabbed a towel and dried himself before wrapping a towel about his waist. Walking out of the bathroom, he picked up his cell phone and selected the number for his contact. Before hearing the second ring, his call was answered.

"Good afternoon, Angus," the familiar voice of Mr. Higgins said.

"Aye, it is a good afternoon," he said. "I understand you have other assets for me to handle?"

The executive sitting in his office in Belfast coughed briefly before he answered. "It seems there's a foreman on the docks who was used as a middleman during my transaction who has knowledge of Mr. Hunt's colleague."

"I see. And you wish for me to discuss his responsibilities, is that it?" Dunbar asked.

"Well, of course I do. You're well aware I can't afford to allow too many individuals to have inside information as to my business dealings," Mr. Higgins said. "As we discussed earlier, you need to find a new and diverse means of negotiating with people in this line of work."

Dunbar closed his eyes and considered the means the Irishman was alluding to but knew he had several methods for eliminating people. "And how will I know I've got the right client?"

"You should get an image shortly."

The phone chirped a moment later as Dunbar saw the icon for receipt of an email on his phone screen. "Aye, I've got it," he said.

"And, Angus, time is very important; don't waste it trying to be perfect," Mr. Higgins said in an impatient tone. "Don't forget to contact me when you've completed everything."

"Aye, if there's nothing else, I've got a few things to prepare for," Dunbar said as he stared at himself in the mirror and the matted hair he'd just cleaned.

"Good day, Angus," Mr. Higgins said, ending the call.

After the screen went blank Dunbar tossed the phone on the bed before returning his attention to his hair, now a dried and tangled mess.

***

Copies of a police photo taken during the booking process stared back at Dunbar. The name was listed below the image: DOYLE, ALLEN. So, he's been added to my list, he thought. The docks were a busy place, with movement at nearly every hour of the day. He was willing to bet this bloke wouldn't be as easily duped the way Baxter was.

Finishing his mince pie, Dunbar drained the last of his cola, washing the greasy goodness from his palette. Going past the dustbin, he swept the papers and cup from his tray before stepping onto the street. Off to his left, he could see the masts of several service vessels, which showed him the direction to take.

After walking three blocks, he approached Regent's Quay, where several service boats laid idle. Wandering along the waterfront, he took up a spot so he could study the dockworkers. In a spectacle reminiscent of mechanical monsters, goods and containers were sent moving between the lorries and boats.

After ten minutes or so, Dunbar soon noticed which chaps were in charge and which ones did all the work. Observing one transition of goods from a vehicle to a boat, he spied a shoddy attempt to pass along a bribe between the lorry operator and the supervisor. He glanced at his phone screen and back at the two men conversing. "It seems I've found my client," he said aloud as he identified Allen Doyle.

"Funny not to see the police about," he said to himself, noticing the hand-off of money. Glancing at the rooflines of the surrounding buildings, Dunbar saw several CCTV cameras pointed in various directions and assumed they were functioning. "I'll need to be mindful of those," he muttered.

Coming back to the action on the docks, he could see a metal cage, half-full of gas bottles, being lifted off one service boat and secured on a lorry. Striding up to the open window, the supervisor handed over a bundle of papers and gave a thumbs-up to the driver. Moments later, the lorry roared off, leaving a trail of black soot exhaust, while Doyle waved at several of the workers, pointing towards the pub across the street.

Noticing an opportunity to wreak some havoc with the police, Dunbar casually followed the men into the pub. This should be an easy mark, he thought. Entering the pub, he chose a seat close enough to keep an eye on Doyle.

Sitting back in the pub, Dunbar sipped his ale while listening to the exchanges of several dockworkers at the adjacent table. Most bar talks centered on football or women, but these two were considering something more urgent.

"What do I tell the lads on the platform tomorrow?" Jimmy Keller demanded. "Ewan was our sole contact to make sure we had the stuff to peddle, and Sammie does nae handle anymore."

"Sammie knows someone else, but after the Apollo got pinched, everybody is keeping quiet," Alvin Doyle said, downing his pint.

"And we've not heard hide nor hair of the Frenchman since the two constables stuck their snout in our meet, either," Keller replied.

As the dockworkers spoke, Dunbar planned a strategy to include a bigger burden to the harried police force. Including an indiscriminate murder to the blend, while having various drugs present on the bodies should make the case to hamper the law enforcement, he considered. Holding up his glass for the barmaid while at the same time pointing to the dockworkers, he gestured for another round of pints.

"Good day, gentlemen," he announced. "My name is Walker, and I'm here to fill in for your young supplier."

Both men stared at Dunbar with a wry eye before Doyle spoke. "I'm not sure I know what you're talking about, mate. Jimmy and I are just enjoying a wee chat about a friend. And who's saying you're not a constable or detective trying to ambush us, heh?"

Before Dunbar could respond, three pints appeared on the table from the hostess. "I can guarantee you, I'm not with any police force," he said. "Who I am is more important, though. I'm the bloke who's capable of furnishing you a supply of product to keep peddling to your associates on the platforms."

"Product? Peddling? What specifically are you getting at?" Keller asked, more guarded now than before. Dunbar walked up to him.

"I'll have two kilos available for you; I need to know when and where to surrender it," Dunbar announced.

"Of what?" Doyle asked, growing leery of this Walker fellow.

"Let's not play games, shall we?" Dunbar said. "I know who you were trading with and what you need," he added. "Your former handler is squatting in a cubicle downtown and you've blokes who need his merchandise. If you wish to stay in good graces with them, I propose we get to the point, shall we?"

"Ok, then, we're off after six; where do you recommend we meet?" Doyle asked.

"To be honest, I'll let you choose," Dunbar replied.

"Sounds sensible. The signal house on the south jetty, then. Say, nine o'clock," Doyle said, deciding the further from the docks the better for him and Keller.

"Then I say we've made a deal, gentlemen," Dunbar said, raising his pint.

Chapter Five

As he thought of the earlier encounter with his uncle, McDermott's temperament didn't improve. Being reminded about missing his mother's funeral always reopened old wounds. It was as if her death was imposed straight upon him. While at his father's funeral, McDermott made a commitment to be near his mother, one his family required him to honor.

However, just six months after her companion passed, Catherine (Gallagher) McDermott succumbed to a massive heart attack and perished alone in her flat. Conor would learn of her passing in the harshest of ways. As the communication officer aboard his ship, he drew the task of receiving the notice from Admiralty and the British Red Cross service first.

Drawing a deep breath, McDermott pushed back the past, rubbing the few tears from his cheek as he stopped before the entrance to the police offices. As he dodged two constables leaving the district building, McDermott entered the lobby, making his way to Superintendent MacCallum's office. "Sergeant McKee, is the chief busy?"

"Aye, he's with Inspector Fletcher," the sergeant said.

Parading past her desk, McDermott entered the chief superintendent's office, tapping on the door as he opened it.

Glancing at his partner with a vexed expression, Fletcher went on. "As I was saying, sir. Mr. St. James thinks the court-assigned barrister has outside support," he said, watching McDermott interrupt the discussion.

"Sorry for the delay," McDermott said.

"Continue on, Inspector Fletcher," MacCallum said, giving McDermott a sour face for disturbing his partner.

"Well, sir, it created the notion that for every query the prosecutor asked while building his argument, the defense had a counter-challenge," Fletcher said.

"Is it possible information about the case is being disclosed from someone in the government's office?" MacCallum asked.

"From what I've gathered about Mr. St. James, the macer, and other barristers during recesses, it sounds remote," he said.

"Sir, has anyone paid Sutherland a call? Or the two seamen, Jones and Campbell?" McDermott asked.

"I'm not sure, but we can consider looking at the guests' journal," MacCallum said.

"I'd still see if we can have someone put an eye on this Mr. Forbes too," McDermott said.

"Who do you think can persuade or exercise pressure to a representative of the Crown's court?" Fletcher asked, looking at his partner.

"For the moment, I'd start with who Sergeant Wallace was chatting with the evening we arrested him," McDermott said.

"I've taken steps towards finding out," MacCallum said. "Chief Superintendent Cameron in Glasgow has begun surveillance on one possible suspect."

"Yes, sir, but haven't we received something from the phone companies themselves?" Fletcher inquired.

Gazing at the young inspector, the senior officer considered the impact of disclosing what his female companion, Inspector Gordon, was preparing and her relationship in the process. "Sergeant McKee is still acting on those with the support of the cadet class," he replied.

"Further, you'll be delighted to learn we've still got the separate evidence from the oil derrick," McDermott said.

"I almost forgot about the evidence from your sojourn to the gas derrick," MacCallum said, his mood seeming to improve instantly.

"Aye, if you recall, we ran across a liquor bottle with traces of hashish still in it. And several cooking pots with butane burners for heating the pots," McDermott said. "Not to mention a pile of suits the first officer from the ship said are needed for working with chemicals."

"Cooking pots and chemical suits?" MacCallum inquired.

"Aye, pots large enough for a few servings of roast mutton," McDermott said.

"What in the world would they need chemical suits for, though?" Fletcher asked.

"I don't know what the suits are needed for," McDermott replied, rubbing his palm on his chin. "The first officer on the *Talisker* suggested the dockworkers wear them when they handle caustic compounds. But, for you and me, it's another portion to the damn puzzle we need to locate a spot for," he said, leaning back in his chair.

"You two best get on with it, then," MacCallum said, dismissing the detectives. "We'll be including your discovery to the post of drug-related issues growing over the last few weeks."

"Aye, shows we're right popular," McDermott said. "Come on, we've some reports to examine." He motioned for Fletcher to follow him out the door.

Back in the detective's office, the two inspectors continued to pore over piles of reports. Gawking over the documents, Inspector Andrew Fletcher stretched and yawned for what sounded like the hundredth time. "Didn't we just finish covering the same damn thing looking for the ship records?" he asked.

"Aye, but it was distinctive information, mind you," McDermott answered as he looked through his listing.

"What about the comments from the spouse? Couldn't she shed some light on the sergeant's actions?"

"To be fair, I've not paid very much thought to them, but you bring up an excellent point. Give Sergeant Giles or McKee a call; see if we can get those too," McDermott said, brushing the stubble on his face.

Contacting the Records office, Fletcher asked for the account files and was soon combing the handwritten remarks, attempting to interpret the information. "Some of these constables need to go back to school and work on their penmanship," he said.

"Looks like the Sergeant received the odd call on weeknights or weekend. But no mention of any names," Fletcher said, noticing the content of the conversation in his notebook.

"Does the wife mention something else?" McDermott asked.

"Oh, wait a minute. Looks like the sergeant's relative, Gordon, would call setting up times to attend soccer games," Fletcher said, scanning the interview notes.

"Nothing amiss with watching soccer, but it allows passing along info without being listened in on," McDermott said, his thoughts surging in every direction.

"Once Sheila comes back from Glasgow, we should be apt to see who the sergeant was calling most regularly. She's expected to have records from the phone companies based on who he was calling" Fletcher said.

47

"Aye, that's splendid, but that hardly answers the disputes about the information leaks in the station. It does nae answer any on the drug trafficking," McDermott said, reminding his partner of their investigation in Aberdeen.

"I suppose it would benefit if some calls were mentioning the Irishman identified in the notes from Portsmouth," Fletcher said, drawing his hair back.

"That's something we did nae consider: calls made through the international operator," McDermott said, taking a pen and jotting down a note. "I'll be back in a minute." He then rushed out of the office and hurried to the room of Sergeants Giles and McKee.

"Giles, do we still have a few cadets to work with?" he muttered, catching his breath.

Glancing at the detective, the sergeant responded, "Aye, we've still got a handful waiting to pass their exams. Why are you asking?"

"Because we need to examine the phone records again. This time concentrate on calls Sergeant Wallace was making or receiving from the foreign operator," McDermott said. "Begin checking for calls from Ireland, starting with Dublin or Belfast codes first."

"And when might you need the information, Inspector?" the sergeant inquired.

"Yesterday might be a wee bit too late," the detective said, stepping out of the room.

***

After he left Inspector Fletcher to swarm over the phone lists, McDermott wound up parking along the curb near Sergeant Wallace's home. From the outside, the two-story house looked much like others in the development—gray slate exterior with a modest stonewall along the walkway. The only splash of color was of crimson roses in bloom along the path to the front door. Wandering past a television news van parked along the roadside, the detective made his approach to the front door.

Picking up the brass handle of the doorknocker, McDermott tapped on the strike plate several times. Tuning in to the shuffling of feet behind the door, he stepped back as it swung free. "What do you need?" the woman who answered asked.

"Mrs. Wallace, I'm Chief Inspector McDermott of Scotland Yard," he replied, holding up his credentials. "I'd welcome a few minutes of your time."

"Another traitor to my Logan, are you?" Maggie Wallace said loud enough for the broadcast people to understand. "Mind you, the labor union has advised me I did nae need to chat with any of you."

"Aye, I understand your reluctance to speak, ma'am, but I'm in need of gaining some clarification," McDermott said. "It might be to your husband's favor too."

"And what might that be?" she asked.

"May I come in?" he asked, looking back at the news crews watching him.

"Aye, down the hall," she said, directing McDermott to the sitting room.

McDermott stepped into the back room, studying the ordinary furnishings and simple belongings. Nothing appeared to show that someone was paying the sergeant a king's ransom for the information at the station. Photos of family gatherings adorned the walls over a small table pushed against it. The furnishings were comfortable but not extravagant.

"So, what questions is it you want to ask me that hasn't been asked before?" Maggie asked. She picked up a packet of cigarettes from the end table before pulling one out and lighting it. Letting out the smoke, she created a brief cloud between herself and McDermott.

"Ma'am, my concern rests in when your husband learned about my fellow inspector and me from being assigned to Aberdeen from Scotland Yard," McDermott said.

"Logan worked in the Admin office of the District; he saw everything," she said, blowing smoke into the air. "If someone called in or a shred of paper moved from one chap to another, my Logan had knowledge of it; he was smart like that."

"Yes ma'am, I'm sure your husband was keen on many things, but my partner and I don't work for Police Scotland. Like I said, we're here from London; we're assigned to Scotland Yard," he said, the cigarette smoke now causing his eyes to sting and water.

"That would nae matter, someone would say something, and my Logan, he's keen at remembering everything."

McDermott nodded as Maggie took another drag on her cigarette. Noticing a few photos of a gentleman holding up a fair-sized salmon, he saw an opportunity. "Did your husband ever talk with any dockworkers or maybe the men working the boats about the best place to fish?" McDermott asked.

"Aye, he'd talk with them all the time. He even went out once or twice when they were just fishing off the coast. Logan went even though he gets seasick something fierce," she said with a laugh. "We were down in the Mediterranean sailing on one of those fancy cruise ships and all he'd did was hug the throne."

"I understand the feeling, ma'am," McDermott replied. "I served in the Royal Navy on a cruiser some years back." In the Med on a cruise ship, he thought. There's possibly a connection to what the French are working. "Aye, I recall some of the young seamen having to try coping with the rough seas too."

A small clock chimed on the mantle, giving McDermott an excuse to end his questioning and return to the fresher air. Glancing over the scribble of words in the notebook he had lifted from Fletcher, McDermott decided he'd never get the sergeant's wife to admit her husband's involvement in wrongdoing. "I apologize for the intrusion, ma'am, and I thank you for your time," he said. He began walking toward the door.

"My Logan did nothing wrong, Inspector. I'd wager my father's pension on it," Maggie Wallace said, closing the door behind him.

After returning from seeing Sergeant Wallace's wife, McDermott briefed his partner on his hypothesis of the drug traffickers and dockworkers knowing about their investigation. Neither inspector was scheduled to testify against the former sergeant, allowing them time to conduct another round of questions with the workboat captains.

Stepping hastily out of the police car, the two inspectors walked along Albert's Quay, heading straight to the support boat, *Nordic Supplier*. As they reached the vessel, they could see a lone petite figure of a deckhand looking away from them and out past the harbor's entrance.

"What makes you so keen on this captain being involved?" Fletcher asked, trotting to keep up with his partner's pace.

"He's got his arm around the good sergeant holding a fifteen-pound salmon," McDermott said. "The last time I spoke with him, he didn't appear chummy like he was with Wallace." Approaching the workboat, McDermott slowed his pace, much to Fletcher's relief, who could now catch his breath.

"Ahoy there! Is Cap'n Duncan onboard?" McDermott shouted across the deck.

Hearing the hail, Seaman Carr spun around to see the two inspectors. One was dressed like a scruffy panhandler in his faded and stained field coat, while the other was more businesslike, attired in sports coat, and pressed trousers. Each man stood side-by-side at the dockside, with a foot on the rail ready to step onto the vessel's deck. "Aye, who's asking, though?" she asked.

"Chief Inspector McDermott, Scotland Yard," McDermott said showing the young woman his credentials.

"Show them to the bridge wing, Seaman Carr," came the voice over the external speakers onboard the boat.

Squinting up at the bridge windows, the seaman could see the faint image of Captain Duncan standing with the microphone in his hand. "If you'll follow me, it's this way," she said, walking towards the ladder leading to the bridge wing. "Mind your step, though." She pointed out several spots glistening with a mixture of spilled fuel oil and water.

Scampering up the steps, the seaman stood to wait for the inspectors to finish making their way to the top. Here she noticed Fletcher's pale complexion and the way he seemed to take each step more cautiously than the previous one. "Are you nae feeling well, Inspector?" she asked.

"I'm fine," he said. "It's just been a while since I was last aboard a vessel." He made his way to the overhanging bridge wing. Each step required him to work keeping the bile down, nausea stemming from his motion sickness.

Captain Duncan opened the bridge door and stepped out onto the platform, his briar pipe in hand, its contents smoldering. "That'll be all, Carr," he said, dismissing the young woman. "Now, what can I do for you today, Inspector McDermott?" he asked, leaning against the rail and looking back at McDermott.

"I'm following up on a comment made by someone we've questioned," the inspector said, looking at the water below the bridge wing. "Have you offered your services or the boat to do any fishing?"

After a deep drag on his pipe, the tobacco sizzling as the air drew past it, Clive asked, "You fancy going out? I can recommend someone if you are, but this boat's not for that type of hire."

Fletcher looked at the captain, steely-eyed and confident, a stream of tobacco smoke wafting from his lips. *He sounds too sure like he knows what questions we'd be asking him,* he thought.

51

Standing downwind, he caught the scent of the pipe tobacco, which reminded him of ceremonial incense used in Buddhist temples.

Maintaining his gaze on the seafarer, McDermott replied to the captain's question. "I was thinking you might have had a few of the local citizens or even some constables out in the past," McDermott said. "Maybe a charity trip of some sort for doing a good job, that sort of thing."

Rising away from the railing, Captain Duncan took his pipe, tapping the bowl on his boot, spilling the smoldering tobacco into the water before responding. "As I said, this boats not hired out for private fishing. I captain this vessel to service the rigs," he said, waving his hands towards the open waters of the North Sea, "not to have someone bring home a fish supper. Now, if there's nothing else, I have a supply run to prepare for."

After hearing the captain dismiss him and his partner, McDermott bid farewell. "Thank you for your time, Captain. If I have any more questions, I'll be sure to contact you before arriving. Let's go, Andrew," He turned to make his way down the ladder to the working deck below and the docks.

Captain Duncan watched as the two inspectors made their way off the boat before he reentered the bridge. He picked up the ship-to-shore handset from its cradle and prepared to place a call to his contact in Northern Ireland.

"He seemed pretty cocksure of himself," Fletcher said as he followed McDermott to the police car, glad to be off the vessel, his nausea slowly ebbing away.

"Aye, too sure," McDermott said. "Didn't we have a list of calls showing the sergeant contacting the vessels?"

"Yes," Fletcher said. "We were to have the listing yesterday, but I don't recall getting anything from the lab."

"Well, then get on the phone and find out from Inspector McIntyre where they are. I want to see who was contacting this Cap'n Duncan," McDermott said, pulling open the car door and sliding behind the wheel.

After returning to the station, each inspector entered the foyer of police headquarters, splitting up before they reached the detective's office. Inspector Fletcher made his way to the forensics lab to speak with Chief Inspector McIntyre about the phone reports. Bumping into him at the counter was Devin, one of the young technicians.

"Afternoon, Inspector Fletcher." he said. "If you're looking for Inspector Gordon, she's out running an errand, I'm afraid."

"I'm not here to see her, Devin," Fletcher said. "CI McIntyre was to have a packet with listings available for McDermott and me; do you know if he's finished putting them together?"

"I'm not sure but let me ask him; he's in the back vault," the technician said, walking away from the counter.

Pacing about the room, Fletcher considered the possibility of the vessel captain still withholding information pertinent to activities relating to the investigation. *If a worker on the docks knows which deckhand is handing off the drugs, and the captain directs the deckhand...* he thought to link each step through a logical sequence. Then the captain is the key behind the trafficking, but who's directing the captain? He was pondering the question as Devin returned from the backroom of the lab.

"Here you go, inspector," Devin said, handing Fletcher a packet of files from under the counter.

"Thank you," Fletcher said as he signed for the evidence.

Fletcher returned to his desk in the detective's office and pulled out the files. Scanning each list of calls, he noted those made by the sergeant to the Coast Guard and Maritime Agency office. As he came across one, he highlighted each instance, trying to find a pattern.

McDermott entered the room carrying two cans of soda and saw Fletcher poring over the files. "Anything jump out and bite you?" he asked, handing over one of the drinks.

"It looks like the sergeant made two calls a week, over a six-week period," Fletcher said, pointing to the highlighted numbers. "And the dates look to line up with our first encounter with the French or Arab gentleman, the dock hands, and Sutherland."

"So, he calls twelve times, but who is he talking to?" McDermott asked, circling the desks in the office.

"All we have is the call from the cell phone to the office; there's no mention of a specific vessel."

"Aye, lad, but we've got the timestamp when the call was made and received. Plus, the office logs from their communication center will show the vessel receiving the call," McDermott said. He recalled how each time he sent a message while on the HMS *Edinburgh* it was recorded at each communication site. "Come on, it's time for more detective work." He grabbed his field coat off the chair and headed out the door, leaving the sodas on their desks.

Chapter Six

Sauntering into the Coast Guard and Maritime Agency building, McDermott went straight to the communications office, with Fletcher a few paces behind him. Opening the door, they found the clerk, Nora Moffett, sitting at the front counter.

"Can I help you gentlemen?" she asked.

"Aye, you can," McDermott said, pulling out his credentials.

Nora sat frozen in her chair, *they've come for me*, she thought. *I'm going to jail for sure.* She was certain they knew she had passed along information to outside sources illegally and someone was paying her for it.

"We've got a need to examine your communication logs, beginning with the ones from the first week of April until last Monday."

Hearing McDermott asking about the logs and not her activities made her relax enough to collect her wits. "And you have a summons from the court?" she asked, knowing she couldn't turn over the information without proper authority.

"They've got the proper authority," a voice said from behind Inspector Fletcher. Turning, both of the men saw Ailene O'Leary, McDermott's love interest, standing in the door, and holding a red folder up in her hands for them to see. "I've just received it, Nora. Let them read the logs for as long as necessary. Mind you, the original logs don't leave the office, though."

"Of course, Miss O'Leary, I'll get them pulled right away," Nora replied.

"Inspector McDermott, I'll need you to sign a copy of the summons for our record," Ailene said, playing the charade for her co-worker. "If you'll please follow me inspector," stepping into the hallway.

McDermott followed her down the hall, leaving Fletcher alone with Nora.

Ailene held the door to her office open until McDermott had entered before closing it behind him.

"What's this all about, hen?" he asked.

"Nora is the one I suspect as the mole," she said. "You are here to gather evidence to arrest her, aren't you?"

"Nae this moment, but if we've got the evidence, we'll be back," McDermott said. "Now let's look at this summons, shall we?" he said, taking the folder from her hands. Upon opening the folder, he discovered it was empty.

"You can go to jail for this, you know," he said. His tone was serious and official.

"Aye, I know. But like I said, when I saw you heading to the office, I thought you were coming for Nora," Ailene said, sounding somewhat guilty.

Back in the communications office, Nora Moffett placed the last of the files onto the public computer terminal for Fletcher to access. "Each file is labeled by date, beginning with calls on Sunday at 0000 hours, finishing at the end of the week on Saturday at 2359 hours."

"Thank you," Fletcher said. He took off his coat and sat down in front of the terminal. He pulled out his notebook and turned to the dates and times Sergeant Wallace called the agency and searched for the corresponding information file. May 11, *Standard-Hercules*, Captain B. McIntosh, 2:30 min was the first communication he found of the calls coincided with a service boat. *We've got the date, the vessel, and the party he talked to*, he thought, *but not the text*. Turning, Fletcher asked, "Do you have any of the calls recorded?"

"Yes, all communications are recorded and kept with call transcripts stored in Newcastle," Nora replied. She got up and returned to the terminal where Fletcher sat. "Here," she said, opening the folder on the computer. "These here are copies of the recordings for the dates you mentioned." She moved the audio files onto the desktop and provided a set of headphones for the inspector. "Hope you enjoy the banter," she said, leaving the inspector alone so he could listen.

Shifting the earpieces over his head, Fletcher found the audio file and hit play. Two voices came through after the communication technician placed the shore-to-ship call. It was the captain of the *Hercules* and Sergeant Wallace.

"McIntosh speaking," answered the vessel's master, Bernard McIntosh.

"Campbell and Jones need to contact Sutherland no earlier than half past three to meet the supplier." It was Sergeant Wallace's voice

Fletcher was hearing, not in a hushed tone, but guarded. He realized this while leaning towards the computer, assuming it would help with the transmission.

"We'll be in the evening of the twelfth. Out," was the captain's response before the recording stopped. Fletcher made note of the names and the time, confirming what they had suspected: the former constable had ties with the drug traffickers.

Reading over his shoulder, McDermott did his best not to disturb the young inspector lest he scare him while writing. Feeling the gentle tap on his shoulder, Fletcher slid off the chair onto the floor, tossing off the headphones. "Damn you, Conor! Give me a warning, will you?"

McDermott could tell Fletcher was embarrassed for being surprised.

"Aye, sorry about that, lad; I'll nae do it again," he said. "So, what have you got there?"

Fletcher pulled the chair back to the computer and sat down again. "Sounds like the former sergeant made a call, two days before we observed Sutherland. He knew of 'the supplier', which the French have identified as Remesy, meaning he had knowledge of the drug trafficking."

Working his hands through his hair, McDermott closed his eyes, mentally attempting to line up puzzle pieces, with Fletcher handing him another piece. "We've got him talking with which captain?" McDermott asked.

"McIntosh, of the *Standard-Hercules*," Fletcher said, referring to his notes on the desk.

"Aye, but not the one we had the call on, but the sister ship," McDermott said, pacing about the small space of the office. "But we've got notices of the captains working in the same area with the French freighter."

"So, maybe they transfer the drugs among themselves after meeting the freighter?" Fletcher asked, trying to decipher McDermott's thoughts.

"We need to find out if the good constable talked with the *Standard-Apollo*," McDermott said. "And I'm considering we add the *Nordic-Supplier* to the list." Cap'n Duncan did nae appear keen to discuss anything at all the other day, McDermott recalled, making the captain a suspect of wrongdoing.

After listening to seven of the other eleven recordings, they had solidified their case against the former constable. On the eighth recording, the inspectors caught a break, hearing a conversation between the captain of the *Nordic Supplier*, Clive Duncan, and an Irishman who identified himself as "Mr. Higgins."

"Are you thinking what I'm thinking, Andrew?" McDermott asked. "Did we just get a name of the buyer?"

"It sounds possible. I mean, our information from Portsmouth mentioned an Irishman being the money behind the drugs," Fletcher said, leaning back in the chair.

"We need to get all the files together and let MacCallum know what we've found," McDermott said. The giddiness in his voice was unmistakable at having a puzzle piece fit neatly into a void.

After dropping off the recordings to the forensics lab for cataloging, McDermott and Fletcher were sitting in Chief MacCallum's office discussing their newfound evidence.

"While questioning the sergeant's missus earlier today, I saw him, arm-in-arm with one of the boat captains," McDermott said. "So, after we rechecked the numbers from the calls he made, we came across several to the Coast Guard and Maritime Agency."

"Sounds odd since we'd rely on our own water patrol for anything," MacCallum said. "What else did you find?"

"Well, sir," Fletcher said, "after we identified specific dates and numbers, we contacted the agency and found they've recordings and transcripts of all calls."

"Recordings? We've got the sergeant speaking to the captain?" MacCallum asked. "Is there anything can be used in the trial?"

"Yes, we've got the lot," McDermott said. "Not only with the captain, but with the Sutherland lad too. And we stumbled across a call from the boat captain of the *Nordic Supplier* alluding to an Irishman named Mister Higgins."

"We'll need to read Hamilton in on this so he can use it against the sergeant," MacCallum said.

"Aye, but we'll need to be careful," McDermott said. "We din nae want to spook this Higgins fella into hiding. He might be the one we heard about in Portsmouth." *Especially if I can prove he had a hand in Edna's death*, he thought.

Fletcher cleared his throat before speaking. "Sir, I recommend we take a day to review the recordings before passing anything to Hamilton," he said. "We've still concerns about possible eavesdropping in the courts from the Sutherland trial we've not closed."

"You're right," MacCallum said, looking over at Fletcher. "I'll have McIntyre and his staff make a list of the recordings. Then we'll list out who he talked to and pass along just what Hamilton needs."

"Just so you understand," McDermott said. "I've taken the liberty of having Constable Smythe make two copies so I can send one set to Mister Collingsworth in London."

"Aye, good call, Inspector. We'd be remiss if we didn't let Will know what was going on," MacCallum said. "I also finished reading your report on the evidence found on the derrick. You're right about the first officer's observations regarding the derrick trespassers. We need to take into consideration the persons operating this supposed drug lab won't be happy seeing someone mucking up their site."

"But didn't we have the Navy policing the derricks after their encounter with the freighter?" Fletcher asked.

"According to your office in London, they have informed the Admiralty, but there are only so many patrol craft to monitor the derricks, not to mention the service boats coming from here and Inverness," MacCallum said. "Still, we need to be diligent with our investigations here. So, both of you get back at it while we've still got a few hours left in the day," promptly dismissing the inspectors.

Chapter Seven

After leaving behind the two dock workers to mull over his offer, Dunbar returned to his hotel and readied himself for the evening's task. He pulled out the large case from the closet and opened it to retrieve his cleaning gear.

Relaxing at the table, he laid his handgun and silencer down and unrolled the container and its contents. Breaking down the pistol, Dunbar went over each part, first with a brush and again with a cloth moistened in lubricant. Whenever he cleaned one of his many weapons, his thoughts turned to his time in the Army and his First Sergeant.

The senior member of the unit was always admonishing him and his squad for having filthy weapons. Insisting it would be their failure if they had to defend themselves. *Cocky little Welshman, for all lecturing he bought the farm in Londonderry when his rifle jammed from using too much lubricant*, he thought to himself. Wiping the last pieces down, Dunbar reassembled the pistol, satisfied with his devotion to being comprehensive and thorough when dealing with all his weaponry.

Several hours passed as Dunbar lay resting in the darkened hotel room. With his head propped on the pillow, he visualized the manner would dispatch the two dockworkers. His normal routine was always to take at least two to three days to plan the ambush of his victim (or victims). However, it wouldn't be in this case.

Dunbar knew the best approach would be to show up after them, realizing they'd be on edge to the encounter. Though he was not familiar with the surroundings of the meeting place, he felt confident his skill and knowledge in close-quarter combat would serve him well.

The worst-case scenario would have him meet the two longshoremen at the same time outside the signal house, without being able to surprise them. His watch chimed as the alarm he set for eight o'clock sounded. "No time like the present," he said, picking up his firearm from the table.

Walking past the valet station, Dunbar waved his arm, signaling a taxi coming up the avenue to the hotel and was relieved to see the driver was older than most. Getting in the back, he directed the driver to head for the south jetty. Pulling out some money from his billfold, he slid one of the bills to the driver. "There's fifty quid now, and fifty more when I tell you to stop," Dunbar told the driver.

As he spied the money and heard the request, the driver gave a wry smile, showing a few gaps where teeth once were, before answering. "Nae worries, governor," the driver said as he pulled his taxi away from the curb.

After twenty minutes of skirting the evening traffic through town, the taxi approached the entrance of the signal house. "Pull into the car park there," Dunbar said, pointing to the lot of gravel with a few cars parked facing the waters of the North Sea. "Here's the other fifty. Remember, I'm a ghost and you're a shadow, understand?" Dunbar asked the driver.

"Aye, I'm a shadow," the driver said, glancing at the fare of nine-quid, but pocketing ninety for his troubles.

After getting out of the car, Dunbar shoved his hands into his pockets and began walking towards the breakwater. Lights glistened and reflected off the water of a passing service boat as it sailed out into the North Sea. The breeze was cool as it swept over the shoreline before rolling over the jetty, its finger of concrete damp as the waves of the incoming tide splashed against the rocks.

As Dunbar approached the signal house, he noticed just one window facing the roadway; with it a glow cast a beam of light in the growing darkness. A few steps away was the door, its paint faded and peeling, a telltale sign the entrance was constructed from wood.

Sidestepping away from the light, Dunbar reached behind his back, pulling out his pistol. With cautious and deliberate steps, he soon found himself leaning against the concrete wall of the building, partially hidden from the roadway and car park he'd just walked from twenty minutes prior. He could hear muffled voices coming from the lone window.

"He's late, and I don't like it," Jimmy said, pacing about the room.

"Aye, I'm nae happy about it either, Jimmy," Allen Doyle said. "But with Sutherland sitting in the jail, we're running out of options for getting the hashish to the dealers. If this fella can get us a wee bit, then we'll keep the lads at bay, heh?" he said, sitting at the only table in the room."

Jimmy pulled a chair out and sat across from his friend. "Still, I'm nae feeling good about this," he said. "Sutherland has only been in the lockup for two or three weeks, and now this fella comes outta nowhere to feed us. Something's nae good about it, I'm saying."

Doyle looked at his friend and felt the same thing but was reluctant to voice it. He was feeling the pressure of being the only person moving drugs about the waterfront. It was after he promised the addition of hashish to his list of illicit drugs that the pressure grew to the breaking point.

Dunbar edged his way along the wall to just outside the window. Glancing at the two men in the room, he began analyzing the scene, pondering his next step. Figuring out where the table was from the sole entrance, he recognized where his shooting lanes would be once he entered.

Crouched down, he duck-walked below the window to avoid being seen by the two men from the docks. Standing up alongside the doorway he stopped and listened again for the voices. Dunbar took one last glance about the grounds, the darkness growing in the fading summer light, making sure no one observed him enter.

Raising his foot high in the air, Dunbar brought it hard against the wooden door. As it crashed open, Allen Doyle and Jimmy Keller both reacted to the noise, making his action that much simpler.

With years of practice on the firing range at the barracks located in Hereford, Dunbar's skill with a pistol showed itself. In a matter of moments, he had dropped both longshoremen, putting two rounds each in both of their heads. Even with his weapon equipped with a silencer, the shooting sounded like cannon fire echoing off the walls.

Dunbar stepped back to the broken door and switched off the lights. Pulling out a small flashlight, he walked back to where the bodies lay, the pool of blood growing larger beneath the wounds. Pausing over the remains, he fired an additional round through the heart of each man for safe measure.

Aiming his flashlight at the floor, he scanned the area around the bodies. Dunbar spied the spent casings from his pistol and picked them up, placing them in his pants pocket, feeling the warmth of the casing through the fabric. Reaching into his jacket, he pulled out a small bag of marijuana and some rolling papers, which he then tossed onto the table. Next, he pulled a small hard case out and opened it, dumping used syringes, two bent spoons and a candle onto the table.

As he bent over the body of Allen Doyle, he reached into his pants pockets, where he found the keys to the car belonging to the longshoreman parked behind the signal house.

Walking to the doorway, Dunbar spied the few cars parked at the pull-out along the street. No one new came in, and no one seemed to notice anything, as he walked along the path running behind the signal house, and into Doyle's car.

After nearly an hour after dispatching the two longshoremen, Dunbar pulled into the long-term car park adjacent to the airport. Once he found an empty space, he parked and locked the car. The roar of a Ryanair flight masked the sound of the spent shell casings being dropped into the sewer as Dunbar made his way to the terminal and a taxi ride back to the city.

***

Most evenings, civilian volunteers making up the Coast Guard Auxiliary had little excitement while executing their duties. However, tonight, the evening patrol would have something to discuss over their pints later.

"Police Scotland, Aberdeen; please state your emergency."

"Aye, this Officer Connelly of the Coast Guard Auxiliary; I've got two dead bodies at the signal house at the south breakwater."

"Excuse me?" the operator said. "You said you have two dead bodies at the signal house?"

"Aye, cool and stiff they are," Officer Connelly remarked.

"All right, I'll dispatch officers; please wait outside for their arrival."

"No worries, Constable," he said, glancing at the busted doorway which led to the corpses lying inside. "I'll nae be going in there anytime soon."

After what seemed to be nearly hour, but was actually less than five minutes, constables from the Victoria Station arrived on the scene. The senior officer, Constable Sergeant McCord began directing the others to cordon off the crime scene. As two officers began extending the familiar yellow tape carried by most agencies around the building, he walked to the civilian patrol and began to take his statement.

It wasn't long before the forensics team, led by Chief Inspector Graham McIntyre, arrived and the grim process of removing the bodies and collecting evidence began. The news of the murders and the location even drew out the senior officer, Superintendent MacCallum of the Aberdeen police.

"Well, Chief Inspector, what do we have?" MacCallum asked McIntyre, stepping into the room and standing beside him.

McIntyre had been crouched down, examining the area where the bodies had fallen, when he heard MacCallum's voice. Standing, he turned to face the superintendent. "Someone was waiting for the right time before taking action on these two," McIntyre said. "We found footprints outside the window leading to the doorway; it looks like just one gunman." He pointed to the remnants of the wooden door hanging on its hinges.

"It was a professional job, in my opinion, that's for sure. We've scoured the whole room inside and the grounds outside, and yet we've not found any shell casings. Nevertheless, each victim is sporting two shots on the forehead and one in the chest. Not to mention they appear to be from a large caliber handgun."

"Based on the spray pattern, the blokes were sitting across from each other at the table, before falling backwards." McIntyre shined his laser pointer on the floor and wall behind the chalk outlines. "Further, we've got what appear to be fresh tire tracks behind the building, but no vehicle. It sounds reasonable that whoever did the shooting likewise has these poor blokes' motor."

"A professional hit, you say?" MacCallum asked with a hint of reluctance.

"Aye, sir, it's the only reason to have a crime scene with nae shell casings, but two dead guys," McIntyre said. "Because of that, I believe it points to a pro cleaning up after himself. When you take in the fact we've got the remains of drug paraphernalia laid upon the table, seems pretty certain."

Before Superintendent MacCallum could ask another question, Chief Inspector McDermott and his partner Inspector Fletcher stepped through the doorway.

"Glad to see your timely arrival, McDermott," MacCallum said.

"Aye, we would have been here sooner, but we were being handed our summons for court," McDermott said. "I take it this has something to do with our investigation from Portsmouth?"

MacCallum blinked at hearing the vague rebuke from the Scotland Yard inspector but held his comments for later. "There's always the possibility this investigation can provide substance to yours," he said.

Fletcher stepped carefully about the room, taking in the carnage, writing down several notes regarding what he saw. "Who were the victims?"

"A very good question, Inspector," the chief said, and turned to the uniformed officer. "Do we know their identities?"

Sergeant McCord stepped forward, opening his notebook. "Aye, sir, one of the deceased was a bloke named Allen Doyle, and the other was James Keller, both residents of Inverness."

"They came a long way from home only to end up dying here in a derelict signal tower," Fletcher said.

McDermott's interest was piqued at the mention of the city. "You said one was Doyle? Do we know what they did for a living?"

"Aye, sir, both are—sorry, were—registered longshoreman working for Chevron-Europe, here in Aberdeen," the sergeant said, handing over their seamen's cards.

"Seems we do have a link to your investigation after all, McDermott," MacCallum said. "I'd think it necessary to look into these two as part of the drug traffickers, don't you think?"

McDermott, fuming over being led by the nose on his own investigation looked at Superintendent MacCallum. "Aye, sir, they might be; but then again, they might not," he said. "But we just had a wee run in with Doyle the other day. He was working the receiving yard when we tailed the supply truck," McDermott added. "Andrew, make a note to look into the fella Keller's' work area. We'll check on it first thing in the morning."

"With the way they died, it suggests they pissed in someone's garden," the senior police official said. "Let me know if there's anything significant, will you, Chief?" He turned away and walked out.

"Do you think it has anything to dae with the young chap's recent assault trial and the drugs?" Sergeant McCord asked.

"Good question, Sergeant," McIntyre said, pulling off his gloves. "A very good question indeed."

"I'd nae be so quick to link the two," McDermott said as he began walking about the crime scene. "Do either of you see this as 'too convenient'?" He gestured toward the table. "It's like the killing of Baxter; he just happened to have some drugs on him too."

"You mean someone is doing the killings as a distraction to our investigation?" Fletcher asked.

"Aye, it's possible," McDermott said, folding his arms across his chest. He scratched his chin and closed his eyes, visualizing the puzzle pieces sitting on a table. Some pieces were scattered while others lay attached together forming brief glimpses of the finished picture.

"The only common thread amongst the recent victims has been the waterfront," McIntyre said, interrupting McDermott's thoughts. "I'll admit the discovery of the drugs tonight seemed a little far-fetched for the victims."

"How so?"

"They looked healthier than most drug users," McIntyre said. "People who use marijuana are more into the drug for its recreational appeal. But the heroin user, that's hard-core, and these two didn't appear to be in that category."

"That feeds your suspicion of the killing being done by a professional," McDermott said. "The killing was done to send a message to someone," he added.

"But who?" Fletcher asked. "Sutherland is on trial along with the three other longshoremen, so they're not a threat."

"They're a threat to the supplier if they talk," McDermott said. "And we're no closer to finding them as we were three months ago."

"You don't think the Frenchman could authorize the killings?" Fletcher asked.

"Aye, it's possible," McDermott said, his voice growing steadily louder. "And it could be this Irish chap we've yet to identify too. Why don't we add the constable while we're at it, just to avoid being embarrassed!" While McIntyre and Sergeant McCord looked on, McDermott made his way outside before he said something regrettable in front of the other officers.

"I'm just thinking aloud, mind you," Fletcher said, following his partner.

"Well, then mind you think clearly and with purpose," McDermott said as he pulled the door open to the car. "Come on, we've enough fun for the night; I'll drop you off at Sheila's flat."

As he drove through the outskirts of town, McDermott's head spun with the number of possible scenarios connecting the drug dealers and the killings. He knew Fletcher was right to mention the Frenchman, Remesy. His frustration grew from not being able to establish a substantial link between their first encounter with Sutherland and Remesy with anything since the first encounter.

As he pulled the car in front of the complex where Inspector Sheila Gordon lived, he turned to his partner. "Don't forget to be at the courthouse early, so we can get a good seat," he said. "And make sure you wear your Sunday best too."

Chapter Eight

Inspectors McDermott and Fletcher stepped into the court where they saw Superintendent MacCallum discussing an issue with prosecuting lawyers, Hamilton and St. James, sitting at the barristers' table.

"Looks like they're about to start," Fletcher said.

"Aye, but I need a minute to let MacCallum know what we've found," McDermott replied. He began walking to the front of the public seating.

Stepping away from the barrister's desk, Superintendent MacCallum approached McDermott, who was standing behind the rail dividing the court members and the public. "You've something to report, Inspector McDermott?"

"Aye, we've found more information that the sergeant communicated with Sutherland and the supply crafts," McDermott said, looking past the chief and at Hamilton and St. James. "It's rough evidence, but we'll have it separated out in a day."

"I'll need to let Hamilton know," MacCallum said, turning back to where the barristers sat.

Just then, Priscilla El-Sayad and Sean Gilmore—counselors for Constable Logan Wallace— entered, pressing their way past police officers before taking their places opposite Hamilton and St. James. As the constables escorted Logan Wallace to the panel's stand, Sean stepped up and murmured something in his ear. This caused Logan to pull back from him, McDermott noticed.

At that moment the macer entered, calling the court to order as Lord Maxwell took his place and the room became hushed. "Is the prosecutor prepared to proceed?" the justice asked.

"We are, my Lord," Hamilton said, standing at his table.

"And is the defense prepared to proceed?" he asked, looking at Priscilla and Sean.

Standing behind their table, Priscilla rose. "We are, my Lord. However, I'd like to request a twenty-four-hour continuance. This will provide for the disposition of witnesses just furnished by the prosecutor." She held up a copy of the revised witness list.

The judge glanced at the young woman and then at Hamilton before giving his direction. "I'll grant your request, Miss El-Sayed. Upon completion of testimony today, the court will reconvene at nine o'clock on Thursday. If that's all, Mister Hamilton, you may proceed."

"Thank you, my Lord. The Crown calls Constable Sergeant Marcus Giles to the platform."

Hearing his name, Sergeant Giles rose from his place and entered the witness box to be sworn in by the clerk. For the next ninety minutes, Hamilton asked mundane questions, confirming Giles's working relationship with Logan Wallace and the other constables.

"Sergeant, when were you made aware Scotland Yard had appointed two inspectors to Aberdeen?" the counselor asked. "And did you know they were in Aberdeen investigating drug trafficking?"

"It was about the first week of June. We'd received a request for help from Chief Inspector McDermott at Albert's Quay," the sergeant said. "That's the first I knew of he and Inspector Fletcher working here in Aberdeen." He then nodded toward the officers located in the front row. "We supported the detention of three men assaulting another that transpired during the inspector's surveillance activities."

Priscilla wrote her notes on the tablet as the sergeant gave his testimony. She wrote in English so Sean could read it: why the mystery by Scotland Yard? Did they know of something developing in the District Office of Aberdeen, maybe? She glanced at Sean, who just shrugged and shook his head.

"That'll be all, sergeant, thank you," Hamilton said.

"Miss El-Sayad, do you wish to dispose of the witness?" the judge asked.

"Yes, my Lord," she said, opening up her notes and stepping to the platform.

"Sergeant before you gave aid, did your superintendent inform you that two inspectors from Scotland Yard had been dispatched to Aberdeen?" she asked.

"No, he didn't," Marcus said, looking over at the senior officer, who just gave a brief nod.

"If the inspectors weren't recognized by the personnel at the district office; where were they working from?" Priscilla asked.

"I heard from Sergeant McCord they'd found office area at the Victoria Road site for them to work out of, being near the docks," the sergeant said.

"And you're saying they never had a reason for being at the district offices?"

"No, ma'am."

As the examination of the sergeant went on, both prosecuting lawyers looked at each other, seeking to understand where Priscilla was heading with her examination of the constable. Watching the woman, Hamilton thought to himself, these sound like simple questions, but what's her game?

"Sergeant Giles. If Inspectors McDermott and Fletcher worked from the Victoria Road location, how come no one saw Inspector Fletcher meeting Inspector Gordon in the district forensics lab?" she asked, reading her notes.

Fletcher sat upright at the sound of the question and his partner's name. He leaned forward in his chair, aching to listen, struggling to capture every word uttered between the barrister and the constable. What is she getting at? he thought. Is she seeking to drag Sheila in on Wallace's traitorous activities?

"Inspector Gordon was just awarded a promotion to the district office from Victoria Road Station because of a vacancy," Giles said. "She's only been there for the last three and half weeks, I'd say. Until then, she was in charge of the forensics lab at Victoria Station."

"I see. Curious that such a junior officer knew of the members of Scotland Yard before someone like yourself," Priscilla said.

"Aye, well, from what I've been told from Sergeant McCord, they've been seeing each other for a fortnight or two," Sergeant Giles answered.

Sean Gilmore sat back, listening to the discussion, recognizing that his employer, Mister Higgins, had condoned the effort to defame the police by pointing out the relationship between the two officers.

"So, it's possible Inspector Fletcher, as a senior officer with Scotland Yard, could have persuaded her when dealing with evidence?" Priscilla asked.

"Not likely, ma'am. Inspector Gordon is a stickler for protocol and policies, she'd nae give in to making errors or skipping steps when it comes to evidence," Giles replied.

Hamilton stood abruptly from his chair. "I object to this line of questioning, your Lordship. It has no relevance to the case," he said.

"Your honor," Priscilla said, "you've already ruled on the evidence presented to the government by Police Scotland. My questioning will point out that the incident evidence in custody by the government is not correct or complete," she replied.

"I'm noting your objection, Mister Hamilton," Lord Maxwell said. "I'm further warning the defense to continue its line of questioning by concentrating on the case and evidence presented and not hearsay."

"Yes, your Lordship," Priscilla said, looking at her notes. Smiling inward, she knew she'd just accomplished planting a seed of suspicion in the minds of the jurors. "Sergeant Giles, from what you know, did Sergeant Wallace have any reason or opportunity to offer others information outside the station?" she asked. "Specifically, did he pass along activities concerning the inspectors from Scotland Yard?"

"Not to my knowledge," Giles said. "We'd never been advised as to their activities until the episode on the dock last month."

"Thank you, Sergeant. I've no further questions for this witness, my Lord." Priscilla took her place next to Sean.

"Mister Hamilton, do you have another witness to call forward?" the judge asked.

"Yes, my Lord. The government calls Chief Inspector McDermott to the platform."

As he approached the witness box, McDermott pulled his slacks up while working to straighten up his shirt under his field coat. Once in the witness box, he recounted the witness's oath before Hamilton began his line of questioning.

"Inspector McDermott, given recent testimony, please tell the court what required your presence here in Aberdeen," Hamilton asked. He anticipated that McDermott's answer would bring to rest the questions about Scotland Yard activities in Aberdeen posed by the defense.

"Inspector Fletcher and I were appointed a case involving possible drug trafficking here in Aberdeen," McDermott said. "As part of our investigation, we were conducting surveillance of several parties identified by Aberdeen's Police Scotland constables working the waterfront."

"Can you offer an account why you and Inspector Fletcher were relegated to work from the post on Victoria Road and not the district offices?" Hamilton asked.

"After being briefed in London about our appointment, we were informed to contact Chief Superintendent MacCallum," McDermott said. "After our meeting, he identified the available workspace for us at the Victoria Road station offices. Nothing more than that."

"And this is when Inspector Fletcher met the forensics technician, Inspector Gordon, during your time at the station, isn't it?"

"Yes, but Inspector Gordon hadn't been promoted yet; that came after she was transferred to the district office," McDermott replied.

"Thank you, Inspector," Hamilton said. "I've no further questions for this witness, my Lord."

"Miss El-Sayad, do you wish to depose the witness?" the judge asked.

"Yes, I do, my Lord," she said, stepping to the dais with her notes.

"Inspector, what evidence have you assembled so far in your investigation that might include Sergeant Wallace?" Priscilla asked.

Gazing at the young woman, and then Hamilton and St. James, McDermott thought about the question. He knew they were unaware that McDermott and Fletcher had just come across recordings that included Logan Wallace and the supply boat captains. *I'm nae ready to admit we've got the transcriptions and tapes with the constable on them*, he thought. He cleared his throat. "In a cooperative investigation with Police Scotland," he said, "we've identified calls the constable made to associations operating in Glasgow who have possible links to criminal activities."

Looking down at her notes, then back at Sean, Priscilla continued. "But, Inspector McDermott, how is it the only charge against Sergeant Wallace is 'conduct unbecoming'?" she asked. "There's no mention of unauthorized calls or any mention of connections pertaining to criminal activities," she said.

McDermott sensed the female counselor was backing him into a corner. He took a deep breath before providing his answer. Looking at the government table, and then the public sitting area where

Superintendent MacCallum sat observing the procedures, he stole a moment before responding.

"The charges against the sergeant are based on activities observed by myself, Inspector Fletcher, and Superintendent MacCallum," McDermott said, attempting not to give away too much detail.

"So, Inspector, you're saying the charge against Sergeant Wallace is not based on an observed action, but something as silly as a phone call?" Priscilla asked. Keep walking inspector, she thought I'll jerk the noose around your feet soon enough.

"No," McDermott answered, raising his tone. "What I am telling you is the evidence to submit the charge was on one action and further investigation. It was found out that the former constable had made several calls to identified members of a crime organization," McDermott replied.

Grasping the possible aggression and pride in McDermott's response, Priscilla pressed on with her questioning. "And what are the names of those crime syndicate members Sergeant Wallace communicated with, Inspector McDermott?"

McDermott blinked. He realized that he had just thrown the woman an opportunity that could contribute to disclosing parts of the investigation before they were ready. "I'm not at liberty to discharge this information, as numerous parties are still part of active investigations headed by Scotland Yard and Police Scotland agencies," he said.

"My Lord, I've asked a direct question of the inspector, who's under oath, and I'd like an answer," Priscilla said, looking at the court.

Before the judge could answer, Hamilton rose, near the podium where Priscilla stood. "My Lord," he said. "I request the continuing testimony by Chief Inspector McDermott be taken in closed chambers owing to the nature of the current investigations which are adjoining to this case."

After viewing each of the barristers, Lord Maxwell nodded in understanding. "Further testimony from the witness will be handled without participation by members of the public." He glanced at his timepiece and did a quick mental calculation. "Court is in recess until nine o'clock Thursday morning."

"All rise!" the macer exclaimed. As the attendees stood, the judge and jury retired from the court, while constables escorted Logan Wallace to his holding cell.

McDermott climbed down from the witness box and started heading out of the courtroom. As he passed by Hamilton and St. James, who had sat down in their chairs, he said, "Gentlemen, we need to have a wee chat."

Priscilla came over after McDermott had gone. "What are you seeking to pull off, Mister Hamilton?" Priscilla asked, stepping up to the table.

"You'll need to summon the good inspector," Hamilton said, gathering his notes from the table before trailing after his associate, St. James.

McDermott and Fletcher stood in the barristers' lounge, waiting for Hamilton and St. James to arrive. Before he pulled out a chair, McDermott gave Fletcher his marching orders. "You need to go and ask Chief McIntyre if they've got anything written up on the recordings," he said.

"What are you looking to get from Chief McIntyre?"

"We need to give Hamilton something on Wallace, based on the calls," McDermott said, "but just a wee bit. Nothing too much until we can nail down who the Irishman is." Just at that moment, the lawyers entered the room.

"Ok, McDermott, what do we need to discuss?" Hamilton asked. St. James was standing behind him.

"Go on, Andrew," McDermott said. "I'll be a few minutes."

"I'll be ready when you get to the office," Fletcher replied, walking past the barristers and out of the room.

"Well?" Hamilton asked, pulling out a chair and sitting.

"Just the other day," McDermott said, "Inspector Fletcher came across recordings of Sergeant Wallace talking with people aboard several ships, and he mentioned Sutherland by name during the communication as well."

"I wasn't informed of that, Inspector," St. James said.

"Aye, neither were we," McDermott said. "The crucial thing is the sergeant was conversing with sorts who are part of our current investigation. You just can't hand over everything to the defense. If this woman finds out about other suspects we're investigating, they might just catch wind and flitter away in the current."

Hamilton massaged his temples, attempting to thwart off his headache, as well as consider his options. "We have to show something to the defense in good faith; it's a matter of the statute. The question is, what do we show and how much." Settling back in his chair, he closed his eyes and let out a moan.

"Can't we just use the information from the phone companies?" St. James asked.

"There's already a concern about the substance; the defense has made it obvious to the court," Hamilton snapped back, staring at his assistant. "You and the others need to find out why our copies of the phone logs from the police vary from the defense's copies."

"These recordings are specific to calls between Wallace and two ship captains," McDermott said. "I propose we use the recordings where he reached Captain McIntosh. He and his crew are already in detention."

"But how do we use it against the sergeant, though?" Hamilton asked.

"We've recovered drugs on the ship, based on an anonymous tip," McDermott said. "If the sergeant called the captain, letting him know to transport the drugs, you've got him as an accessory to trafficking."

Hamilton looked at the inspector. He was beginning to see the picture he was producing. "Of course. If we link the sergeant to the confiscated drugs, then you can return to your investigation against the others," he said.

"But what about these 'crime syndicates' you mentioned in court?" St. James said. "They're a matter of record now; you have to disclose them when the judge asks."

"Aye, but it'll just be a handful in the room, nae the town folk sitting in the pen," McDermott said. "And you've already advised the court his cousin will be present, too, I understand?"

"He's expected to appear during the next session," St. James said, checking his notes.

"You think someone is communicating the results of proceedings to these criminal types in Glasgow?" Hamilton asked.

"Aye, I spied the young fella who bested St. James here sitting in the back of the room."

"You mean Forbes?" St. James said bitterly. "How can you be so certain?"

"Aye, trust me, sure enough, it's him," McDermott said. "So, tell me, why would he be sitting in the back? Shouldn't he be getting another case ready? Or maybe even go out and have a wee celebration for getting his client off the charges?"

St. James was ready to defend the point of celebrating when Hamilton waved his hand, cutting him off. "I've got a colleague in the Public Office; I'll inquire—discreetly, of course—what Forbes's caseload is for the coming weeks."

McDermott got up from the table and headed for the door. "Then we better get on with it; we've only got one day."

***

With a steady push on the massive oaken doors, Inspector Fletcher stepped out of the sheriff's office. As he made his way toward the police station, the recognizable note of metal striking metal caused him to duck through sheer instinct. It was the same noise he heard countless times when Marine snipers he commanded practiced hitting metal discs hidden in the brush.

As he took shelter behind a parked lorry, Fletcher pulled his service pistol from its holster. Glancing around the bottom of the truck, he caught sight of Ewan Sutherland, the drug trafficker, being ushered out of the building by two constables. Before he could call out a warning, a woman shrieked as the side of Sutherland's head burst from another bullet's impact.

"Everybody, take shelter!" Fletcher shouted. "Get down!" He drifted along the truck's side while looking up at the rooftops. "Constable, are you injured?" he called out to one of the escorts.

"No," the officer exclaimed, "but where the hell did the bullets come from?" They both looked down at the face of the other escort. They could both see the unresponsive eyes staring upwards and the pool of blood widening beneath him. It wasn't long before the sound of sirens was reverberating through the streets as more police and emergency crew arrived.

In a tentative fashion, Fletcher stepped away from the truck, gun pointing toward the roofline of each building he looked at. He held his gaze upward sweeping his eyes from the sheriff's office down Union Street, when he paused at the tallest building.

Within minutes after the first shot, McDermott had forced his way past security, going out the entrance to see Sutherland's body behind the constables. "He's dead," McDermott said, more as a proclamation than a question.

"Aye; one shot, one kill," the constable said, kneeling over the body.

Staring up the avenue, McDermott noticed Fletcher making his way towards one of the store entrances. Before he could step off and follow his partner, Sergeant Giles arrived with other officers from the district office.

"Bloody hell, Inspector," the sergeant muttered, looking at the body.

"Go up Shiprow Lane and into the alley, but be careful," McDermott said to the sergeant. "You two," he said, pointing to the other constables, "come with me." They followed him as he made his way towards his partner, who was hurrying towards a row of buildings in the distance.

Chapter Nine

The gunman cursed at his complacency, having mistimed his shot when the proposed target appeared outside the courthouse. As he dismantled the rifle, Dunbar covered the gunstock with a cloth before laying the piece in the mason's bag sitting next to him.

With his back against the roof façade, he searched the gravel, spying the two spent shell casings from the rifle and picked them up. *Damn reflection off the bus*, he thought. He mentally played back the scenario: the chimes of the clock from the chapel, a person pushing the door forward, and the image of a man with sandy-blond hair exiting. However, it was the sudden glare of the morning sun off the bus's windscreen which caused him to squint. His first shot wasn't off its mark by much as it caught the ornate metal railing a half-meter from the entrance. *Good thing it missed*, he thought. When he realized his proposed victim might have accidently become Inspector Fletcher rather than Ewan Sutherland.

With the leather straps pulled together on the weapon bag, Dunbar made his way down four flights of stairs to the alley. As he paused at the bottom, he moved the door open, in order to steal a hurried glance for any police officers who might be milling about. The distant howling of sirens became louder as he stepped out of the building. Dunbar opened the door of the rented panel truck and climbed in, setting the bag next to the seat.

He glanced in the mirrors and started the truck. As he pulled out of the parking area, he saw Sergeant Giles and two other constables enter the alley. Speeding away in the opposite direction, Dunbar pulled out his phone and issued a predetermined note. It read: CLEANING COMPLETED, MOVING ON TO NEXT MEMBER ON THE LIST.

***

Kneeling down, Michael Connelly felt the wind whip across the dunes and cause his golf ball to shift somewhat. His pants fluttered in the gust, delivering a slight chill across his calves. With his putter in hand, he took his stance, maintaining the picture of the ball rolling into the cup in his mind's eye.

"Twenty quid says you miss," one of the playing partners said to him.

"Good enough," Connelly responded as he backed off from the ball.

Going back through his putting routine, he once again stood over the ball, just as the wind died down. With a gentle and steady stroke, he sent the ball rolling until it tumbled into the bottom. "You can pay me at the pub," Connelly said, pulling the ball out of the hole.

As the men paraded to the next teeing ground, Connelly's cell phone chirped in his golf bag. He paused on the walkway, pulled it out, and tapped the message icon it displayed. It was from Angus, letting him know he had disposed of another potential exposure to his project.

His playing partners noted Connelly stopping to look at his phone.

"I'll just be a moment," he said, waving them on while he typed the response: CONTINUE WITH YOUR DUTY, KEEP ME INFORMED. *Two down and two more to go*, he thought as he put the phone back into his bag.

The other golfers stood waiting for him. "Come on, Mick, it's your honor," one said.

"You know we don't want to go against protocol," another piped up. "It's rotten luck to hit before the man who made a birdie on the last hole."

"All right, then," Connelly said, pulling his driver from the bag and teeing his ball up. After several practice swings, he noticed the direction of the wind coming off the Irish Sea. He made sure his alignment was correct as he took his stance. Finally, with a well-timed stroke, he drove the ball, sending it flying down the fairway. "You mean something like that?" he asked, dropping the club back into the bag.

"You need to invest more time in your office," one opponent said. "It's evident you are on the practice ground too much these days."

Michael Connelly just smirked at the compliment. If his golfing friends and fellow Irishmen only knew what he was doing while at the office, they would probably change their minds. After the last man finished teeing off, the four men strolled down the fairway, each one heading towards his golf ball and next shot.

Out of the corner of his eye, Connelly spied a solitary figure trudging through the native shrubbery and grasses, making its way towards him. As the two men approached each other, he could just make out the facial features of his driver Geoff Brennan, who was coming to greet him where his ball had settled in the fairway.

"Sorry for the intrusion, Mr. Higgins," he said. "But Erin received a call from a Mister Liam Finnegan in Dublin. She said he wanted to speak with you about a recent affair."

Connelly stood following the ball of one of the other players as it sailed through the air. A gust of wind came up just as the ball descended, shifting it offline and into a sand trap next to the putting surface. Turning his attention back to Geoff, he held out his golf bag. "Hold this for a moment," he said, and then pulled out his eight-iron from the bag.

After several practice swings, he studied the wind's direction coming off the water. Once he was properly aligned with his target, he stepped up and struck the ball, sending it flying towards the green. With just two hops, the ball stopped before spinning back towards the flagstick, ending a mere six inches from going in the hole.

"Excellent shot, Mr. Higgins," Geoff said.

"We'll head back to the office after I've tapped in," Connelly said, handing Geoff the eight-iron and pulling his putter from the bag. Wandering down the fairway, his mind raced, as he contemplated the need for Liam to contact him. He knew his chemists at the labs in Limerick were already evaluating the consignment of hashish.

As Geoff stood off to one side, Connelly's playing partners stood on the green, producing a round of mock applause at the shot he'd just pulled off.

"Double or nothing on whether I make the putt this time," Connelly said, smirking.

After lamenting to the others for having to leave the match early, Connelly and Geoff were soon on their way back to the office in Belfast. Sitting in the backseat of the vintage Jaguar, he pondered what his operations supervisor in Dublin needed from him. They had devoted several days assessing the method to secure the hashish from the French-Algerian and test it so his pharmaceutical company could produce a counter-drug to fight its addiction.

Geoff maneuvered the executive car to the front of the office building. Before he could get to the passenger's door, Connelly had already stepped out and was making his way through the rotating doors.

In moments, he had entered the offices where his secretary, Erin Malone, met him.

"Was it a satisfactory round, sir?"

"Good enough to steal twenty pounds," he said, opening the door of his personal office. After shedding his windbreaker, he snatched his coffee cup and poured some of his special blended mixture. "Geoff told me Mr. Finnegan called recently," he said.

"Yes, sir," she acknowledged. "But he was hesitant to give me a reason. It was odd; he sounded out of breath like he'd just run a marathon or something of that sort." She passed him the note she'd written.

Connelly took the slip of stationery and gave it a brief glance as he sat down. "I've his number, so I'll see what he requires. Please see I'm not interrupted for the time being."

"Certainly, Mr. Higgins."

Connelly pulled his desk-phone over and dialed the number for his associate. As he took a sip of his coffee, he heard the familiar chirp of the cell carrier signal as his call crossed the imaginary border into Ireland. With just one hundred and four miles separating him from his party to the south, the call was acknowledged after the first ring.

"Hello?" the young Dubliner answered.

"Good afternoon, Liam, it's Mr. Higgins returning your call."

"Thank you for getting back, sir," Liam said. "I thought it would be necessary to update you of an issue the chemists have come across with the latest material."

"You were right to contact me," Connelly said. "Please, go on."

"It would suggest that the blend of hashish has a supplement. It's something the chemists are having a relatively hard time decoding. Their hedging their speculations on some type of hallucinogen was combined by the originator, possibly PCP," he said, taking a deep breath. "They'd like to know what you wish for them to do, seeing you established a deadline of October first."

Connelly closed his eyes upon hearing the statement. His intention was to not only overwhelm the drug cultures in Aberdeen, Edinburgh, and Glasgow with the hashish cocktail, but likewise make his rendition of an antidote ready. If his chemist couldn't detect the specific type and portion of the foreign drug, then he'd have no remedy to market to the hospitals or clinics.

Connelly took a drink of his coffee, mulling over his next remark. "Liam, have the chemists focus on studying this drug as if it were the most common hallucinogen being exploited today." Connelly knew this direction was a long shot, but he was pressed for time to make the release to the numerous drug dealers.

"Certainly, sir," Liam responded. "I'll make sure they know of your wishes."

"And, Liam, let them know there will be a thousand-euro bonus to the first one determining what this drug is," Connelly said, hoping the cash would inspire his chemists to concentrate on their work.

"Yes, sir," Liam said.

"I don't recall hearing of any complications when the material was transported to Dublin. Did everything go as designed?"

"It was rather steady," Liam said. "The only issue I came across was the ship captain expressing a concern with what he carried and when his next task would come about."

"I see," Connelly said. He thought of his discussion with Captain Clive Duncan in Edinburgh when he asked about a responsible captain who could be called upon to move the drugs. The captain said his protégé, Brodie Fraser, was more than capable of accomplishing the task without asking questions. *Seems I'll need to have Angus pay the captain a visit*, he told himself. "I'll see to having the captain reminded about being more restrained," he said.

"If there's nothing else, sir, I need to be getting back to the shop floor," Liam said.

"You're absolutely right, we've got a business to keep afloat," Connelly said. "I'll expect a call from you if there's anything else we need to discuss."

"I'll be sure to ring as soon as possible. Good day to you, sir."

As he sat in his office, Michael Connelly considered his options. He could tell the chemists to strip out the 'unidentified' drug from the hashish so he had a 'saleable' product to keep to his timetable. However, he knew this would just add more of a familiar drug to the metropolises and drag down the cost. It would also preclude his business from selling the countermeasure for the addictive nature of the drug.

He guzzled down the last of his coffee and stabbed the intercom button, summoning his secretary.

"Yes, Mr. Higgins?"

"Erin, could you please contact Mr. Gilmore and have him call me on my private line, oh, let's make it four o'clock this afternoon," he said, looking over his journal.

"Yes, sir. Will that be all?"

"No," he said. "I'd also like you to arrange for a table at the Ginger Bistro for six o'clock."

"Consider it done," Erin said, and clicked off the intercom.

Connelly turned his chair around and gazed at the view of the harbor below. The news that Liam had told him about the mystery substance the French-Algerian supplier, Louis Remesy, had added to the hashish was troublesome. *Why did he do this? What benefit did the drug receive from this addition?* Some questions he knew would be better suited for the analysts and chemists working in the pharmaceutical plant in Limerick.

The flicker of sunlight reflecting off the windows of an approaching jet to the city airport made him squint. *How shall I deal with the young captain Liam mentioned*, he thought? Connelly knew the usefulness of maintaining his anonymity from men like Brodie Fraser was to maintain the upper hand. It was a question of how much pressure to emit so his message would be accepted and adhered to without creating any resistance or retaliation.

"Captain Duncan vouched for the young man; he can be the one to receive the message," he said aloud to the empty office. He went to where his windbreaker hung, reached into the pocket, and found nothing. "Damn!" he blurted out. "Where the hell did I leave my phone?"

He marched out of his office and found Erin shredding files in the corner.

"Erin! Do you know where Geoff has gone?"

She gasped, startled by the sudden intrusion. "He left to put some petrol in the car and get it cleaned up."

"Let me know as soon as he returns, please," Connelly said, clearly distracted.

"Is there anything I can do?"

"No, thank you. I've misplaced my mobile phone, and I'm hoping it just fell in the boot of the car."

He returned to his private office, poured himself another cup of coffee, and began pacing back and forth, bracing for the discussion he would have with Dunbar. He knew Dunbar would ensure the ship captain understood the repercussions. The trouble lay in whether Captain Duncan could influence his protégé in Glasgow before Dunbar would be required to point out the young seafarer's mistake in questioning his position.

Chapter Ten

Chief Inspector McDermott and the two constables accompanying him caught up with Inspector Fletcher just as he was preparing to enter the ground floor of the building. Behind them, the chaotic scene surrounding the sheriff's office had grown larger with the addition of emergency vehicles.

"What are you thinking, lad?" McDermott asked, gasping from the thousand-meter run from the sheriff's office.

"I heard the original shot miss," Fletcher replied in a flat, disciplined tone. "Metal on metal. After a got my bearings, that's when I noticed the second round hit Sutherland." His memory of the impact moved in slow motion, frame by frame. Impact, entry, and suddenly the explosive exit as the sniper's shot did its destruction. The carnage was now a bloody splatter across the stonework of the sheriff's office entrance. "I figured the shots had to have come from above," Fletcher added. "And seeing that this shop is the tallest structure with a perfect line of sight, it looked somewhat obvious to start here."

"Aye, good call," McDermott said, his breathing returning to normal. He turned toward the constables. "You two stay here and make certain no one shows up behind us." He opened his field coat and took out his gun. Once they were able to force the door open, they moved inside the building. Both inspectors proceeded with caution as they stepped through the shop, making certain it was clear before heading towards the next floor.

After carefully searching every story of the building, McDermott and Fletcher reached the rooftop thirty minutes later. As he treaded out of the darkened stairwell, McDermott was overwhelmed by the glare of the morning sunshine. Fletcher exited the doorway next, turning in the opposite direction, gun at the ready for the suspect or suspects. McDermott made his way along the rooftop until he came across a section of disturbed gravel which concealed the underlayment of tar. With care, he moved up to the roof's edge. McDermott looked out and saw that from this spot there was an unobstructed view of the entrance to the sheriff's office.

"Andrew, over here," he said, holstering his pistol.

As Fletcher came over from the other side of the rooftop, he paused a few feet short of where his partner was standing. "The gunman was here," McDermott said, squatting down and pointing at the gravel and exposed tar.

"Seems so," Fletcher responded. Scanning around, he couldn't make out anything out of place except for the gravel. "It appears the shooter knelt here and here," he added, pointing at two spots where someone had forced the gravel away.

"But no brass lying about," McDermott said. "No burned fags to indicate the assassin was waiting longer than a few minutes."

"So, how did the murderer know to be here? Moreover, how did he discover Sutherland was being discharged? I mean, the court suspended his release a day because of a botched set of documents," Fletcher said. "And how was it Sutherland was the victim anyway?"

"Aye, right. Good questions," McDermott replied, looking over the edge again down toward the pavement. "Someone's tidying up a few loose ends. You remain here; I'll go down and have Sergeant Giles fetch one of Inspector McIntyre's team," he said. The increasing wail of sirens signaled the arrival of other officers and an ambulance, which would prove worthless with regard to the fatality.

***

Inspectors McDermott and Fletcher stood behind the crime tape strung across the walkway. Looking on, they observed Chief Inspector McIntyre and Inspector Gordon at the doorway searching for bullet fragments that had killed Ewan Sutherland.

"Seems surreal to watch Sheila working a crime scene, doesn't it?" Fletcher said to McDermott.

"Aye, here's assuming they can discover a useable slug."

"Inspector Fletcher," CI McIntyre said, "where were you standing when you heard the original shot?"

Fletcher slipped under the yellow tape as he approached the forensics chief. Fletcher looked around the walkway and walked away from the entrance. Peering between the parked lorry and the doorway, he recalled his bearings. "About here. I was walking towards the corner," pointing away from the entrance.

86

McIntyre noted where Fletcher stopped in proximity to the door before speaking. "Inspector Gordon, turn to your left and look above you at the window grill."

Sheila followed his directions, raising her arm up to shield her eyes, when she glimpsed an irregular fragment of metal just beyond her reach. "I've got something," she said, "but I'll be needing a ladder."

McDermott moved closer, looking at the spot she had pointed to, and saw the bullet embedded in the rustic iron lattice. "I'll be damned; it looks relatively intact."

McIntyre got the small stepladder, took out his forceps, and opened a specimen bag before climbing up. Reaching above him, he gripped the slug and tugged it out of the metal, then slipped it into the pouch. "Thank God for seventeenth-century wrought iron," he said, stepping off the ladder.

"If that was the original shot taken, then the kill shot should be along this route," he said. He attempted to depict the trajectory of the bullet from the rooftop to the entrance, employing the forceps as a pointer. "How tall was the victim?"

Inspector Fletcher got out his notebook and thumbed through several pages before pausing. "He was six feet, four inches. Just a touch taller than you, I'd estimate."

"Here," Inspector Gordon said, pointing at the granite block near the window. Lodged in the crook of masonry sat the flatten projectile. Using her spatula, she extricated the metal from the block, allowing it to tumble into the open evidence bag McDermott held open for her.

"Does nae look like much help," McDermott said, staring into the pouch.

"We'll tear into it," Chief Inspector McIntyre said. "It might just be suitable to identify the type, and if we're successful, the manufacturer, as well."

"Pardon me, sir," a voice said. It belonged to Devin, the forensics technician, now joining the group. "We've finished canvassing the rooftop. Can't say we have much to go on," He held up half a dozen evidence bags. "We came across an odd fabric print near the spot where the shooter knelt, though."

"In the gravel?" McDermott asked.

"Not actually, Inspector, it was in the tar pitch below it. Like the person pushed himself to his feet," Devin said. "We've prepared a casting of it so we can look at it in the lab."

"Seems you've got your hands full, Graham," McDermott said. "Give us a ring if you need something from Andrew or me." He turned to Fletcher. "Come on, Andrew, we've got paperwork to fill out and submit."

They reached the police headquarters a short while later. McDermott and Fletcher entered the foyer and showed their IDs to the pair of uniformed constables standing guard.

"Be advised: the super is a bit on edge, gentlemen," one said as he looked over their credentials.

The two inspectors shuffled into the detectives' room, each arriving at his desk. McDermott took off his field coat, tossed it over his chair, and paced about the corner of the small office.

"We've one dead drug runner, a Frenchman with an Algerian connection, and three blokes in lockup for assaulting the dead one. What in the hell are we missing, Andrew?"

Inspector Fletcher contemplated what McDermott was saying and was working out his own thoughts before responding. "We've still not turned up the fifth fella from our first surveillance last month. In addition, the seaman—Jones, is it? —he alluded to 'Sammy' during Ewan's hearing. That could be our fifth person."

McDermott took out a pen and paper from his desk and began scribbling. "Five chaps at the docks, the constable Wallace, and the ship captains. That's eight possible leads."

"I'm glad to learn you've taken to writing things down," Fletcher said. "Don't neglect the Irishman from the recordings."

"Aye, the Irishman; he's an 'unknown' for the moment," McDermott said, patting the pen against his chin. "We've got to turn up a weak link in all this. The recordings, they're a benefit, but they don't give us the who," he said, closing his eyes.

"What about the barrister?" Fletcher suggested. "St. James was quite sure the young chap Forbes was in over his head during Ewan's trial. Maybe the sergeant was supplying him information about our surveillance to apply during the proceedings."

"Aye, you're on to something," McDermott said. "He'd been in the rear during the sergeant's trial. We'll need to get Constable Howe and the cadets looking at the phone logs to determine if he made calls to the barrister's office."

"Didn't Superintendent MacCallum secure a warrant for us?" Fletcher asked.

"With all the commotion over Wallace, he's doubtless forgotten about it. Not to mention the bit about constables being objects for a rogue shooter," McDermott said.

"What about constables and objects? Where did you learn of that?"

"Didn't I mention it to you?" McDermott said. "MacCallum got a demand note in the mail. If Wallace isn't freed in one week, one constable will turn into a target each day until he's absolved of his crimes."

"You're suggesting the original bullet was meant for me?" Fletcher asked as an icy shiver coursed through his body.

"No, of course not. You're a Scotland Yard inspector, not a constable with Police Scotland," McDermott replied. "We've still got two days before the conclusion of the week to satisfy the shooter's deadline. Now, come on, we've got accounts to compose." He sat down in front of his computer.

***

As he maneuvered the van into the complex next to the hotel, Dunbar grabbed the bag which bore the pieces of his sniper rifle and went to the lift. In a matter of minutes, he was re-entering his room, where he promptly began cleaning the weapon.

For approximately an hour, he toiled over each part, scouring the residue from the metal, wiping smutches from the walnut gunstock. After cleaning each section, Dunbar placed it back in the carrying case, but only when he was convinced the task was completely finished. After shoving the rifle scope into its foam cut-out, he drew the case closed, locking it.

He slid the chair clear of the desk before sitting down. Here he pulled out a pencil and his weathered moleskin notebook, turning to the last entry. Just below the names of 'Allen Doyle' and 'James Keller' he recorded the date and name of 'Ewan Sutherland' just as he'd done on over fifty other occasions during the preceding years. Closing the notebook, Dunbar sighed, knowing he'd added another demon to his nightmares.

His cell phone jarred him from his thoughts as it resonated. Picking it out of his pocket, Dunbar recognized the familiar number of Mr. Higgins.

"Good morning," he said after the second ring.

"Good morning, Angus," Michael Connelly replied. "I'm calling to notify you of another task I need you to undertake."

"And what might that be, sir?"

Savoring his coffee, Michael presented a few details on what he received from his man in Dublin earlier about the ship captain, Brodie Fraser. "Since this gentleman was seconded to me by an operator in Aberdeen, I need you to pay the captain a call. His name is Clive Duncan, and the ship is the *Nordic Supplier*."

Dunbar noted the name and ship's moniker as the Irishman spoke. "I understand, sir. To what degree am I to confer the issue with the good captain?"

"I need you to advise the good captain about our agreement," Michael said. "He needs to recognize the repercussions, not only to himself but likewise, his associates. Moreover, this includes every crew member of his ship too. Not to mention the captain and his crew in Glasgow."

"I'll see he is accorded a proper warning, Mr. Higgins," Dunbar said.

"I'll dispatch a picture to you in a minute," Connelly added. "Now, then; how are you coming along with negotiating with the other members on your party list?"

For the next ten minutes, Dunbar gave Connelly a meticulous narrative of his efforts against the longshoremen. He emphasized to the Irishman of his desire to include several other crimes, which could be connected to other criminal groups, who participated in the illegal narcotics business in Aberdeen.

"As of this morning, I've seen to removing Mister Sutherland," Dunbar said. "However, I'm sad to say I was a bit clumsy on this one, though. I required a second shot to accomplish my task." The tone in his voice sounded trite and apologetic.

"It's not like you to be clumsy like that, Angus. Do you suppose the police will be more attentive with the other members of your party?"

"No, sir," Dunbar said. "I'm confident they'll be chasing themselves for quite some time. I've been thorough in choosing my positions and practices. You know I've never performed a task the same way twice," he said. "Specifically, when you've given me more than one item to correct."

"I'm quite aware your methods," Connelly said. He smiled, knowing full well what Dunbar was alluding to. As a former

Legionnaire, he too was taught different techniques of overcoming an adversary or objective. "If things don't proceed sufficiently in the coming week, I may need to add to your tasking. Would that be a problem?"

Dunbar sat in the hotel room, looking out the window at Aberdeen's skyline before responding. He knew staying too long in one place would raise the potential for him to be challenged. *If I need to stick around longer, I'll need to switch hotels soon*, he told himself.

"Angus, is that a problem?" Connelly asked sounding slightly agitated.

"No, sir. I'll nae have a problem," Dunbar responded. "I'll make arrangements to change later in the day." He pulled out the city directory from the drawer.

"Very well, then," Michael said. "Keep me advised as to your progress."

"Aye, I'll be in contact with you after I pay my respects to the captain," Dunbar said, observing the shadows grow as a summer squall began passing over the downtown.

"Until then," Connelly said, hanging up.

"Aye, until then," Dunbar said, looking at his silent cell phone. As he leafed through the pages of the directory, he discovered the listing for the hotel southwest of the train terminal in the Ferryhill district. He knew it would do if he needed to escape in a rush.

Looking outside, he saw the passing shower had not increased, and decided he would pay a visit to the docks. He knew the benefit of disposing of a threat lay in gaining the upper hand. In his case, it would be in learning where he could position himself considering the berth used by the Nordic Supplier.

Bundled against the breeze and drizzle, Dunbar walked along the quay looking at the boats tied alongside the docks. *How do you do it, Alistair?* he thought. *Plenty of spots on a boat to plant the drugs, but only in small lots*. Having done research into the Glasgow criminal's endeavors, he struggled to imagine the numerous spaces to hide the drugs as he looked over the Nordic Supplier.

"Can I help you?" a voice asked from behind.

Spinning around, Dunbar came face-to-face with a robust figure of a man. The sailor had done what most men couldn't do, wander upon the criminal and catch him off guard. In this case, he'd shown up after coming from the local eatery next to the docks and not from one of the ships.

"Oh, I'm sorry; no, I was just marveling at the crafts," Dunbar said, glancing backward at the supply boat, then the captain.

"Mind yer step about the docks, most of the ship captains don't take to tourists very nicely."

"I'll keep that in mind; thank you, eh, Captain . . .?"

"Duncan, of the Nordic Supplier," the man said, nodding to the craft secured to the dock in front of them.

"Aye, I'll do that, sir, and thank you again for the warning," Dunbar replied, walking away from the docks and the captain. So, the image from Michael doesn't do you justice, Dunbar thought, recalling the picture his employer sent to him previously in the day.

As the shower subsided, Dunbar stopped at the end of the quay, spying several warehouses with rooms on the second floors sitting along the south jetty. *Perhaps, just perhaps*, he thought. He glanced between the buildings and the opposite shore while looking past the channel's opening. "Might just be under seventy-five meters. Close enough not to need the scope," he said to himself. He turned to wander back to the roadway and the bus stand. Higgins was clear in his instructions: eliminate loose ends, as needed, Dunbar recalled. Standing under the cover of the bus stand, he started sorting out the details in his head, in the event he had to kill the good captain.

Chapter Eleven

The summer squall drifted through downtown, ultimately falling on the barristers as they were leaving the courthouse and dashing to Priscilla's automobile. Skirting passed several pedestrians, they were soon standing along the lawyers' car.

"What other evidence do you suppose this Inspector McDermott has on the sergeant?" she asked, unlocking the car with her remote.

"I'm not certain," Sean replied as they slid into their seats. "We know the sergeant called his cousin Gordon. And he passed along information to several others outside the agency, just based on the cell phone records alone."

"Oh, what others? Who are these individuals?" Priscilla asked as she pulled into traffic, provoking an approaching bus to trumpet its horn at her.

"Other people working for my employer," Sean said, looking straight ahead.

"So, this employer of yours, he prefers keeping secrets more than revealing the truth," she said, shaking her head. *What in Allah's name have I conceded to?* she thought as she navigated through the traffic.

"Priscilla, as I said before, our burden is making certain specific entities aren't called to testify," he said, turning to look at her.

"You need to let me know who they are, Sean," Priscilla said. "I need to be ready to negotiate with something other than a pledge from your employer." She pulled into the hotel entrance and halted in front of the valet podium before stopping the motor. "You've my word, Sean. I'll do my best not to let something happen."

"Let's get inside, and then we'll chat," Sean said, stepping out of the car. He entered the hotel foyer and paused for a moment. He glanced at the nearby hostess standing at the entrance to the hotel bistro and then turned toward Priscilla. "Shall we order lunch and have it brought to the room?"

"Fine," she said. "I might need a bottle or two after what's developed this afternoon."

They each selected a lunch from the menu and Sean payed. "Please have the meals brought to room 514," he said.

"Certainly, sir," the hostess said. "It'll be about twenty minutes."

They headed for the lifts, Sean leading the way. When it arrived, he held the door open for Priscilla to enter first. After pressing separate floor buttons, Sean and Priscilla stood in uncomfortable silence, each absorbed in their own thoughts.

"I'll meet you at your room in fifteen minutes," he said as the lift stopped at his floor and the doors opened.

"Fine," Priscilla said, pressing the button again to close the door behind him. In moments, the lift stopped again, and Priscilla stepped out and headed towards her room. She unlocked the door, made her way inside, tossed her briefcase and handbag onto the bed, and went to use the bathroom.

She was sprucing up soon afterward. She untied the hijab from around her head and began brushing out the waist-long hair concealed beneath it. After ten minutes of tussling with her matted-down hair, she heard a tap at the door. "Just a minute," she said, straightening her blouse before leaving the bathroom.

She opened the door to find Sean standing there with his briefcase in hand, his shirt loosened at the collar.

"Punctual to a fault, you are," she said, letting her colleague into the room.

"I'm not the sort to keep a woman waiting," he said, stepping past her. "I see you've not cut your hair since school."

Before she even closed the door, a member of the hotel staff came out of the lift with their meal on a serving cart.

"Your order, ma'am," the attendant said when he approached the open door.

"You can set it on the table, if you please," she said.

Sean pulled out some cash for the tip.

"Thank you," Sean said, handing a couple of bills to the server before he left the room.

After having a seat at the table, Priscilla lifted the cover from the food. She twisted the cap off the miniature bottle of Chardonnay and dumped its contents into a plastic cup. She respected her father's Muslim culture, but she wasn't as devout as he would like her to be at times, notably when it came to consuming liquor.

"Now, who else do I need to be concerned about?" she asked. "Who is it your employer wishes to protect?"

Sitting across from Priscilla, Sean took a deep breath before speaking. "There are several key individuals you need to become acquainted with," he said. "The first one is a bloke named Alistair Hunt. He's the major mover of products in Glasgow and was drawn in by my employer for a transaction here in Aberdeen." He opened his bottle of Heineken and took a swallow before proceeding.

"The other principle is a boat captain by the name of Clive Duncan. Not only does he make certain the product arrives on shore, but he moved a portion of the product from here to Glasgow. From there, one of his confidants moved it to Ireland."

Sitting back in her chair, Priscilla sipped her wine and took in the remarks that her acquaintance was disclosing. *I'm certain "the product" he's talking about could only mean drugs*, she thought. "And we need to keep these chaps from being ordered to court?" she asked.

"Yes. And if they get called, we're required to do whatever is needed to keep them from implicating my employer," Sean said, stabbing his salad with a fork. "You should likewise know my employer has a chap he's paying to keep the peace."

"By 'keep the peace' you mean eliminate the miserable bastard who sings." Just discussing it sent a shudder through her body, being privy to learning of a potential murderer.

"Regrettably, yes, it wasn't something I was made aware of until the other evening, I'm afraid."

"Well, if that's the case, the poor sergeant and his relative will get roasted by Hamilton," Priscilla said. "That is, unless we can prove the police of botching the records, which sounds like a slim defense if the Yard-types have other substantial evidence. Because as of right now; we've nothing to protect him."

As he continued burrowing into his salad, Sean felt his cell phone vibrate in his pocket. He took it out and could see the call was from Ethan Taylor.

"Something interesting?" Priscilla asked.

"Yes, looks like we've got a notice of when the inspectors were appointed from London."

After they both got up from the table, Sean pulled the computer from his satchel and turned it on. Moments later, he was downloading the report from his email.

"So, how do we work this against Hamilton?" she asked, pacing in front of the window.

"I'm not sure," Sean said. Tapping on the console, he soon had the file open and read. "The memorandum is dated April twenty-fifth from a Chief Superintendent Collingsworth at Scotland Yard in London. Moreover, it's addressed to MacCallum here in Aberdeen. Strange that it didn't go to Edinburgh and the Commandant, don't you think?"

"That would be the first chink in their armor for me to expose," Priscilla said, jotting down the information into her notebook.

"The other piece is the relaxed nature of the memo itself," he said. "Even though it's on official stationery, this Collingsworth fellow addressed MacCallum as 'Bruce'; somewhat chummy, isn't it? Ah, here's something interesting," he said, looking back at Priscilla. "Seems this chief inspector got himself reprimanded after his last investigation. His reassignment appears to be a form of penance." Scrolling down the screen, Sean read on: "From there it's basic correspondence; findings from a drug investigation in Portsmouth outlining three deaths, confiscation of evidence, the mention of a document relating to . . ." his voice trailed off.

"To what, Sean?" she asked, stepping towards him.

"It turns out a document they seized during their investigation in Portsmouth referred to an Irishman and an impending meeting in Aberdeen with the French supplier," Sean said, the color fading from his face.

"Do you think they're referring to you? Or maybe they know of your employer, then?"

"I'm not sure," he said. He gulped down the rest of the beer and opened a second bottle. He wiped his brow and proceeded. "I need to make a few calls and hope my contact can get something more on this." Pulling out his phone, Sean thumbed through the contacts before coming across Ethan Taylor. Soon he was texting his message: CALL ME. IN NEED OF MORE INFORMATION, MOST URGENT. SG.

"So how do we use this against the police?" Priscilla asked, feeling a surge of adrenaline as the excitement of the duel took hold of her.

"If the prosecution uses this against the sergeant, we must be quicker with our rebuke," Sean said. He then drained the second beer in one draw. *How in the goddamn hell did the police get that information from the Portsmouth affair?* he thought.

"Do you only have the one contact, Sean?" Priscilla asked.

"What?"

"You're involved in something, and I reckon it might be more dangerous than you imagined," Priscilla said. She finished the rest of her sandwich and chased it with a mouthful of wine. "Who else is out there you can call to get answers regarding this Portsmouth incident?"

Sean thought back to earlier dealings with the French-Algerian drug trafficker Nazim Aziz, whom he knew as 'Louis Remesy.' He knew the man would be reluctant to help after losing his last shipment. *His partner, Adrian Richelieu, might be more willing, though for a cost, I'm sure*, Sean thought. "There might be someone I can contact," he said to Priscilla. "I've your word you'll not mention anything at all about this call?"

"My word, Sean, not a peep," Priscilla said as she refilled her wine. The alcohol was warming her to the contest.

Sean snatched up his phone from the table and thumbed the register until he found 'Papillion Transport' and its proprietor, Adrien Richelieu. Punching the call button, he walked to the window and looked out at the metropolis.

***

Sixteen hundred kilometers to the south in the French city of Marseille, the counselor's call was being answered in a typical-looking industrial building near the harbor. Sitting in the freshly established office of Papillion Transport, Claudette sneezed for what seemed the hundredth time. Since transferring from the older building to this one, the smells of new carpet and fresh paint assaulted her senses. As she tossed the tissue into the trashcan, her phone rang.

"Papillion Transport, how may I direct your call?" she answered.

"This is Monsieur Gilmore; I'm calling for Monsieur Richelieu," Sean said. "It's very urgent that I speak with him."

"I'm sorry, but Monsieur Richelieu is out of the country on business," Claudette said, reading the prepared manuscript for the day. "I can forward your message to him if you'd like."

Priscilla watched Sean as he conversed with the person on the other end of the line. She saw beads of sweat forming on his forehead and began to understand the significance of the information being furnished by his contact.

"Please inform him that there seems to be an issue with one of their vessel captain. His name is Duncan, and he is need of assistance in Aberdeen. I would appreciate that," Sean said. "Please pass the following name and number to him." He then recited his name and cell phone number. "And let him know he can call any time it is advantageous to him."

"Of course, Monsieur Gilmore, *Au revoir*," Claudette said taking down his information. She looked up to see Louis Clement standing over her. As soon as she hung up the phone, she turned and passed the message to him.

"I'll see he gets this; you may go home now," he told the receptionist.

Walking into the back office, Louis began dialing the private cell number for his partner, Gregory Arsenault. On the second ring, his partner answered.

"Bon jour, Louis."

"Bon jour. We've a slight problem, Gregory," Louis said.

"What is it?"

"We just received a call from the Northern Irishman's lawyer," he replied. "I believe something may be happening that could have an impact on our operations. He was expressing his concern for his and the ship captain's safety. I'd like a few days to go and see if I can resolve the problem before it gets out of hand."

"Which captain?"

"Duncan; the older one we dealt with on the last transaction," he said. "He's the one who helped McIntosh and McKenzie obtain their vessels, remember?"

"I do. He was the one who identified the abandoned oil derrick we allowed Nazim to obtain," Gregory said. "The three of them are good men, so you're right to want to help out."

"I shouldn't be more than a couple of days," Louis said.

Gregory looked out at the water from his hotel balcony, considering their options. "Has Claudette finished with your travel documents yet?" He knew the police would still be looking for him after the shoot-out at the docks last month.

"Yes, she finished them the other day," Louis said. "And I must say, I look very distinguished with a beard and longer hair."

"Ok, but don't go alone," Gregory said. "Take one of the men with you."

"I was planning on having Hector and Pasqual join me, in the event there's more than just one issue," Louis replied. "Plus, they've both been here in Marseille the longest; I think they could use a little break from the routine. I'll also contact our friend in Manchester to prepare some bags for use, so I don't have to test my arm in a fight," he said, flexing his right elbow.

"Good call," Gregory said, sipping his wine. "But keep me informed. I'll tell Julien to be ready to travel if you need more help."

"I'll keep your number on speed-dial, Mon Ami," Louis said, ending the call.

***

News of the murder soon littered the airwaves of every television and radio service. Sitting in the hotel room with Priscilla, Sean was numb to what he was watching until his cell phone chirped with a text message.

"A reply from your contact?" she asked.

"No, something else," Sean said, reading the message: ONE LESS POSSIBLE LEAK TO WORRY OVER. Reading the message again, he realized Ewan Sutherland was just the first of several victims being suppressed to protect his employer.

The uncomfortable silence building between them was soon disrupted by the ringing of the hotel phone on Priscilla's nightstand. She grabbed the receiver and answered.

"Hello?"

"Yes, Miss El-Sayed? This is Mister Jenkins calling from the sheriff's office. I apologize for the short notice, but all the court sessions have been postponed for the rest of the week, owing to an unexpected event," he said. "Your hearing will continue at 9:00 a.m. on Monday."

"What unexpected event?" she asked.

"There was a shooting outside the building. A participant from a separate case was murdered, I'm afraid," he said with a tremble in his voice.

"I understand," she said. "Thank you for the call." She then hung up the phone.

"What was that all about?" Sean asked.

"Seems someone was shot outside the sheriff's office."

"Oh, I see," he said, remembering the text he had just received.

99

Priscilla stepped to the miniature bar and poured herself another plastic cup of wine before swallowing it in two gulps.

"It won't be the last," Sean muttered.

"What did you say?" she asked, turning to face him.

"I said it won't be the last. I didn't know the victim, but I can assure you my employer made the decision to have it done."

"Your employer condones the homicide of an innocent person?" she stammered. "My God, Sean, what in hell has happened to you? You were never this cold or insensitive about people before."

Sean stared at the carpet to avoid looking at her. "Several years ago, I made a pledge with this man for the chance to see my country unified. I was foolish because I was blinded by nationalism rather than governed by conscience." When he lifted his head, Sean could see the look in the astonishment in Priscilla's eyes. She couldn't fathom the actions he had agreed to or felt obliged to support. All he could see now was disbelief and shock, something he hadn't planned to cause.

Priscilla walked around the bed and opened the door. "Sean," she said, "you need to go back to your room and give me some time alone."

As Sean got up from the table, he picked up the notes and computer before shoving them into his briefcase. "Can I call you in the morning for breakfast?" he asked as he walked past her.

"I'll let you know," she said stepping behind him. Closing the door behind him, she slid the lock against its stop, as if the action would separate her from the evil lurking outside. At the window, with its view of the harbor and the North Sea in the distance, she slid the drapes together, sending the room into blackness. Collapsing onto the bed, Priscilla curled up, clinging to a pillow as she convulsed and cried at her dilemma.

What am I expected to do now? She thought. Whom can I turn to, if I can't trust Sean to tell me the truth? She rolled onto her back and stared at the ceiling as tears crawled down her cheeks. Who is the strange man Sean is working for, anyway? Wiping the streaks of moisture from her face, she perched up in the bed and took a deep breath. With or without Sean, I'm good enough to win this case. She walked into the bathroom and saw the results of her sobs. Dark streaks of mascara showed trails of where her tears had flowed on her cheeks, as well as her hands.

"Looks like it's shower time," she declared to the empty room. Turning the spigot, the spray from the shower soon produced a sparse cloud of steam. After removing her clothes, she soon felt the warmth of the water cascading over her skin. Using every drop of shampoo, she devoted the next five minutes to lathering her waist-length hair before rinsing. Next, she grabbed a washcloth and scoured the remnants of makeup from her face.

After thirty minutes, she materialized from the bathroom and put on an oversized t-shirt before settling onto the bed. Grabbing her notebook, she proceeded to make out her questions for the next court session, determined to win the case and perhaps her client's freedom.

* * *

After his unexpected dismissal from Priscilla's room, Sean made his way upstairs to his own room to ponder their next course of action. He slipped his key card into the lock, entered the room, and dropped his briefcase at the foot of the bed. He opened the small refrigerator, pulled out a bottle of ale, immediately opened it, and took a long gulp. Sitting in the easy chair, he closed his eyes and reflected on how he could regain Priscilla's faith without placing her in harm's way.

He wondered why Mister Higgins was so keen to have the young Scot killed. He knew the Frenchman wanted them to intervene on behalf of Captain McKenzie, but he didn't think Higgins had known about Sutherland. After another gulp, he grabbed his notebook from his briefcase and proceeded to jot down notes as he organized his thoughts.

He knew the Frenchman Remesy had met with Sutherland to move more of the drugs onshore. Nevertheless, what about the dockworker and the two deckhands from the boats? Why did they accost him? Was it only about payment?

Tipping the bottle back, he drained its contents, dribbling a few drops down his chin and onto the page in the process.

"How many times did Wallace contact Sutherland?" he asked himself while scrawling several question marks across the page. Was Sutherland a key piece against the sergeant? If he was, who would have seen that information?

He returned to the fridge and grabbed another bottle and opened it but was mindful not to splash more on his remarks.

"The simplest way to figure this out is to call Mister Higgins," he said aloud. He pulled up the office number on his cell phone and selected it. On the second ring, he heard the familiar voice of Mister Higgins's secretary, Erin.

"Callaghan & Higgins Limited, how may I help you?" she answered.

"Erin, it's Sean Gilmore calling for Mister Higgins."

"Oh, hello there, Sean. Mister Higgins isn't in; he's left on holiday for the rest of the week," she said. "And he asked I keep all calls and correspondence until he comes back on Tuesday."

"Oh hell, I forgot about his trip," Sean said. "Did Geoff go with him by chance?" He knew Higgin's driver was also a bit of a pseudo bodyguard.

"No, he gave Geoff a few days respite," Erin said. "At the moment, he's off fetching lunch for the two of us."

"When he comes back and you're done eating, can you have him contact me?"

"Of course, I can, Sean. Is there anything I can do besides relay the message?" Her tone became slightly annoyed. Why would he ask for Geoff's help and not hers?

Not considering the repercussions, Sean continued with his questioning. "Do you know if Mister Higgins has been in contact with a gentleman by the name of Dunbar, or maybe a Mister Walker in the past few days?"

"No, he didn't mention a Mister Walker," Erin said. "But how do you know of Mister Dunbar? Mister Higgins had an extremely spirited conversation over the phone with him the day you flew out to Aberdeen. You know, I've never heard him use abusive language in the office before, Sean, but he was touching every syllable."

"Do you recall if he cautioned Mister Dunbar about making a rash decision or requesting him to undertake a particular task?"

"You need to understand, Sean, I was working very hard not to listen in on his call. However, he was insistent about wanting Mister Dunbar's activities to be conspicuous and impressive. Those are his words Sean, not mine. Oh! Geoff just stepped in the door with our lunch."

"I'm not surprised," Sean said, imagining the exchange between his employer and who he speculated was Ewan Sutherland's killer. "Let Geoff know to call me when you're done eating; I'm not going anywhere for the rest of the evening."

"All right, then," she said, and hung up.

"Who's on the phone?" Geoff asked, laying out several small packages of Chinese food onto the desk.

"It was Mister Gilmore. He needs you to call him after we're done."

"Did he say what he needed?"

"No, just to give him a call. Said he'll be in his room the rest of the day. Now, where's my orange chicken and pot stickers?" she asked, snapping her chopsticks apart.

Chapter Twelve

Chief Inspector McIntyre and his forensics team were earning every penny of their proper wages. *Four murders in two weeks,* he thought. *You'd think Andrew Walker was back in business.* He walked passed the constables milling about in front of the victim's flat. "Who's in charge here?" he shouted, stepping over the wrecked front door and into the sitting room.

"I'm senior man, Inspector," Sergeant McCord said.

"Good evening, Sergeant. Looks like the city is gaining quite a list of odd deaths. How did you come to discover this one?" The body in question was tied up and sitting on a chair. The throat had been slashed from ear to ear.

"Couple of the neighbors out walking their dogs caught sight of someone barreling through the door. By the time they got close, the bloke had turned out and driven off. We've got details of the killer and his motor out to the patrols in the city." The sergeant then took out his notepad and stood next to the corpse.

"This unfortunate fella was Ian McLeod of Aberdeen. He'd been living here for the last two years after leaving Glasgow. The proprietor of the flat claimed he was civil, no issues with neighbors, settled his rent on time, all on the up and up, it suggests." He flipped his notepad shut.

"So, you've already identified that the fella busting through the door is our suspect?" McIntyre asked, looking forlornly at the constable. "Need I remind you, Sergeant, everybody gets a proper hearing regardless of the circumstances."

McIntyre tugged on his gloves and used a tongue depressor to inspect the gash. "This actually looks like a surgical reduction," he stated, peering at the bared flesh. "Sergeant, hand me that torch if you would, please," he said, pointing to his kit bag.

Shining the light on the wound, he didn't see any tearing of the skin, an indication the knife had a straight edge without serrations. "Notice how the laceration is high here on his right, Sergeant?"

"Aye. So, what are we looking at?" McCord asked.

"Well, the reduction begins high and subsequently exits lower on the left. It asserts our assailant was behind the casualty when he slit the throat, and most likely left-handed."

Walking around the torso, McIntyre spied his assistant Devin standing in the front room carrying his gear and a folded body bag. "Devin, have the medics lay out the bag and bring back the gurney. When they're done, you can dust for prints. Best if you start with the front door and make your way in towards the kitchen."

"Yes, sir," Devin said. He turned and walked out to escort the medical unit to the crime scene.

"This looks familiar," McIntyre said, staring at the knots binding Ian's wrists. "Sergeant, can you have someone fetch the files from the signal tower murders from last week?"

"Aye," McCord said. "I'll give the station a call and have them collected. Anything specific you need to see?"

"The crime scene photographs and the rope found at the scene, for starters. We may have a clue connecting the two homicides."

***

As the hours passed, the city grew dark and lonely; though the roads surrounding the harbor were still abuzz with movement. Emerging from the shadows, a solitary figure walked along the waterfront. Under floodlights casting an eerie glow on the concrete, the figure continued walking towards several containers waiting to be loaded.

Glancing at the door of one, the person stopped, reached down and grasped the handle upward, swinging it free. Squeezing into the dark void of the metal box, the individual closed the door before turning on a small flashlight, finding the storm lantern that had been left earlier.

Under the dim glow of the lantern, the occupant shed his outer garments. He reached into a sports bag on the floor and pulled out jeans, a t-shirt, work boots, and a hammer before stuffing the bloodstained clothing he had taken off into an open crate. Sweat seeped from his pores, as the air grew stagnant inside the metal shipping box.

With the clothing pushed inside, he added bloodstained surgical gloves on top. After securing the crate's lid with the hammer, the individual put on a sweater before tossing the bag over his shoulder and exiting the container.

***

105

Inspector Fletcher pulled up behind the forensics van sitting outside Ian McLeod's flat. Turning to his colleague, he asked, "Do you think this murder has anything to do with the shooting from this morning?"

McDermott glanced at him before speaking. "Aye, it might. But then again, it might not." Stepping onto the pavement, he greeted the constable positioned behind the security line, and presented his credentials.

"Here you go, Inspector," the constable said, handing over a pair of cloth booties to McDermott. "Chief McIntyre is particular with his crime sites."

"Aye, he is now, isn't he?" McDermott said, slipping the coverings over his shoes. Ambling up the walkway, McDermott and Fletcher noted the busted door, its handle, and the surrounding woodwork covered with dust from where fingerprints were raised. "Evening, Devin. Is the Chief about?" McDermott asked.

"Aye, he's in the kitchen."

After entering the flat, they found their way to the modest kitchen, and noticed the chair filled with the remains of the slaying. The stench of the crime still hovered in the air, dried blood from the victim, now a mahogany brown, had stained the chair fabric. Several envelopes lay strewn on the dinner table, showing splatter stains of blood. Fletcher squatted down to inspect the rope bound around the legs of the chair.

"This is a brand of parachute cord," he declared.

"You sure?" McDermott asked.

"Yes. We used it in the Royal Marines to attach just about everything down with our containers. Comes in various thicknesses, each spool has one hundred meters. Simple to find at most outdoor outlets."

"I'm glad some of your colleagues' trade has rubbed off on you, Inspector Fletcher," Chief Inspector McIntyre said as he entered the kitchen. "But we don't rely on conjecture when it comes to evidence."

"No, sir, I'm just relating to my previous knowledge, using the evidence," Fletcher said.

"So, we've got a person drawing up the victim before executing him?" McDermott asked.

"Based on my initial examination of the body," McIntyre said, "the securing of the victim came after the assault."

"Is it conceivable the victim knew his assailant?" Fletcher asked.

"Yes, it's feasible, but I'm guessing the aggressor was lying in wait, not welcomed in, as it were," Graham said. He took out a pen and began using it as a pointer. "The table was shoved aside when we showed up, but the blood splatter proves it was closer when the slaying took place. We also discovered what turned out to be someone's lunch," he said, pointing to the stomach contents splattered next to Fletcher's foot.

"Which means the killer was already in the flat before the victim," McDermott said, rubbing his head. "Was there anything discovered in the back; prints, fags, something of value?"

"The door lock looks to have some recent scrapes on the keyhole where it was picked open. A few boot prints are just outside the door. We've made casts, and we'll compare them to those of the victim," the chief forensics officer replied. "My suspicion is that they won't match, but we might have something to associate this with the homicides at the signal tower."

"Andrew, we'll need to see if there were any communications between those dock workers and this fellow," McDermott said. "And along the way; check to see if Ewan Sutherland's lawyer ever had dealings with our victim."

"Forbes? You think he has something to do with all this?" Fletcher asked.

"No. He's nae sharp enough, but someone might pluck a few strings, making him the fall guy." He turned to face the forensics officer. "Graham, how quickly will you have something on the two scenes?"

"If the murders can hold for a night or two, I should have something prepared by the end of tomorrow. If not, the next day for certain."

"We'll leave you be, then. Come on, Andrew," he said, tugging Fletcher's elbow, "we've got a couple of blokes to chat with before they get hauled off to Grampian"

"The dock workers?" he asked, falling in behind McDermott as they left the flat.

"That's right. I've got a notion they know something about this killer," McDermott said. He paused to lean on the police car as he ripped off the booties.

After driving for ten minutes in complete silence, the inspectors arrived back at the police station. McDermott pulled the police car into a vacant stall behind the police station and doused the headlights. "We'll talk to them, starting with Jones," he said as he and Fletcher exited the vehicle. "He sounded the most set off by Sutherland's discharge. Not to mention he believes someone planted the drugs."

"Besides trying to figure out if they knew the victim, what else do we ask them about?"

"Well, it couldn't hurt to see if any of them had dealings with the sergeant," McDermott said.

When they reached the caretaker's window, McDermott offered his credentials. With a buzz, the security door latch opened, allowing the officers to enter the jail.

"Evening, Inspectors," the corporal on duty said as they checked in their firearms. He slid a dilapidated logbook towards Fletcher. "Don't fail to sign in, please."

The two inspectors stalked along the corridor, its bleak appearance stressed by the garish white enameled surfaces, until they reached the access point to the interrogation rooms. Knocking his knuckles against the window, McDermott announced their presence. "Hello? Anyone hame now?"

Shuffling around from the corner, the civil constable sauntered to the security glass window and peered at them over his horn-rimmed glasses. "Is there something I can do for you?"

"Aye, we need to have a wee talk with a Mister Willie Jones," McDermott said, holding up his credentials for the constable to see. "And when we're finished, we'll need to have a talk with . . . oh hell, what are their names?" he said, turning to Fletcher.

"You need to start managing your own damn notes," Fletcher spat back, taking out his notebook. "Ian Campbell, Stanley Dunnigan, Reginald Brown, and Clyde Smith."

The constable glanced at his roll-call sheet. "We've got your initial three, but we freed the other two earlier today." He pointed down the hallway. "If you'll have a spot in room number four, we'll deliver your first fella to you."

"Thank you, Constable," McDermott said and turned away from the window.

Trailing behind McDermott, Fletcher quickstepped to match his colleague's stride. "I take it you'll do all the speaking," he said.

"Aye, since I've nae notebook," he said with a sneer. "Yes, I'll do the talking, and you do the drafting."

The interrogation room was bleak and sparse. The only furniture occupying the space consisted of a metal table and three chairs. The floor was a checkerboard of black-and-white tiles. There were two closed-circuit cameras set up in opposite corners of the ceiling. Fletcher stood with his back against the wall, watching the middle chair, waiting for the constable to bring in the convict from his cubicle. He thumbed through his notebook, finding the next available blank page, and waited in anticipation for his partner to start the examination.

"He's been sentenced already," McDermott said, "so we've got that in our favor"

"How so?" Fletcher asked.

"We can bargain with him. Offer a few months off his time, maybe," McDermott said. "I'm sure there's something we can get by having him talk."

Before Fletcher could ask another question, the door swung open and Willie Jones was escorted to the chair opposite the Scotland Yard detectives. The chain surrounding Jones's waist clanked against the metal chair as he sat. The chains connecting his wrists to his waist were long enough to allow his palms to rest on the surface of the table. "Come to see me off, have you?" Jones asked peevishly.

McDermott looked sternly at the former seaman, yanked the opposing chair out from under the table, and sat down. "It looks like you've got a few months ahead of you to contemplate if your crime was worth doing," he declared. "For the record, I don't go for 'druggies,' Mister Jones. And you now qualify for that group. As far as I'm concerned, you're a step above a pedophile in my book. However, you've had your time in court, and the judge has passed down her decision. So how 'bout you and I have a cordial conversation for the moment, man-to-man?"

"After what took place the other day, I'm rather looking forward to my time at Grampian. Least I'll fare better than the sod Sutherland has." Jones said smugly. "If you think I had something to do with the slaying, you're daft." He sneered as he stared into the detective's eyes.

"So, all the bluster in the courthouse was just you swinging your 'boaby' for the judge, was it? You and Campbell both said

109

Sutherland would get his, and now he's dead, isn't he? That's all fine, Willie. I believe you too," McDermott replied. "I'm needing to hear who else you've conferred with at the docks. Understand, we've got a chance to help you see the Highlands sooner if you help."

Fletcher glanced up from his notebook, soaking in the back-and-forth exchange between McDermott and Jones. *A name, just throw us a name, will you?* he thought himself as he scribbled down the responses.

"You've nae business cutting my time," Jones argued. "Now you bring me a barrister here, then I'll consider your display as legitimate. Until then, you can deal with the court directives and see all the details from me you need."

"You're quite the smart one, aren't you?" McDermott said. "You do recognize your friend Campbell; he talked very highly of you. After a few hours, he knew, by extending a hand, he'd be gaining his license back so he can work again. Moreover, he's keen to help, that one is. Such a nice fella to dae business with."

Jones scoffed at the detective. "Ian's not that foolish. He'd nae say a word against me."

"You can choose for yourself when he saunters out of Grampian six months ahead of you," McDermott said, glancing at the image of the clock in the window. "All I'm asking you for is where I can locate your colleague 'Sammy' you spoke of in court. A flat number, the vessel they work, just a wee morsel to whet my thirst."

Jones glared at the inspectors, contemplating his future if he exposed 'Sammie' to the police. Over the last sixteen months, she'd handled his drug money while he peddled small portions of marijuana and cocaine amongst other deckhands and platform roughnecks. It wasn't until he overheard Ian Campbell discussing an arrangement for hashish aboard a French freighter that he became further entangled with the drugs.

"If I help you," Jones said, now more calmly, "I need assurances, you see. Maybe even a nice flat in the south of Ireland for my efforts. I'll never work a platform or boat again if the characters I've dealt with ever found out I snitched on them."

"I can't guarantee anything, you know; I'm just a constable. But I'll vouch for your help, provided it yields the apprehension of the next two members in the drug ring," McDermott said. He waved his hand at one of the cameras and soon afterwards, Robert St. James came into the room. "You've heard the young fellow; can you see his concerns are considered?"

The barrister bristled at the statement. He had just spent weeks getting Jones committed for his crimes, and now here he was haggling for a reduction in his sentence. "I'll see the necessary documents are created tomorrow." Turning to the convict, he said, "Mister Jones, after you reach Grampian, but before your parole, you'll be afforded a chance to discuss things with a civil lawyer before signing anything of this agreement. Do you understand?"

"Aye, I do," he said, setting his head on the table.

"Inspector McDermott, I believe we have an agreement in place," St. James said. "But simply in principle, that is." He turned to leave the room.

"Thank you, Mister St. James," McDermott said. "I'll be out shortly." He turned back to face Willie Jones. "So, where can we locate this bloke 'Sammy'?"

Willie straightened himself in the chair and cleared his throat. "Known to the lads on the ships as 'Sammie,' but Samantha Atkins is her formal name," he said.

"Sammy's a woman?" Fletcher asked, clearly surprised.

McDermott grit his teeth upon hearing his partner speak out of turn, but let it slide for the moment. "And where can we locate the young lass?" he inquired.

"She works the support ships. She's a second engineer on the *Standard-Hercules*," Jones replied. "Quite the fireplug, she is. She's tough as they come, too; can drink most lads under the table when she's parched. However, she's nae keen on any of us; she's got a lady friend from what I've been told. But I did nae know what her name is."

Fletcher was noting everything as quickly as Jones spoke. Hearing the felon describe the young woman, he reflected about the latest crime and the chance that she could have subdued Ian McLeod.

"So, you've nae idea about her flat, just the ship?" McDermott queried.

"I've only dealt with her while on the docks or the boats," Jones said. "Oh, and a few times at the pub after a voyage when both our boats came in at the same time."

"I'll do my best to maintain my end of the arrangement," McDermott said, standing up. "But, if I'm out chasing my tail for nothing, the agreement is no good, you understand?"

"Aye," Jones said.

He was then escorted out of the room, back to his cubicle.

McDermott left Fletcher and stepped out of the room behind Jones to find the bespectacled constable heading to the holding area for Ian Campbell. "We're done, for now; you can cancel the other interview."

"All right, Inspector," the officer said as he shuffled away.

Sticking his head back into the interrogation room, McDermott said, "Come on, Andrew. Let's have a chat with this young lass, shall we?"

"What about Campbell?" Fletcher asked, closing his journal.

"I've got a notion he'd be less apt to comply with our questioning," McDermott said. "And I'm curious to see if this lass is fit to handle a fella like McLeod." He began heading towards the command room to leave the jail.

"I had the same thought," Fletcher replied, scurrying after his partner. "The victim appeared considerably robust, like a weightlifter. This young woman might have plied him with sex to get him to let his guard down, don't you think?"

"Aye, it's a possibility, as sick as that sounds," McDermott said, climbing behind the wheel of the police car. The inspectors tore out of the car park and made their way back across town towards the harbor.

After making it through the Commercial Quay, McDermott and Fletcher arrived just as two boats drifted out the channel. The one closest one was the *Nordic Supplier*, but they couldn't see the other vessel's name. "Damn," McDermott said, his hand beating the car's bonnet. "We've missed them, Andrew. Now it'll be a week or better before we can grill the lass."

"But Jones said she was on the *Standard-Hercules*," Fletcher said.

"But the initial boat is undoubtedly the one we needed to board," McDermott replied, exasperated.

"Can't we get the Coast Guard patrol to have the boat turned back to the harbor?"

"Not if they're set to supply a platform," McDermott said, pointing to the containers lashed to each craft's aft deck. "The companies provide a substantial amount of currency to support their derricks in work; they'd nae take kindly if we screwed with their schedules, would they?"

As the *Nordic Supplier* made its way out to sea, it passed the last boat tied up at the Regents Quay. The familiar red and blue hues of Chevron-Europe adorned the superstructure, and the name reproduced in dazzling white enamel on the blue steel surface read *Standard-Hercules*.

"Conor, she's still in port," Fletcher said, pointing out the boat across the water, a wisp of exhaust spiraling upward from her funnels.

"Aye, but nae for too much longer," McDermott said. "Come on, we best hurry if we wish to catch them!" They hurried down the dock towards the supply boat.

Fletcher trotted after his partner, his limp more prominent and peculiar to spectators as he made his way along the concrete surface. Dodging a cargo lift placing crates into a container, he caught up with McDermott, who was already preparing to set foot on the deck.

Suddenly, a voice roared over the ship's bullhorn. "Hold fast, there! No one comes aboard without my permission!" Turning toward the bridge exit, Bernard McIntosh stepped onto the narrow platform looking over the dock. Leaning on the rail, he looked down at the two officers. "I've got two minutes before I shove off!" he called down. "What do you need?"

"I'm Chief Inspector McDermott with Scotland Yard!" McDermott shouted back. "We need to talk with your second engineer!"

The twin diesel engines thundered to life.

"You might see they've got their hands full, now," Bernard replied, hoisting a thumb at the exhaust stacks bellowing the sooty black plumes skyward. "I'll give you one minute, but not one second more." He retired to the interior of the bridge where he picked up the ship's phone.

"I don't like this, Andrew," McDermott said as he turned to Fletcher, who was rubbing his knee.

"You don't think he's being trustworthy?"

"What I'm suggesting is, he'll send someone up from the engine room, but I don't think it'll be the lass," McDermott said. A moment later, the hatch swung open, slamming against its blocks, and a lone figure materialized from the passage. Wandering through the maze

113

of crates, pallets, and two shipping containers attached to the deck, the crewmember headed their way, walking toward the railing. McDermott and Fletcher stole a glimpse at each other. The person walking towards them wasn't what they imagined or expected.

Second Engineer Samantha Atkins, a hearty and well-rounded woman who could've played half-fly for the national rugby club, strolled across the deck. She was clad in oil-smeared blue overalls and a red bandana, already darkened with sweat, wrapped around her head. Strands of hair, black as coal, slipped out. All the while, she was rubbing her palms on a rag. The arms of her overalls were cut-off, displaying a pair of muscular biceps most fellows would covet, with the one on the right sporting several colorful tattoos.

Keeping her distance from the rail, Samantha called out to the two inspectors standing on the dock. "You've got a question for me?" She now stood with her hands jammed into the pockets of her coveralls.

"Where were you on Monday evening, say, about eight o'clock?" McDermott asked.

"I was here," she said, twirling her hands around the packed deck. "It's an 'all-hands' effort making her ready to sail!" She had to holler to be heard over the revved-up engines. "I'd let you check the log, but the Cap'n said you've only got a minute, and well . . ." Before she could finish, a buzzer sounded and four deckhands emerged. With a mock salute, Samantha waved off the inspectors while the crew took up the mooring lines, allowing the boat to edge away from the dock.

"We'll call the Coast Guard to notify us when she's back," McDermott said, resigned they just missed an opportunity which might not come back. Squinting up at the bridge, he spotted the captain raise a mug towards them. "Aye, we'll meet again," he said with a mock wave back.

"Can't we call upon Captain Kincaid again?" Fletcher asked as he kept pace with his partner.

"Aye, and what would we have him do?"

"I don't know offhand, but we just can't let them go. Can we?"

"We'll have our chance, lad," McDermott sighed. "Here, your turn." He tossed the keys to Fletcher and slid into the passenger side.

"You just want me to fill it with petrol, don't you?"

"Can't say I like the stink of it when I splash some on my hands," McDermott answered, looking out the window. With a deafening burst of its air-horn, the Standard-Hercules cleared the harbor entrance and made its way out to the North Sea.

"I'm guessing the lass could just about handle any bloke she wanted," he said. "When we get to the Coast Guard office, have them draw her documents to see what we find." He slouched in the front seat as Fletcher pulled away from the docks.

Chapter Thirteen

The hotel café was lively, but not cramped. People appeared to be chatting about the day's earlier killing. Sipping her drink, Priscilla El-Sayad looked over the notes she'd written last night. How can I disprove the appointment of two Scotland Yard's inspectors against the prosecution? she thought. If the chief for Police Scotland was privy to their assignment, why not let his organization know sooner? Before she continued, she caught one of the porters standing next to her table. "Can I help you?"

"I'm sorry for the intrusion," the youthful fellow said, "but I was requested to present this to you." He held out an envelope.

She paused for a moment, then held out her hand. "Thank you," she replied.

As she held the envelope, she saw that it was fashioned in an old-world style, employing thin-weight paper with a blue tint. Looking at the front, she saw her name was composed in beautiful calligraphy, in English and Arabic.

Turning it over, she observed the seal fixing the flap, and saw it was a narrow golden ribbon looped under the maroon-tinted wax. She donned her glasses and examined the seal, recognizing it as the French fleur-de-lis.

"From a secret follower?" someone said.

The voice startled her. Glancing up, she saw Sean Gilmore attired in active wear, his hair all a tussle standing across from her. "I'm not certain. I likewise didn't expect to meet you before receiving a call," she stated.

"I apologize for that," Sean said. "But I went for a stroll to do some thinking, and I saw you sitting alone. By the way, I discussed matters with our client's cousin last night, and we might have a few points to employ against Hamilton. Nevertheless, I can see you're busy, so I'll leave you be. Give me a call when you're ready to get back to work." He spun around and quietly walked away from the table.

After watching her colleague walk away, Priscilla picked up a table knife and slipped it under the flap, breaking the seal. She drew out the folded note within and read it.

On Monday you will offer evidence showing your client agreeing to provide information which culminated in a successful capture of drug smugglers. The circumstances of the evidence will single out a French National by the name of Louis Remesy. The court must be assured this man is the mastermind behind the drug trafficking. It is essential for your client to persuade the court his process of moving along information was warranted. If not, your personal security will be put in peril. If you or your gentleman assistant fail in this task, then your futures will be no better than the young man's outside the sheriff's office.

Clenching the note, Priscilla's hand quivered as her eyes darted about the room from face to face. She set it on the table and picked up her drink, hoping no one saw her hands shaking. She sat guzzling the cold liquid, attempting to purge the taste of deceit and panic from her mouth.

Staring down at the handwriting, a sense of vulnerability swept through her, and her stomach fluttered. Feeling unsettled, as if each individual glancing at her could have been this mystery author, Priscilla's body tingled as if she knew she would be the next fatality in some horror show. She seized the note and envelope off the table and shoved them into her handbag. She read the receipt for her breakfast, pulled out several bills totaling thirty euros, and dropped them on the table before hurrying towards the lift.

Meanwhile, Sean had paused at the desk clerk. "I was wondering if there's a parcel for me," he said. "The name's Gilmore; I'm in room 610."

"Just a moment, sir, I'll check," the young woman said. She turned around and picked through several large envelopes before selecting one near the bottom. "Yes, we do, Mister Gilmore," she said, passing him the parcel.

"Thank you," Sean said. As he began walking towards the lift, he saw Priscilla. She was visibly shaken, fidgeting with her handbag, and glancing around at the patrons in the vestibule. "Everything, okay?" he asked, walking up to her.

"We need to talk, now," she stammered as the lift doors opened. As occupants stepped out, she clutched his arm and didn't let go.

Once the lift was empty, she dragged him inside and immediately pushed the DOOR CLOSE button.

"What's the matter?" Sean asked.

"Before you stepped up, I was given a note," her voice was cracking as fear displaced the disbelief of what she had read.

"What was on the note?" Sean asked.

"I'll let you read it, but after we're in the room," Priscilla said.

The lift halted at her floor and as soon as the doors opened, she dashed into the corridor towards her suite. Outside the door of her room, she fumbled with the key card, dropping it in front of her.

"Relax, I'll get it," Sean said, reaching down to pick up the card. As soon as he slid the card through the reader, she clutched the handle and thrust the door open, allowing them both to enter. Before he could even take two steps, Priscilla had closed the door behind them and engaged both locks.

She moved over to the desk and thrust down her handbag upon it. She reached inside, fished out the note, and handed it to Sean. "This case is getting out of hand," she said. "Your employer isn't paying me enough for this shit, Sean."

He unfolded the note and read it. "Um, Priscilla, I'm not quite certain this was produced by my employer," he said.

"What do you mean?!" she wailed. "He had someone murdered the other day, didn't he?" Tears were welling up in her eyes.

"Priscilla, we're an asset to my employer, not a burden," Sean said matter-of-factly. "The police officer is a liability because he's privy to other activities, which makes him unimportant."

The look in her eyes showed him the coldness of the statement did little to calm her down. "Remember, our sole purpose is to make certain my employer's status doesn't become public. Everything and everyone else involved is fair game."

"Including me and you, according to that letter," she said, pacing about the room.

"I'll not let that happen," Sean said, putting his hand on her shoulder.

"Oh, and what's your suggestion to protect us?"

"I've got a few associates that I'm going to call upon to help us," he said, holding the parcel up in his hand. "Over the last three years or so, I've made a few . . . acquaintances, shall we say, who have the means to undertake business not always located in advertisements."

"You've your own gunman-for-hire, have you?" Priscilla chortled. "You've seen too many spy movies on the telly, you have."

"No," he replied, "I'm not sure if they would acknowledge themselves as 'assassins' per se, like the one who murdered the young fellow yesterday. But they can handle themselves without fear of opposition." He reached into the envelope he received earlier and pulled out a short stack of files. He sat down at the table and flipped open the first, labeled ADRIAN RICHELIEU.

"A Frenchman?" Priscilla queried, looking over his shoulder.

"Yes. He controls a shipping organization, but I've discovered his former life consisted of time spent with the Foreign Legion, which still means he knows friends capable of accomplishing things others won't." He continued turning pages of the portfolio until he fell across the service histories. "But like most fellows in their line of work, it'll come with a price."

"Are you going to hire mercenaries to protect us?"

"Not quite. I'm not sure they'd want to hear themselves called that," Sean said.

"Then what are they going to do for you?" she asked, picking up the last bottle of Perrier from the miniature fridge. "If it's not for security, who are you sending them after?"

Sean held up the second file in answer to her question. "It would be this chap." He handed her the second folder labeled ANGUS DUNBAR.

Priscilla opened it and read the pages as she thumbed through them. "Angus Dunbar, born in Dundee, Scotland. Former British Army, Special Air Service type, experienced as a scout and sharpshooter. The prime suspect in the disappearance of an officer and senior enlisted man within his unit while serving in Bosnia, but never charged. Was discharged from service when he was found guilty of beating and raping a young woman in Londonderry during a routine patrol . . ." she murmured, her voice trailing off.

Flipping to the next page, she continued reading. "Dunbar escaped custody while being moved between the maximum-security prisons at Frankland near Durham and Wakefield in Yorkshire and is still at large." She closed the file. "You had this on him and did nothing?" Priscilla said, tossing the folder on the table. "You knew he was out there ready to kill someone?" She stared directly into Sean's eyes.

119

"I've been gathering the information in the hopes of never needing to wield it like this," Sean said. "My employer has, on occasion, approached him privately to solicit work. He's never had me telephone him, just as he did in this instance. What you have there, it's what I've assembled together over the last few years. The most significant element I require is a photo, since I've no inkling what this chap looks like."

"But you assume you can use the French to ferret him out, is that it?"

"Yes, I do," Sean said. "I've learned that both Richelieu's French Legion unit and Dunbar's SAS unit trained together on several occasions, and he might have a means of tracking him. Military types like Dunbar tend to establish patterns, and though they may be odd to you and me, they are readily detected by others."

Priscilla gulped down the last of her water, struggling to purge her mouth of the putrid taste lingering from what she had heard. "If that's the situation, how do we push on with the case?" She wanted so badly to turn her concerns to something she could concentrate on and control.

Sean picked up on it. "Based on this," he said, "we need to persuade the court that the sergeant was acting for a 'higher authority' his superior wasn't cognizant of. And after my discussion with his cousin last night, I might just have a notion how to do that."

"His cousin? What did you learn from him?"

"The good sergeant was passing along patrol schedules to the young fella who was murdered yesterday. Specifically, when it was clear to plan talks with the dock workers and deckhands on the ships," Sean said. "The sergeant's cousin also revealed one date was of specific relevance because the French supplier of the merchandise was planning to meet with Ewan."

"Oh hell, Sean, just say it. Drugs, they're dealing in drugs," Priscilla said in frustration.

"Yes, it's drugs," he said. "And that's all you'll hear from me. Anything else you learn could be your undoing."

"And your 'employer' is the cash behind it all?"

"He's got an agenda, as perverted as it sounds," Sean said. "Not only does he see the demand but feels he can produce the treatment." He went to the miniature fridge and took out a bottle of water. "And, you know, he just might do it in the end." Sean said.

Sitting on the corner of the bed, Priscilla dropped her head into her hands. "And we're to get the good sergeant freed, knowing all this?"

Sean glanced at her and recognized he was putting her life at risk by keeping information from her. "I know it all sounds absurd, but if we keep our wits about us, we'll do fine," he said. "Now, let's get our notes together and prepare for Monday, shall we?"

***

Sitting at the examination table centered in the police lab, Inspector Sheila Gordon was studying the contents of a report from Aberdeen University's School of Pharmacology. As she sipped her tea, she read over the school's evaluation of the drug sample obtained by Chief Inspector McDermott's search on the gas derrick, three weeks prior.

Sheila turned in her chair and peered at her colleague who was typing away on the computer. "Devin," she said, "are you done evaluating the hashish that was collected from the young lad at the airfield?"

"Aye, I've just finished," Devin said. "Here you go." He handed her the printout.

Sheila took the paper and laid it alongside the one from the university, and then slipped the one furnished by the French police in Marseille next to it. "Appears we've got a number of the same indicators," she said. "The same coding for the hashish and the resin extracted from the cannabis . . ." Her voice trailed off.

Chief Inspector McIntyre entered the lab. "What does it indicate for the 'unexplained' material?" he asked.

"Well, the French report lists it as a probable 'hallucinogenic' substance," Sheila said. "The university's report describes it as a genetically modified form of PCP."

"Well, that certainly falls into the group of 'hallucinogenic' drug, doesn't it?" McIntyre said.

"So, we've got essentially the same drug found on the support boat, on a bloke arrested at the airfield, and from a suicide in Marseille, France," Sheila said. She opened the evidence folder from Chief Inspector McDermott's visit to the gas derrick and pulled out the analysis report. "And the same for the liquor bottle found on a derrick in the North Sea. And they all look to be linked with the drugs from the Portsmouth investigation Scotland Yard was engaged in as well."

"It turns out we've got a consensus, then," CI McIntyre said. "The drugs all came from the same laboratory. But just where that laboratory is and who is working it remains to be clarified."

"And how much of this drug is still out amongst the public here in Aberdeen too," Sheila said.

"That, young lady, is for your gentleman friend and the other policeman to figure out." He gave her a subtle wink. "Now then, what do we have on the ballistics from the murder outside the courthouse?"

"Devin's been studying the slugs from all the recent victims," she said. "The ones from the signal house don't match the one from the sheriff's office."

"Have you figured out the caliber of each weapon yet?" CI McIntyre asked, turning to the young technician.

Devin nervously stepped forward and cleared his throat. "The bullets we retrieved from the two remains at the signal house came from a 40mm pistol. Doctor Quincy recovered one bullet nearly intact during his autopsy. Turns out it was a standard hollow-point round. It can be purchased at any gun shop with the appropriate licenses."

"Go on," McIntyre said, passing his hands through his hair.

"The bullet fragments you and Inspector Gordon recovered from the sheriff's office turns out to be of a .303 caliber. It must have been hand-packed because it didn't deform like a high-velocity type normally fired," Devin said. "Because of the caliber, it lends itself to be shot from a rifle."

The chief inspector closed his eyes and sighed, knowing the young technician had just opened Pandora's Box. The young man was recounting the specifications of the popular rifle and caliber used by sharpshooters in most militaries throughout the world. "And the rifling on the slug had a right-handed twist to it, I presume," McIntyre sighed.

"Yes, sir," Devin said, turning the page of the report. "It showed traces of that."

"Why is that significant?" Sheila asked.

"The rifle wielded by sharpshooters in the British Army and SAS is based on an American adaptation. They are a bolt-action with rifling in the barrel having ten twists per inch," McIntyre said. "In the competent and reliable hands of an experienced sniper, they can regularly strike an objective at approximately twelve hundred meters."

"But the shot that murdered the young lad in front of the sheriff's office was fewer than eight hundred fifty meters," Sheila said, peering over her notes.

"Which makes the gunman missing the first shot even more baffling."

Sheila's heart quickened at the recognition that the first shot might have been fired at her admirer. "Do you think the first one was meant for Andrew—I mean, Inspector Fletcher?" she asked. "If what you are suggesting is correct, a normal shot wouldn't have missed."

"With what's taking place on the trial and the sudden incursion of the hashish, I'm not sure," McIntyre said, recognizing the worried look in her eyes. "But, I'm quite positive Inspector Fletcher and Chief Inspector McDermott and the rest of the constables will do their level best to find out who's responsible."

***

An energetic group of young men were involved in a rugby match in the field across the park from where a solitary figure relaxed. Couples walked hand-in-hand, professing their affection for one another, while sporadic citizens jogged along the pathway.

After thirty-six hours of handling his ship in the North Sea, the skipper of the Nordic Supplier always reserved time to take in the simpler comforts of city life. Clive Duncan sat quietly on the bench watching the few families and their children playing in the park.

"It's peaceful, isn't it?" a voice from behind him said.

The captain turned and saw Dunbar standing behind the bench, hands clutched in front of him.

"You're the same bloke from the other day at the berths, aren't you?" Clive asked.

"Yes, I am."

"Is there something you need from me?" the captain asked, reaching for his knife fixed to his belt.

"Easy, Captain, you'll lose the fight before it's begun." Dunbar opened his jacket to reveal the pistol in his waistband.

"I'll ask my question again: what is it you want from me?" Clive asked. "And how am I to address you? What's your name?"

"There's nothing I need from you for the moment, Captain," Dunbar said. "And you may call me Mister Walker, for the time being. Now, getting down to business, I've been asked to talk to you—caution you, really—about your allegiances and who matters in your world."

"I'm not sure I follow," Clive said, twisting on the bench to get a better look at Angus.

"Our employer," Dunbar said, "aspires to remain anonymous. Moreover, he's asked me to spread the message to those who need to hear it. He's ready to keep his anonymity at all costs."

"Our employer?" the seaman asked. "Do you mean to tell me you're also working for this Higgins character?"

"Let's say he's arranging for my present and subsequent lifestyle expenses," Dunbar said with a snicker. "And in doing so, I provide him with the security not regularly found or overpowered. One young lad found out the hard way this morning not to make Mister Higgins uncomfortable."

"Is that so?"

"And I'm to caution you that the advice I'm providing goes for your associates as well," Dunbar said. "So, when you have a chance, remind Captain Fraser—your former first officer, I believe—what he's agreed to and what is demanded of him."

"Oh, and how did you manage to scare off this 'young associate,' if you don't mind me asking?" Clive asked, trying to hide his apprehension.

"You'll see in tonight's edition of the Evening Express," Dunbar said. "And for the record, I'm mindful of your flat location and your routine. Please, don't decide to cross me." He tilted his head and touched the brim of his hat before turning and walking away.

Watching this "Mr. Walker" as he strolled through the park, Clive Duncan whispered to himself, "We'll see how much you know about me and my routine." The captain stood up and pulled his cap down over his eyes before heading off toward his flat.

Walking the few blocks to his flat that he retained for occasions when he wasn't at sea, Clive pondered his next action. He got a sense that this fellow named Walker was not to be taken casually, but likewise that he had the means to undertake any action. He saw from his body language that he was confident, bordering on arrogant, in what he said he did and what he said he could pull off. His first step was to arrange for the delivery of his guest to a passing ship.

He made his way up the stairs and entered the small flat. He then went to sit down and relax at his desk. He drew out a leather journal, opened it, found a certain name and number, and picked up the phone to dial.

Before the end of the second ring, Sean Gilmore answered.

"Mister Gilmore, it's Captain Duncan, and I need your help."

"I'm listening."

"Can you arrange for an emergency resupply action for the *BP Platform Orion*?" Clive asked. "They'll be needing more 'drilling mud' and three medium bits."

The lawyer wrote down the information as the seaman dictated the material. "Is that all?"

"That's enough," he said. "It'll get things in motion to let me sail this evening."

Sean had a strange sense this would only be the beginning of his work helping the captain. "And who am I contacting to set this in motion?"

"Just call the Maritime office and convince them you're working for BP in Inverness. They shouldn't question you."

Sean pulled out his laptop, looked at his file containing the Maritime work schedule, and saw the name he was hoping to find. "I'll have this taken care of shortly," he said.

"Good. I'll be heading to the docks. I'll know if you were successful when the harbormaster delivers the manifests," Duncan replied. "And, Counselor, mind yourself from this point forward."

They hung up simultaneously.

Scrolling his list of names, Sean found the one for Nora Moffett and selected the number. In a minute, the call was answered.

"Coast Guard and Maritime, how can I help you?" the woman answered.

In just under three minutes, Sean Gilmore had relayed the message for Captain Duncan, setting a series of events into motion. The message would allow for the immediate sailing of the next available support boat, which just happened to be the Nordic Supplier, to deliver the material.

Chapter Fourteen

As the last of the supplies were secured, Captain Duncan signaled the engine room and the *Nordic Supplier* eased away from its berth. Getting the entire vessel resupplied and underway in only ninety minutes after receiving the message to do so was nearly a record for the crew.

Louis Clement was below taking a shower. The hot water spilled down his gaunt, powerful back, rinsing off the soap. Steam continued gathering near the ceiling even after he turned off the flow. Just as he stepped out to dry off there was a knock at the door.

"Just a minute," he said.

He reached into his duffle bag and pulled out some clothes. He tugged on a pair of slacks and a t-shirt before unlocking the door and opening it. It was Duncan.

"We've passed the breakwater," the captain declared.

"Excellent. The *Bonaparte* will be finishing up in Hamburg later this evening; which means we should be in position for the transfer by daybreak tomorrow," the Frenchman said.

"That's if the Royal Navy doesn't show up searching for the freighter again," Duncan said. "They've got a description of her and a probable claim of drug trafficking to link it to as well."

"Your Navy merely has a vague notion of what's going on, Captain," Louis said. "The other support vessel had finished goods on her when the police conducted their raid. They've nothing on you or your craft."

"And your business ashore, there's nothing the police will discover or suspect?"

"Hardly, my friend. I've done clandestine visits in places much more perilous than your city. Besides, the dispatching of the young fellow is meant to frustrate the police," Louis said. "The tougher challenge is if my associates and I can locate this elusive Mister Walker before you return to the harbor."

"But he's working for this Mister Higgins, who pays for quite a portion of my trade," Duncan said. "If Higgins learned of my concerns or my contacting you, I'm afraid my crew and I might be the next victims."

Pausing outside the cabin in the passage, the former Legionnaire looked at Clive Duncan and understood he was a man who was not afraid, but actually concerned for the welfare of those sailing with him. "Your consideration for your crew is commendable, Captain," he said. "But, I needn't remind you this Higgins fellow is responsible for my associate and me losing a profitable part of our business due to his last action. He'll be made to answer for his mistake, I assure you. Now, is it possible to have something to eat?"

Captain Duncan stared at the Frenchman and wondered if he'd made a mistake contacting the two clandestine owners of Papillion Transport for aid. "Aye, come on," he said. "We'll see if the cook has fixed supper."

They wandered along the passage, making their way to the galley where the aroma of garlic, rosemary, and olive oil on roast mutton filled the interior of the ship.

"Don't worry, Captain; I suspect that in fewer than seventy-two hours, this will all be over," Louis said. "Your description of this gentleman you saw in the park sounds vaguely similar to a British soldier I came across in Wales during a training mission. If that's the situation, he won't be hard to locate."

Peering over the serving counter, the sight of a roasted leg of lamb, potatoes, and vegetables greeted him. Alongside these were salad greens and other condiments, completing the first day's meal for the crew. "You've got a splendid cook," he said, taking a plate and making his supper.

Louis looked about the cramped galley, scrutinizing the faces of the men as they came and went. The time put in on the supply boat had weathered them as they carried out their tasks of replenishing the various derricks dotting the North Sea. After completing his meal, he rose and set his plate on a cart before heading out on to the working deck.

Shuffling past a container onboard the Nordic Supplier, Louis Clement pulled out a cigar from his pocket, snipping the point before wetting the tip. Such a fashionable vice to have, he thought as he fished for his lighter. After striking the flint, he allowed the butane flame to scorch the end until it flared red as he sucked in the mild Caribbean tobacco smoke.

Pocketing his lighter, he next took out his cell phone and scrolled through the listings until he came across the number for his companion, Hector Pichon. He selected the name to initiate the call. On the second ring, he was promptly answered by a recognizable voice.

"Oui, Louis," the Frenchman on the other end said.

"Are you in town yet?"

"Oui, Pasqual, and I just showed up. We'll be starting our way about the city in a short while. Do you have anything further on the objective?"

"No, but I'm confident it's the same man we dealt with in Wales," Louis said, taking a draw on his cigar. "You have the names of the two contacts; I would start with them before checking the taverns for him."

"But if they've traveled on since our last contact, we might not have an option," Hector said as he sat watching his companion, Pasqual, outfit his firearm with a silencer.

"I trust you'll encounter at least one of them."

"If you are so certain, then offer up a box of your brother's Cuban cigars as collateral, then."

"Fine. A dozen of Yves's finest. And what will you bring to the table?" Louis inquired.

"My cousin has one of the few remaining bottles of one-hundred-fifty-year-old Napoleon brandy; I'll coax him to hand it over as a gift," Hector replied, noticing Pasqual chuckle to himself at the exchange he heard.

"Then it's decided. Now, go and find Stuart and have your conversation. When you're done, don't forget to text me."

"What about Gregory?"

Sensing someone nearby, Louis turned to discover Captain Duncan a few meters away, puffing on his pipe. "Don't worry about him, he's got his own issues with his niece and the Italians," Louis said. "Don't forget to contact me. *Au revoir*." He turned to face Captain Duncan,

"My apologies for the intrusion," Duncan said, "but my first officer was concerned about your safety."

"Not to worry, Captain, this is not my first time on the open seas," Louis said. "Plus, where else in this world can you stand and see such an impressive sight such as those?" he said, looking upward and waving his arm at the shimmering forms of the stars.

***

Across town from the harbor, a local pub was preparing to see its business pick up. A throng of students—regular patrons from the university—were settling in for their own adaptation of Britain's Got Talent karaoke. The owner of the pub agreed to their entertainment since Thursday evenings were quiet, unless a cricket match was being aired.

Unwinding at the end of the long counter, a solitary figure sat, head hunched down with an empty shot glass upturned in front of him. As the designated emcee announced the participants for the night's acts, the patron motioned for another drink.

Strolling through the door, the former members of the French Foreign Legion, Hector Pichon, and Pasqual Sequin, arrived. They were soon jostling with the locals as they jockeyed for seats in front of the impromptu stage. Staring past the front row of chairs, Hector spotted their mark.

"In the corner," he said to Pasqual. "Locate a spot behind him while I have a chat."

After splitting up, Hector saw his companion discover a vacant chair at the last unoccupied table along the wall. Turning his attention back to the target, he quickly stood next to the former army corporal and current Glasgow criminal, Stuart Ross.

"You don't look so well, Stuart," Hector said, noticing the empty pint and shot glasses.

Lifting his head, Stuart Ross saw the face of a man he'd swear was a ghost. With the fog of whisky lifting with every flutter of his eyes, he recognized the face didn't belong to a ghost, but his former adversary.

"Where in the hell did you come from, Hector?"

"That doesn't matter for the moment. What matters is our need to have a civilized conversation," the Frenchman said. Searching around the pub, Hector knew this would not be the place to have an altercation; there were too many witnesses.

Grasping the whisky placed before him, Stuart contemplated his choices. "I assume you're not alone, are you?" he asked. "Is Louis behind us, or are you braving this encounter by yourself?"

"You're clever to ask, Stuart," Hector responded. "No, I'm not alone. I've brought Pasqual with me." He nodded in the direction of the corner where Pasqual was sitting. "He wished to visit the highlands of your beautiful country."

Turning in his chair, Stuart saw the other Frenchman lifting his water glass in recognition.

"What do you want?" he asked, concentrating his gaze upon Hector.

"We're searching for your friend," Hector said.

"I've got a few of those, you know. You'll have tae be more specific."

Hector wasn't in the mood to play games with the Scotsman. Drawing his dagger from his boot, he leaned in and spoke under the cover of the singing of a young woman doing her best to imitate Madonna.

"We're looking for the Scot, Angus Dunbar. Where is he?" He touched the point of his blade against Stuart's ribs.

Feeling the edged weapon against his side, Stuart sobered up enough to realize he was in trouble if he lied. "Dammit, I don't know. I'm telling you the truth, Hector. I've nae seen him since last year. It's possible he's had a touch of surgery to change his looks by now."

"We've been made aware he's becoming busy here in Aberdeen. Is this true?"

"What do you know?" Stuart asked, wondering how the Frenchman was getting his information. It had only been two days since Ewan and Ian's murders had taken place. Moreover, he previously considered the possibility of the killings being accomplished at the hand of Angus.

"Someone passed along a kit to him in the last few days. He's used it to dispatch a young Scot just the other day," Hector continued. "It's even possible there's a second victim by now. And I want to see he's stopped before he targets the wrong person."

Signaling the barkeeper over, Stuart ordered a cup of coffee for himself. "All I know is, he gets contacted by an Irishman who goes by the name 'Mister Higgins' nowadays. I'm told this Higgins fellow is in Dublin or even Belfast most the time. Rumor has it he might have been a Legionnaire at one time."

"I don't care about the Irishman," Hector said. "I'm only interested in Angus."

"I've got a mobile number in my wallet," Stuart said, moving his hand from the bar.

"No sudden movements; you don't want Pasqual to get excited, now."

Stuart slowly opened his billfold and took out a business card out which had nothing except a phone number written on it. "This was the last number I had for contacting him," he said, placing the card on top of the bar. "It was good six weeks ago," Stuart grasped the mug of coffee the barkeep had brought.

Stuffing the card in his pocket, Hector said, "I'll be around long enough to know if you're lying to me." He slid the weapon back into its sheath. "I suggest you grab yourself something to eat and sober up so you're capable of defending yourself. You're a better man than this," he said, nudging one of the empty shot glasses.

Angling away from the Scotsman, Hector made his way outside. Accompanying him, Pasqual hesitated long enough to hear the last lines of a Dire Straits song being sung off-key by several drunken patrons.

***

Remaining alone in the detective's office, the former naval officer felt the sensation of the ship's motion as he recalled his time in the communications suite of the cruiser, Edinburgh. Just as he did ten years earlier, he held the headphones close against his ears. The static of the radio transmission filled the headphones before he could hear a voice responding to the call.

Leaning back in his chair, McDermott screwed his eyes shut; attempting to discern whose voice he was hearing. In moments, a woman's voice came from the recording: "Aye, this is the *Standard-Apollo*, send your traffic." Over the next five minutes, the caller to the vessel spoke, relaying a list of gear and perishables they would transfer to the platform being serviced. "Copy all, *Apollo* out," the woman replied before the transmission ended.

Ambling into the office, Fletcher noticed the concentration edged across his partners face, and smiled at the notepad he was using to scribble his thoughts on. About time he took his own damn notes, the young inspector thought.

Opening his eyes, McDermott saw Fletcher grinning at him. "What? You find something funny, do you?" he asked, pulling the headset from his ears.

"Just glad you're writing the few tidbits down, that's all," Fletcher replied. "Mister McIntyre said we might have something on the fingerprints tomorrow. So, are you hearing anything that matters?"

Reading the notepad, McDermott answered. "The *Standard-Apollo* has a woman for a first officer. Her name is Alison Reid. She was with them when we found the cylinder last month, remember?"

"Yes, but, what makes this a significant issue?"

"Our friend Jones mentioned the Atkins girl had a lady-friend. I'm thinking it might be this first officer," McDermott said. "If the captain and first officer know about the drugs, then the engineer is conspiring with the dockworkers. This means we've got a triumvir to charge with a crime."

Fletcher looked at his partner and blinked hard. "You're daft, you know. The Atkins girl, she's an engineer working a separate boat; how is she supposed to manage what happens on another one?"

"I'll wager a tenner they talked about whom to trust. How else do you think Jones folded so easy in court, and Campbell was a mute?" McDermott asked.

"All right," Fletcher conceded. "Say you've got the ladies discussing which bloke to trust, what about the captain's role in all this? He's the one in charge, you don't think he'd have a say in all this?" Fletcher asked, folding his arms.

"They'd be in it up to their necks, all right," McDermott said. "And if we follow along that line, it puts the crew of the *Apollo* out of the mix. I mean, we've got the captain—what's his name?"

Fletcher removed the file from their arrest and flipped it open. "Dillan McKenzie," he said. "And as you mentioned, the First Officer is Alison Reid, and we have the deckhand, Campbell."

"Aye, so we have those three locked up. Now we need to confirm the three working the *Hercules*. And I'm nae including Jones; he was too simple," McDermott said, scrawling the names on the easel next to his desk.

"You don't suppose one of the two blokes killed at the signal house was part of the *Hercules* crew, do you?" Fletcher asked. "Getting rid of them might have been a way to send a message to the others. McIntyre said they found drugs amongst their belongings."

"We know Doyle was nae; we met him on when we followed the gas supplies," McDermott said.

"Which leaves the other bloke, then." Fletcher replied. "He doubtless was the one with the drugs."

"Aye, but it wasn't hashish they found, it was marijuana and prescription-grade amphetamines and barbiturates," McDermott said, scratching his chin with the pen.

"Did you catch any other mention of the Irishman while you were listening?" Fletcher asked, pointing at the headphones.

"Not on the last five transmissions," McDermott said. "Did you note the transmission date or recording number when you were listening at the Maritime office?"

Leafing through the pages of his notebook, Fletcher glanced at the annotations before stopping. "It was the fifteenth. Two days after the sergeant mentioned their meeting with the Frenchman."

McDermott sat behind his computer and scrolled through the files before selecting the proper one. He adjusted the settings to play the recording over the computer speakers, so Fletcher could listen.

"Maritime Exchange, what is your party's number?" came the operator's voice over the speaker.

"This is Captain Duncan, I wish to place a ship-to-shore call to the following number . . ." They listened as Duncan recited the phone number.

"Play that back," Fletcher said, grabbing his pen. McDermott restarted the recording, allowing it to play past the captain speaking. They waited patiently as the connection was made, and a different young woman's voice answered. "Callaghan & Higgins Limited, how can I help you?"

"Is Mister Higgins available?"

"I'm sorry, but Mister Higgins is not available at the moment. May I take a message?"

"Please have him contact Captain Clive Duncan of the *Nordic Supplier*. He can reach me at the following exchange . . ."

The inspectors continued listening as the vessels captain gave the receptionist the communication link.

"I'll pass it along, sir," she said.

"*Nordic Supplier* out."

The communication ended.

McDermott stopped the recording and sat grinning like a fool. "Let's see where that number leads us, shall we?"

Fletcher peered at the clock. "How about we tackle that tomorrow?" he asked. "Sheila and I have plans, and I'm sure Ailene would like you home at a reasonable hour."

"Aye, you've got a point," McDermott said. "Let's get everything picked up and we'll go at it again tomorrow, like you say."

Chapter Fifteen

Ambling into the Police Scotland building, Inspector Fletcher gave his companion, Inspector Sheila Gordon, a brief peck on the cheek before entering his office. "See you for lunch?"

"Aye, if I'm nae too busy," she replied as she headed to the forensics lab.

Opening the office, Fletcher found things on his desk just as neat and organized as he had left them, which was in stark comparison to that of his colleague. "It's like I'm his bloody nursemaid," he murmured aloud. He began picking up the wadded papers from around McDermott's chair and tossing them into the rubbish, along with several empty Styrofoam cups. He clutched the now full bin and walked it to a large trashcan in the corridor.

"Did the night watch forget our office?" McDermott asked as he approached. Fletcher finished unloading the contents of the bin.

"I don't think our office is on their docket."

"Well, come on, then, we've got a puzzle to figure out," McDermott said.

"You and your bloody 'puzzle' descriptions. Did you ever finish one when you were a boy?" Fletcher asked, sliding the waste bin behind McDermott desk.

"I don't recall if I did or not, but it's not relevant at the moment," he said. "Since we've got a few minutes, give the Maritime office a call and see if you can obtain the return date for the *Hercules* like a decent fellow."

Grabbing the phone, Fletcher began dialing the number. After a few brief minutes, he'd gotten an answer to McDermott's question.

"The ship returns the day after tomorrow," Fletcher said. "They've checked in from the second-to-last platform and should leave near three o'clock this afternoon. The Maritime office doesn't have a specific arrival time, but their best prediction will be after six in the evening."

"We'll need to make a note to tell Mister MacCallum so we've constables at the ready when the ship returns then," McDermott said. A soft knock on the door stopped their conversation as Sergeant McKee stuck her head in the office.

"Morning, gentlemen," she announced. "I've last night's activity sheet for you to study. Suggests we've another contact with someone handling your drugs," passing over the report.

"They're nae my drugs, lass, so mind your tongue," McDermott said, chiding the police officer as he accepted the sheet from her. She left without another word.

Leafing through the document, McDermott observed the suspect was an undergraduate at the university caught trying to sell near a prominent club. He imagined this was how his niece Edna had been exposed to drugs while studying in Portsmouth.

Fletcher, noticing the concentration McDermott was giving the sheet, was reluctant to violate his partner's thoughts. "Is there just the one occasion?" he asked.

McDermott blinked as Fletcher spoke but didn't hear the question. "What did you say?"

"I asked if it was merely one arrest," Fletcher answered.

"Aye, just the one. Near the mosque off Sunnybrook," McDermott said. "After worship the mullah was standing outside with several of the worshippers and saw the activity. He called for a local patrol and pointed out the suspect. The policemen found three balloons of hashish, a wee morsel of marijuana, and practically a thousand euros in small bills."

"It wouldn't hurt to see if the hashish matches what came off the ships, don't you agree?" Fletcher asked.

"Aye. And while you're at it, go ask Sergeant Giles to check for a correlation of this fellow to the dockworkers. We might need to look at expanding our investigation into the trafficking beyond the waterfront."

Meandering down the hall, he soon came to the senior constables' space. "Sergeant, have you got a minute?" Fletcher asked, standing in the open doorway of Sergeant Giles's office.

"Aye, Inspector Fletcher, what can I help you with?"

"Chief Inspector McDermott and I need help from the detectives who made the arrest last night of the drug pusher. Can you have them check to see if he has any possible contacts with dockworkers or crew members from the ships?"

"Aye, I'll add that to their list for examination."

"Thank you, Sergeant Giles. Let us know what they turn up when you can," Fletcher said and headed for the forensics lab.

While Fletcher was conducting his rounds, McDermott sat in the office staring at the whiteboard containing their remarks, mentally piecing together his proverbial jigsaw puzzle. *The Frenchman, Sutherland, Campbell, Jones, and a mystery client*, he thought from their first meeting. Add the Irishman, three ship captains with their first officers and engineers or deck hands to the blend. He rose, drawing a path from each suspect he established. "And if we include the three bodies to the crowd, we've twenty possibilities or better." He groaned just as Fletcher returned.

"Which parts don't fit?" Fletcher asked as he looked at the lines across the board.

Turning, McDermott's lips twisted on his face before he responded. "I don't think it's a 'fit' like a squiggly puzzle piece, but more like rings in a tree trunk." He stopped at the Irishman's mark. "And he's at the center of it."

"But only if we go on the assumption he's the cash behind the trafficking," Fletcher said. "And if we place him in the center who takes up the next ring, the Frenchman?"

"I'm nae sure," McDermott said. "I'm considering him the supplier. There's someone else on our end that fits next to the Irishman." He glanced at the list of names. Suddenly he exclaimed: "Where are the documents from Glasgow?"

Fletcher dug through the file cabinet, removing two files from the second drawer. "Here they are: Hunt and Wallace," he said, holding the files stenciled with CONFIDENTIAL across the front.

McDermott took the one for Hunt and began flipping through the pages, examining the text from the police officers' surveillance. Pausing at one page, he glanced up at the whiteboard and then snatched a pen. "It's Hunt, he's the next layer after the Irishman. The statement claims he was meeting with Wallace just after we pinched the sergeant."

"So? It doesn't confirm he's the next cog, though," Fletcher said. "All the papers say is that they had supper, that's all."

"You've looked at the documents; Hunt is giving the orders," McDermott said. "And Wallace has been there taking them. We need to find out other associates of Hunt who might be here in Aberdeen." He picked up the phone and punched in the number for the sergeant's desk.

"Giles here," the sergeant said.

"Sergeant, this is Chief Inspector McDermott," he said. "I need you to contact the Glasgow office and see if they have any other contacts associated with an Alistair Hunt. What . . .? Yes, I need it right away; everybody who's working for him and who might have reason to be here in Aberdeen."

Just as McDermott placed the phone down, it buzzed back. "Aye, McDermott speaking," he responded. "Aye, hen, I'll send him in a minute." He hung up and looked at Fletcher. "Go on, Sheila needs to see you in the lab."

Wandering out of the office and down the hallway, Fletcher was left speculating what Sheila would want after just starting work a while ago. Nudging open the door, he caught sight of her, eyes fastened to the microscope, analyzing something. "You needed to see me, Inspector Gordon?"

Hearing Fletcher's voice, she twisted in her chair. "Aye, Inspector Fletcher," she said. "We've got a preliminary report on the drugs from both the airfield and mosque arrests." She shifted the chair across the floor to her desk. Picking up the top file, she got up and handed it to Fletcher. "Each one was an identical make-up to the original from Portsmouth," Sheila said. "But, by handling each lot, it becomes weaker somehow."

He opened the file and stared at the computer printout, his eyebrows rising as he read halfway down the sheet. "I'm not a chemist, Sheila, what do the figures mean?"

"Sorry," she said, taking back the folder. "See how the hashish and cannabis-resin numbers stay pretty steady?" She pointed to each column. "But the 'unidentified' drug drops incrementally when analyzed. Mister McIntyre and I suspect this breaks down in the saline somehow."

"I'll accept your account for it," Fletcher said. "Glancing at this nevertheless, you're suggesting the first two drugs came from the same source."

"Yes, absolutely," she said. "Quite like starter yeast for the dough in a bakery."

"I'm not certain if this is favorable news or bad," he said. Turning to leave, he paused after the first stride. "Oh . . . just so you're not caught by surprise, Conor is having Sergeant Giles contact Glasgow. We think we might have discovered a link to our buyer."

"Ok, I guess," Sheila said, puzzled.

"Sheila, he feels the link is Alistair Hunt," Fletcher whispered. "And he wants the names of everybody associated with him." He looked into her eyes. "That means your mom will be on the list, I'm sure."

"Thank you for thinking of me and Mum, Andrew," Sheila said. "I've already discussed this with Mister MacCallum, though. He said he'd deal with it if she was called in, and I trust he'll do the right thing." Leaning over the counter, she kissed him on the cheek. "Go on, run back to work."

Moving past one of the detective constables, Fletcher made his way to McDermott, passing over the forensic report of the hashish that had been confiscated. The look on McDermott's face did not alter from Fletcher's as he studied the file on the drugs. "I was nae good working to interpret codes as an officer, Andrew, and I'm nae better with age," he said. "What does it all mean?"

"According to the evaluation, the hashish and cannabis-resin we've seized at every instance come from the same shipment," Fletcher said. "As Sheila explained it, the 'foreign' chemical added to the resin breaks down each time the drug is tested," he continued. "So, if we regard someone in Marseille as the originator, they made the truest batch." He paused to catch his breath. "And then someone on the freighter split the shipment to make more money, and the drug got weaker. And when your lot from the gas derrick was testing weaker than what we have in the lab in London."

"So, you're suggesting it's like someone taking a rare single malt and adding ice," McDermott said. "The first sip is okay, but in the end, the last sip is thinned down."

"Yes. Which makes locating the lab manufacturing the drugs essential for the French," Fletcher said, resting back in his chair. "What we've come across, both here and in Portsmouth are tarnished goods."

"Aye, but the drugs are nevertheless out there," McDermott said, pointing to the door. "And they're being hawked by someone working the docks or boats." He reexamined his list on the whiteboard. Past the names, he could see the ghosts of Kyle Smythe and his niece, Edna Gallagher, staring back at him. "And if we did nae get our shit in one sock, we might end up with another casualty on our hands."

***

139

The clamoring of steel pipes and equipment working at different speeds echoed off the structure of the gas derrick. While the movement above continued at a constant pace, the *Standard-Hercules* was fighting the ocean swells to maintain its position below the deck-mounted crane.

Several deckhands scurried across the open space, hooking cables to a cluster of fuel drums for delivery to the derrick's generator. This took place under the observant eyes of First Officer Blake Young and Second Engineer Sammie Atkins standing a safe distance away along the rail.

"What do you think the police wanted with you?" Blake asked over the commotion.

"I'm nae sure," Sammie said.

"You're nae worried it has something to do about Ewan?" the officer asked, glancing at the young woman for a clue.

"I don't think so, Blake," she said. "Last I picked up from him was just before his meet with the Frenchman. Alison and I were on a wee shopping trip for a few days in Edinburgh right after passing him his notice."

"Nevertheless, Bernard and I are concerned we might lose you to the police; so, now's the time to have your version right."

"I've been piecing the moments together as best I can, you know," she said. "All I can come up with is a wee slice of time I had with Allen Doyle. He was worked up about Ewan's arrest and demanded to know if we'd be keeping up our deliveries."

Referring to the former dockworker caused the first officer to turn and face the ship's engineer. "When did you meet with him?"

"Oh, must have been two—no—three days before we set off," Sammie said. "Why?"

"You didn't hear?" Blake asked. "The police found Doyle and another bloke dead in the signal house the night before we shoved off."

The color left Sammie's face as she heard the news. "I was busy seeing the ship ready. Mister Fischer was allowing me to do all the start-up operations, so I was onboard the last three days before leaving the harbor," she said. "Do you know how it took place? I mean, have the police said anything more about them?"

The crash of a freight container on deck interrupted their exchange. The deckhands were all pointing and yelling at the derrick's crane, while the derrick crew behaved in a similar fashion.

"Who in the hell's handling the deck?" came the voice of Bernard McIntosh, captain of the Hercules over the deck's loudspeaker.

Lumbering up to the senior deckhand, First Officer Young soon found out the newest member of the deck crew was giving hand signals to the crane operator. "Sorry, Mister Young, I thought the youngster needed a little practice," the deckhand explained.

Watching down from the bridge, Bernard McIntosh watched his senior officer speak to the crew, recognizing he would remedy the situation. What he didn't see was his Second Engineer, Sammie Atkins still standing near the rail. Picking up the intercom, he signaled the engine room. "Mister Fischer, is Miss Atkins back on station?"

"Aye, she's back in the control suite."

"Very well. After your break, have her come up to the bridge and see me. Out."

Sammie picked up on the exchange and acknowledged the senior engineer. "I heard; go ahead, I've got things handled here," she said. Turning her attention to the countless dials and gauges, she would have to worry about what was to come later.

"All ahead one-third," Captain McIntosh announced as he ordered the *Standard-Hercules* away from the drilling rig. Feeling the vessel surge ahead and away from the complex, he commenced setting his return voyage to Aberdeen Harbor and their berth along the Regent's Quay.

Soon, deckhands were securing the gear they'd taken onboard from the derrick. With skills honed over years of repetition, each group accomplishing their tasks, securing material to the seventy-three-meter-long ship.

"Engineer Atkins to the bridge," Bernard said into the ship's intercom. "Clear the bridge, gentlemen," he said, in order to the watch operating the navigation and steering components. Moments later, the ship's Second Engineer, Samantha Atkins entered.

"You wished to see me, Captain?"

"Aye, I did," the broad-shouldered captain said. "Blake spoke to you about the police, didn't he?"

"Aye, he did. And like I mentioned to him; I've no clue what they want from me," she said, her voice steady with confidence. "Blake also mentioned Doyle and his mate being murdered, but I've nae had any dealings with him before Sutherland's meet with the Frenchie."

Bernard McIntosh paced the span of the bridge while contemplating what his engineer had just said. "I'd hate to lose you tae something stupid, Sammie," he said. "You're sure there's nothing from when the *Apollo* was searched leading back to you? Anything at all?"

Hearing her captain's concerns, it was Sammie's turn to pace the bridge, stopping at the open window long enough to enjoy the cool breeze as it traveled through her dampened scalp. "Nothing, Bernard, I swear to you," she said. "I'd nae put you and Blake in a position like that. I'd not put Ali in a spot of bother, either," she said, alluding to her companion, Alison Reid.

"Good enough," the captain said. "But, I think you need to remain aboard for a day or two." He placed his arm around her. "I'll feel better seeing you're safe here than by yourself at the flat. Agreed?"

Looking into his gentle blue eyes, Sammie Atkins knew why she loved sailing with this crew, and it showed in her captain's character. "Aye, I'll stay aboard for a few days," she said. "Mister Fischer mentioned checking on the auxiliary generator, so I'll have a wee sample of work to do anyway."

"All I'm proposing is three days, Sammie," Bernard said. "Afterward, I'll give you three with payment."

"Nae worries, Bernard, I'll be okay," she said. "If you dinnae mind, I'll see to arranging for the shutdown now," turning away and heading to the ladder well.

Chapter Sixteen

It was the third time in two weeks he sat alone working through each fragment of evidence, each clue of those involved plaguing McDermott's thoughts. Sipping cold coffee did little to spark his thinking as he pieced his puzzle together.

Carrying out on his concept of a tree ring, he drew a silly stick figure of the sergeant with a watering can, showering the rings. This was his interpretation that the sergeant was furnishing intelligence to each member on the drug movements. "How does he know what tae tell them?" he asked loudly.

Drumming his pen on the desk, he sketched a spider web, associating the suspects. "Always Hunt," he said, muttering to himself as the lines crossed the board. "Never this Mister Higgins."

Opening the report of associates related to Alistair Hunt, McDermott placed each character in a job. "Who has the most tae lose, I wonder?" He continued reading off the names. Near the bottom of the list, he noted the name of his secretary. "I wonder," he muttered to himself.

"Wonder about what, Inspector?" the voice came from the doorway.

Surprised, McDermott flinched at hearing the question. He turned and saw Constable Ames standing halfway inside his office. "What are you doing, lass?" he asked. "I nearly peed myself."

"Sorry, I was just making my rounds of the rooms and saw your light on," she said. "You've quite the puzzle there." She pointed to the whiteboard and colored lines crisscrossing it.

"Aye, looks a wee bit messy for the time being," he said. Looking at the young woman gave him a notion. "Do you have access to the personnel files, hen?"

"I've got the master keys," she responded. "So, I suppose I have access. Why do you ask, Inspector?"

"I've got a hunch I need to follow up on for our case, but I need to check one officer's service record," McDermott said. Andrew will nae like the idea, he told himself, but I need to know something before we meet.

"Well, I need to go back to the foyer and check in, then I'll see you in the admin office," the young constable said, leaving him alone.

Closing the file, McDermott made his way to the admin office where he stood by for the constable's arrival. In minutes she arrived, keys swinging from a ring, the clinking sound reminding him of the prison guard in a motion picture.

Going in, he went straight to the cabinet holding the personnel files and opened the "G" drawer. Leafing through, he found the one-tagged S. GORDON and pulled it out.

"Is Inspector Gordon a suspect now?" the constable asked, noticing the folder he pulled.

"No, she's not," McDermott replied. "I'm just verifying an acquaintance, that's all." He began flipping the pages until he found her family record. Scanning over the entries, he saw her next-of-kin entry. "Janice M. Gordon, mother. Current residence, Hillhead district, Glasgow." Closing the file, he replaced it and closed the drawer. "Thank you, Constable Ames, I've seen what I needed."

After wandering out of admin and back to his office, McDermott sat in his chair. *How do I let Andrew know Sheila's mother is an individual of concern?* he asked himself. And what part does she play in Alistair Hunt's business, and another question demanding to be clarified? Peering at the time, he saw it was nearing midnight. Closing his desk and locking the file cabinet of evidence, he made his way to the flat he shared with his companion, Ailene. The knowledge of what he had just reviewed would make for an uneasy few hours of slumber.

***

Sitting back with the evening paper, Dunbar studied the patrons of the hotel milling about the foyer. Several young women sat together at the small bar sipping drinks. He directed his attention on one with auburn hair, speculating how eager she would be if he took her for a stroll. Or if she would put up a struggle like the others he'd picked up in the past before he had his way with her.

Flipping the page, he came across a minor story on a young man's murder in the Kincorth district. Reading the material, it said a flat occupant was found dead, from a supposed break-in and robbery gone bad. Police were still conducting their investigation. "You need to watch yourself, Angus," he said to himself as he sipped his tea.

Shifting his weight in the chair, he felt the barrel of his pistol dig into his back, reminding him of his business. *The ship captain will be a challenge*, he thought. *I can't use the signal house; I've ruined that location,* briefly recalling his earlier work on the two longshoremen. *I can't rely on him to always going to his flat either, he'd avoid it since we had our little chat*, he told himself.

An attendant came to where he was sitting. "Another cup of tea, sir?"

"Please; and just include it to my room tab," Dunbar said, handing over his empty cup. He turned to the sports page and was about to check the rugby scores from the 7-Nation competition, when his cell phone warbled. Glancing at the display, he thought it was the number of Stuart Ross and acknowledged the call. "Good evening, Stuart, what can I do for you?"

"Bon jour, Monsieur Dunbar," the member of Papillion Transport said.

A cool sweat appeared on Angus's brow at hearing the Frenchman's greeting. Moving his gaze about the room, he sought to determine who was on the other end of the call. "Who is this, and how in the hell did you learn this number?" he demanded. Stuart has turned against me, he thought.

"Mon Ami, I've been asked to discuss your ongoing work," Hector Pichon said. "It appears you've taken extra steps which are not part of your arrangement with your employer."

"My business has nothing to do with you," Dunbar said, smiling graciously at the waiter bringing his tea back. "What I'm doing is well within my employer's wishes." His hand was shaking as he put a measure of sugar into his tea and stirred.

"This employer you're contracting with, he can't be trusted, you know. He's isolated others, and when necessary, disposed of those no longer associated with his business," the Frenchman said.

"Is that so? I've done business with Michael—" He stopped himself before he could utter the last name. Dammit, I need to be more vigilant, Dunbar thought, chastising himself for the lapse.

"Enjoy your tea, Mister Dunbar; I'll be in contact tomorrow," Hector said, ending the call. Keying the switch on his microphone, he spoke to his partner. "Do you see him?" Pascual asked while he remained outside the lobby of the hotel, listening on his earpiece.

"Oui, he's quite nervous right now."

"Don't forget, we need his room number," Hector said. "Do your best not to alarm the hostess this time, we need to maintain close tabs on Dunbar or we'll miss our moment."

"I'll be polite," Pasqual said, pocketing the small receiver before strolling past Dunbar sitting in the parlor, and into the hotel café, picking up a menu.

Lingering in the chair, Dunbar sipped his tea, his mind scrambling with schemes of how he had been compromised tonight and who was responsible. *It can only be Stuart Ross. He dispatched me to tidy-up for his two chaps*, he thought, recalling their meeting in Glasgow. But he's nae seen me in the last three years, and only his man Reggie Brown has contacted me since then.

Pasqual watched the server preparing his order, and when her back turned, he shuffled the receipts. Identifying one with orders for two drinks, paid for by an 'A. Walker' and listed under room 415. The hostess turned around and handed over the order, which Pasqual paid for with cash.

"Thank you, and have a delightful evening," the Frenchman said as he strolled through the lobby past the nervous Scotsman again.

Making his way down the lane, he quickly caught up with Hector walking back to their hotel in silence.

***

Early afternoon drew into the late evening hours as the two counselors for the disgraced sergeant assigned to the Aberdeen office continued to organize their approach for court. Nibbling the tip of her pen, Priscilla El-Sayed read over her questions for what seemed to be the tenth time before talking them out. "Based on the correspondence your informant provided, we can't explain the sergeant having any communication with outside jurisdictions. All he did was pass along the memo."

Sean Gilmore let out a groan. "The evidence of the sergeant's call to his cousin is serious," he said. "And this Inspector McDermott from Scotland Yard has alluded to 'current investigations' that carry evidence against him. Which causes me think it must be another series of recordings."

"If that's true, we're fighting a strenuous battle, Sean," his colleague replied. "Unless we can cite Hamilton's unwillingness to

146

make the evidence accessible for our analysis," Priscilla said, wrapping her fingers through strands of her hair.

"The sheriff's office might be closed because of the murder, but we can still request the police for copies of their evidence," Sean said. "And if they refuse, we'll cite the superintendent for interference, which supports your opening statements."

"I like the way you're thinking, Sean," Priscilla said, waving her pen in the air. "But that will only work for the evidence they've collected as part of the prosecution against Wallace. This Chief Inspector bloke said they're conducting ongoing investigations, which means they might not have other recordings of the sergeant listed under his case."

"It's worth a go in my books," Sean said. "If nothing else, we might make Hamilton nervous, and have him considering something about what we might know. Who knows? It might provoke him to make a mistake we can take advantage of when it comes along."

"Even if we have nothing?" she asked, raising her eyebrows.

"Come now, Priscilla," he said. "You recall the card games from school; part of the thrill is bluffing your way to winning the pot. I'll wager just having to pass the other evidence to us will have the prosecutor's knickers in a twist. And they'll be stumbling over themselves, trying to work a new tact during the trial."

She regarded her colleague with a suspicion. *He's sporting a game of high-stakes poker, he is*, she thought. *Daddy would just let loose a few missiles and finish the job*, recalling her father's career with the Saudi Air Force.

"Okay, say Hamilton refuses to agree to hand over the recent evidence," Priscilla said. "We can press the matter their manuscripts are wrong as a gesture of dodgy record-keeping," she continued. "And from that position, we can proceed to hammer that the only true piece of evidence was the sergeant making a legitimate call to his relative."

"I like your train of thought," Sean said. "Do we lead with that come Monday when the trial resumes?"

"It all depends on the reply from the police tomorrow when we make our request for the evidence this Scottish inspector declared," Priscilla said. "Until then, I propose we wash up and catch a bite to eat. I'm quite famished after all this conversation."

"I agree," Sean said. "I'll meet you in an hour." He headed for the door.

147

Thinking of the mysterious message from this morning, Priscilla felt an unusual chill course through her body. "Sean, do you mind staying here until I'm ready? After this morning, I don't think I'm ready to be by myself after reading that note."

"Sure, I understand," he said. "You can find me settled right here." He pointed at the comfortable chair by the window.

"Won't be long," Priscilla said, gathering her panties, bra, and stockings from her suitcase. Within moments of entering the bathroom, she exited. "Helps to have these, too," she said, reaching in the closet and grabbing a hanger containing a blouse and skirt.

Priscilla returned to the bathroom, leaving Sean to his thoughts as he sat listening to her shower.

Closing his eyes, he tried to imagine Priscilla standing naked in the shower. He fantasized water cascading over her breasts and down her figure before splashing into the drain. Accompanying this vision was one with her swirling a lathered hand-towel down her shoulders and towards her crotch.

What seemed like an hour became just five minutes as Priscilla finished in the bathroom. "Sean, I'm ready," she said, snapping him out of his thoughts.

"Sorry, just dozing off," Sean blurted out, hoping his brief fantasy wouldn't turn into a nightmare. Rising from the chair, he was relieved to see the lack of an erection, though he was sure he would have had one. "I'll do my best to be as quick as you," he said, grabbing his notes from the table.

Showing her out of the room, they hastily made their way two floors above to his room, where he experienced the endless supply of chilly water.

After getting showered and dressed, the two lawyers exited the lift, stopping at the front desk to ask about the local eateries that might be open at this late hour. After a few questions and remarks, the clerk suggested a small restaurant nearby.

The small Italian restaurant was busy but not crowded, even though it was nearing eleven o'clock at night. Most of the patrons were couples or groups of businesspersons ending their harried day. Priscilla and Sean located a spot in the cramped dining room and were soon looking over the menu.

"I wonder how their calamari is?" she asked, catching a glimpse of the appetizer at a table nearby.

"You're joking, right?" Sean asked. "Tiny octopus for supper? No wonder you're a thin as a rail."

"Don't be foolish, it's just a starter," she said. "Plus, when they're cooked in the correct manner, it's quite delicious."

After a few minutes, they had placed their orders and were enjoying a chilled bottle of chardonnay. Sean softened a piece of bread in the olive oil and herb blend and took a bite before initiating their conversation about the case. "For tomorrow, we need to ask not only for the files this Chief Inspector McDermott alluded to, but likewise a list of names," he said. "So far, Hamilton has only selected people we know of to testify against the sergeant."

"You think he's holding someone back?" Priscilla asked, dipping her bread in the warm marinara sauce. "If he is, we'll be hard-pressed to obtain the upper hand. Doesn't your other contact have the capacity to dig up something on the inspector? Something we can use against him," she asked, lifting her eyebrow.

Sean glanced at his colleague, pondering on how much he should confide in her. "My contact," he said with a chuckle, "is not privy too much in the way of direct information these days. I'm surprised we've got what we have so far." Enjoying his wine, he thought about how much Alistair Hunt's nephew, Ethan Taylor, could supply from his position in London.

"You're telling me he's sweeping floor in the men's loo. That's how he picks up his information?" she asked, giving him a Cheshire-cat-like grin.

"No, I'm not claiming he's a custodian. It's just . . . He got himself into a spot of trouble and he's still working it off," Sean said. "When he's done serving his penance, my employer was hoping he'd move a little closer to where we can use his services more readily."

"I'm overjoyed to hear you're not shagging some clerk typist for your information," she snickered. "Still, finding a chink in the inspector's armor would give me someplace to dig at him, make him uncomfortable—you know."

There's a first, he thought. *She showed interest and kindness for me, who knew?* "When I get back to the hotel, I'll send my contact your question and see what turns up," he said. "Now, when the trial starts up, I'm thinking we need to advance the sergeant's position as a community servant."

"How so?"

Sean brought his hands together, propping his elbows on the table. As he laid his chin on his knuckles, he took his time gathering his thoughts. "As the senior officer who worked in admin, I'm sure he had reason to talk with whoever called the station." He paused to sit back as the waiter brought out their meal. "He needs to admit on the stand that he talked with everyone."

"I'm not following you," Priscilla said, stabbing a tentacle from her plate and dipping it in marinara sauce. "Why do we want him admitting that?"

"They're basing this trial on him making a single call, right?" Sean asked. "Then we flood the jury with every possible instance of calls he would have made or taken—schools, church groups, senior centers, the lot of them. We make it more than just a call to his cousin, passing information."

"You're mad as a March hare, you are," she said. "But, you may also have a tact Hamilton might not be ready for. We've got him worried about the listings. And like you say, we can point out every call with the good citizens of Aberdeen to wash it out."

Chapter Seventeen

Once again, Fletcher found himself to be the first to the station, or so he thought. Dropping his coat on the chair, he heard the door open as McDermott came rushing past him holding two mugs of scalding hot coffee.

"Mind your back," he said.

"I didn't think you'd be in yet," Fletcher responded.

"I could nae sleep," McDermott replied. "Have a seat; we need to chat." He handed one of the mugs to Fletcher. "You're not going to like what I have to mention but wait till I'm finished before you speak."

"All right," Fletcher said as he sat down. "Go on, then."

Over the next ten minutes, McDermott described his theory of using Alistair Hunt's associates from Glasgow to obtain information on his illicit drug movements. He described the known associates like Wallace and his cousin, Ewan Sutherland, and Clive Duncan, the skipper of the Nordic Supplier.

"So, you think one of these individuals will turn on him?" Fletcher asked.

"Aye, maybe," McDermott replied, scratching the back of his head. "But there's one other suspect we can meet with . . . and it's Sheila's mum." He stared at Fletcher, anticipating a reaction.

Fletcher sat stone-faced in front of his colleague. He and Sheila had previously considered the potential for the police questioning her mum. Therefore, it came as no shock that McDermott had established the connection or contemplated using her to get something of substance against her employer. "You wish to have Janice Gordon brought in for questioning?" he asked.

"I can't think of anybody else who hasn't faced hard questions," McDermott replied. "I'm nae proud of needing to do this, but we need to find a means to have at this Hunt character." He sipped his coffee, and then practically spat it out. "Dammit, it's hot," he said, rubbing his chin with the back of his hand.

"You'll be happy to know Sheila and I already discussed this earlier," Fletcher said.

"Aye, when'd you do that?"

"Just after she came back from Glasgow," Fletcher said. "It's why she was speaking with Superintendent MacCallum before us that morning. She was letting him know about her mum working for Hunt. According to what Sheila said, Mister MacCallum said he'd deal with any questioning too."

Hearing this helped settle McDermott's nerves on the matter but didn't diminish the harshness of the case. "We must get her to reveal that she was privy to the calls with Wallace," he said. "And if we're lucky, she'll pitch in this Irishman as well for good measure."

"Which of the Wallace's, though?" Fletcher asked.

"It does nae matter, does it?" McDermott said. "If they're both guilty, it's all good. The elder one by a partnership with Hunt; and the cousin for being a snitch in the station." He took another drink of his coffee, this time more carefully. "Ah, much better," he said. "Being the intellectual-type, what questions do you think we should be asking her?"

Closing his eyes, Fletcher thought for a moment. "The questions need to be asked along the timetable of affairs," he said. "From there, we can hone in on either Gordon or Logan, whichever one she mentions first."

"Aye, I like the way you're looking at things, lad," McDermott said, getting to his feet. "You put together the questions just like you said; I'm off to the loo," He strolled out of the office.

"I'm doing it again," Fletcher groaned. "I'm a fucking secretary for him." He pulled out his legal paper to jot down his ideas.

When McDermott returned, he glimpsed over his partner's shoulder at the notes Fletcher had composed. "They sound rather simple, don't you think? I mean, don't you need to be asking about the Wallace's and Hunt being chummy?" he asked.

"Like I said, we need to maintain the questioning along the time each event took place," Fletcher said, handing his partner the pages of questions. "When are you taking off for Glasgow?"

"Ah, I'm nae going, you are," McDermott said with a smirk. "I've already cleared it with Mister MacCallum. He's arranged to have you picked up at the station. You'll need to rush though; Sergeant McKee booked you on the 0945 express to Glasgow." He stood Fletcher up and began leading him by the elbow toward the door.

"I've no bag packed or nothing," Fletcher protested, knocking the chair over as he snatched his coat.

"Superintendent Cameron will watch after you," McDermott said as they made their way to the building exit. "Look at it as an excuse to finally meet your future in-law," he chuckled as Fletcher got into the waiting patrol car.

***

After sitting and fuming over his sudden exit, Inspector Fletcher was soon stepping off the express train in Glasgow's City Centre station, where Constable Weir was waiting. "If you'll follow me, Inspector, I'll get you to your meeting," the petite officer announced, showing him to the waiting car. In ten brief minutes, Inspector Fletcher was being ushered into the Glasgow offices for Police Scotland.

The chief superintendent of the Glasgow office, Grace Cameron, sat opposite of Janice Gordon in the examination room. "I appreciate your assistance, Missus Gordon, we'll do our best not to squander your time."

"I'm always happy to give a hand to law enforcement," Janice said. "My daughter is a sergeant on the force, too." She smiled as she said this, but there was a trace of uneasiness in her speech.

Turning to the inspector to her left, Grace said, "You may begin, Inspector Fletcher."

Fletcher felt more nervous asking questions of Sheila's mother than having to address the service members in his first act as a newly commissioned Royal Marine officer.

"Thank you. Good morning, ma'am," he said. "How long have you been in Mister Hunt's employment?"

"Oh, it must be well over fifteen years," she said. "After my husband and I settled in the city, he encouraged me to find something to remain active, so I answered an advertisement for an assistant," Janice explained. "Of all the lasses, Mister Gordon picked me. He said it was my being a mature woman and all."

"Of course," Fletcher said, making a note. "I'm going to ask you several questions about specific dates. We'd appreciate it if you could give your best recollection of those circumstances if you could," he said.

"Aye, I'll do my best," she said.

Fletcher nodded politely to her before commencing his questioning. "Now then, on May seventh, do you recall getting a phone call from a Mister Gordon Wallace for your boss, Mister Hunt?"

"I might have," Janice responded. "But then again, I get all the calls for Mister Hunt as the sole secretary in the office."

"I understand, Missus Gordon," Fletcher said. "Please do your best to recall, though; it will help us to determine the level of involvement your employer has with our investigation."

"As I said, Inspector, I'll do my best."

"Thank you," he said. "Now, on May eighteenth, do you remember receiving a call from an Irishman who addressed himself as Mister Higgins? Or from his business, maybe? A business called Callaghan and Higgins Limited?"

"No, but I recall getting one from his barrister," she said. "I think his name is Gilmore. Yes, it's Sean Gilmore," she said, tapping her finger on the table several times.

Finding out the name of the barrister caught Fletcher by surprise. Editing his notes, he wondered if it could be the same one representing Sergeant Wallace. Turning the page in his notebook, he cleared his throat before proceeding.

"I see," Fletcher said with a forced smile on his face. "On the day of June fifteenth, did you meet with Mister Wallace at the request of your employer?"

"Yes, I did," she acknowledged. "Mister Hunt wanted me to extend an invitation to Mister Wallace for dinner."

"And this was the only thing you discussed with him during your encounter?"

"Yes, Alistair wanted to discuss a work proposal with him," Janice said. "He's always conducting his one-on-one talks over a meal or drinks. His physician has pointed out to him to be mindful of his habits. He's got a touch of diabetes that passes through his family."

Janice closed her eyes and took a deep breath before proceeding. "He likewise had a call from a somewhat dapper gent on that day, too. His name was Dunbar. Yes, Angus Dunbar, I remember him handing me his business card. Stewart tartan with gold stamping, it was quite a lavish way of announcing himself, if you ask me."

"And do you recall for how long they talked?"

154

"It was only twenty minutes or so," she said. "And after Mister Dunbar left, Alistair seemed flustered the rest of the day."

"I see, Missus Gordon." Peering over his notes, Fletcher decided he'd have enough to pass along to McDermott. "I'd like to thank you for your cooperation, ma'am," he said, closing his notebook. "I've no more questions."

Grace glanced over at him, trying very hard to hide her expression. She got up from her seat and motioned Janice to the door. "Constable Weir will show you out and thank you once again for your help." They politely shook hands, and Janice left.

She closed the door and looked at Inspector Fletcher. "Is that all you needed to ask her? Four or five questions? My sergeant could've managed it for you," she said. "Did any of what she told you make it worth coming all the way from Aberdeen?"

Fletcher looked up at the senior officer, gathering his thoughts before speaking.

"Superintendent Cameron, this woman just gave us a significant piece of evidence," he said. "She singled out the barrister for the fellow who's responsible for the drug trafficking through Aberdeen. But this fella Dunbar, that's the first time his name has come up in our investigation."

"And how is it that one name of a barrister is that significant?" she asked.

"It's because Mister Gilmore's been present in the courtroom representing Sergeant Wallace for the last week," Fletcher said. "Chief Inspector McDermott and I can now offer him as a co-conspirator to the drug-trafficking, based on Missus Gordon's testimony."

Grace looked at the young inspector so full of enthusiastic spirit, assuming he'd gotten a fish on his hook. "Your problem rests in the fact that she didn't have a proper representative present today, Inspector," she said. "She can refute the lot of her discussion today because of it."

Fletcher leaned back in his chair, mortified by her announcement. "You're right. I should have asked if she wanted to have someone present first. Dammit, I'm such an idiot!"

"All is not lost, Inspector Fletcher," Grace said. "I was present during questioning, remember? I can swear to her responses if they come into question. That is, if your barrister in Aberdeen places her on the platform."

Lingering in the interrogation room, Fletcher contemplated telling Grace Cameron that their suspect, Janice Gordon, was the mother of his love interest. Better to let sleeping dogs rest, as they claim, he thought. "Is the next individual available?" he asked, changing the subject.

***

McDermott stood before Superintendent MacCallum's desk waiting for the senior officer to speak. His expression told him everything he needed to know about his summons. It's nae going to be a happy wee chat, he thought.

Setting down the journal entries from the earlier night, Bruce MacCallum was none too happy with what he read. "Where in the hell do you get off perusing an individual's personnel file, Inspector? We've got enough on our hands with Sergeant Wallace's investigation, don't you think?"

"Aye, sir," McDermott said. "But I've been working on a theory and Constable Ames helped me with solving part of it."

"Don't drag the constable into this, McDermott; you're the senior officer," Bruce said. "My God, you of all people know enough to follow the procedures. I took you on as a favor to William; he told me about your little muck-up in Southampton. You're lucky you weren't terminated on the spot. And I've got a fair mind to send you packing now."

McDermott cringed at being reminded of the incident. "I'll mind myself from now on, sir," he said. "And for the record, Constable Ames was with me the whole time; I was nae alone." He hoped this would ease the supervisor's fear of compromising Sheila's information.

The superintendent bowed his head and let out a sigh as he passed his hand through his hair. Waving his hand at the inspector, the senior officer said. "Take a seat and tell me about this theory of yours."

"I was looking over the list of associates for Alistair Hunt, which made me consider one of them as a potential soft target," McDermott said. "I mean, someone saw or heard something I think we can apply during the trial. We already have the sergeant speaking with his cousin and the ship captains; we just need one mention of him communicating with Hunt before we seized the drugs."

Listening to the inspector, Superintendent MacCallum understood why his friend William Collingsworth of Scotland Yard kept McDermott on the force. For all the peculiarities and controversial choices, his outside-of-the-box thinking was winning him over.

"And why stop at this Hunt fellow?" Bruce asked. "Don't we have something from the Coast Guard office about this Irishman from the ship communications?"

"Aye we do, but it's Hunt making decisions to move the drugs here in Aberdeen," McDermott said. "I'm betting we'll find out it was him sending Ewan Sutherland to meet with the French supplier back in May."

"And by putting Inspector Gordon's mother on the hot seat, you hope to learn all this from her, do you?"

"I'm not sure what the missus will state," McDermott admitted. "We might get a gold mine of information, or we'll be handed a gunnysack full of coal. Inspector Fletcher's questioning is what I'm banking on, though; he'll get something for us, I'm sure."

"I hope you're right about this, Inspector," Bruce said. He turned on the intercom and called for Sergeant McKee.

As the female officer came into the office, Superintendent MacCallum handed her a piece of paper. "Sergeant, see that this counseling letter gets put in Inspector McDermott's file."

"You still need to endorse it, sir," she pointed out.

"Just see it gets entered," he said. "We'll make sure this is dealt with through appropriate channels when the time arrives. You're both dismissed."

McDermott strolled towards the detective's office but stopped short when he saw Constable Ames emerge from the duty room, accompanied by Sergeant Giles. "Constable Ames, I want you to know I did nae expect you to be called out for last night," McDermott said. "I'm sorry, hen."

"It's no worry, Inspector McDermott," she said, glancing back at her sergeant. "I've learned from my mistake. But to be honest, it felt good to get me nose a bit dirty, digging for clues."

As he entered the office, the usual commotion of conversation died down as the constables noted his return. Word had circulated through the ranks about McDermott's rifling the personnel files the night before, and several of the younger constables weren't too happy. Their exchanges became hushed and restrained.

Producing the notes from his desk of the theory he'd scribbled on the whiteboard, McDermott thought about the earlier conversation with Superintendent MacCallum. "He's right, it was ridiculous to twist the rules again," he mumbled at the sheets hanging in front of him. "But I was right in Southampton, and I'm right now, too." He began jotting down the dates for each event when the phone rang, interrupting him.

"Chief Inspector McDermott," he answered.

"Inspector, this is Moira Collins at the Coast Guard office. You asked us to tell you when the platform support vessel *Standard-Hercules* came back to harbor."

"Aye, I did," he said. "Where are they berthed?"

"The ship is tied up at Berth number two, along Regent's Quay."

"Thank you, Miss Collins," he said and hung up the phone. He immediately discarded his notebook and his theory, seized his field jacket, and lumbered out of his office. Pausing at the sergeant's office, he caught Sergeant Giles back at his desk. "Sergeant, I need you and three constables to accompany me to Regent's Quay."

"Aye, another incursion on a craft, is it?" the constable asked.

"No, I want to make sure I've got someone I can trust watching out for me," McDermott said. He recalled how much bigger Dillan McIntosh was than himself. "Which motor do you have?"

"Number Two, Inspector," Giles said as he trotted behind him to the car park. "We'll radio the lads on patrol to follow in as we go." They climbed into the patrol car and quickly headed towards the harbor. "Mind telling me what we're in for, Inspector?"

"Aye, there's a lass onboard I need to question," McDermott said. "And the last time I chatted with the captain, he was nae too pleasant, either." He took out his handgun and checked to see it was loaded.

"You're frightened of the wee lass and the captain, are you?"

"Aye, I'll let you decide for yourself when you see her," McDermott replied.

Rounding the corner towards the docks, they saw the other patrol car sitting off to the side. McDermott and the sergeant pulled up behind it, and then got out to meet the other constables. "Gentlemen, you're to block anyone from leaving the boat," he said. "And if someone tries to go onboard, you'll hold them up on the dock, is this understood?"

"Aye," Sergeant Giles said for them. "Okay, lads, you know the drill by now, let's get our kits ready." The men began proceeding to the back of each car and were soon cinching up their bullet-resistant vests and slinging weapons over their shoulders at the ready. "All right, Inspector, we're set," Giles said.

Striding across the roadway, McDermott approached the aft section of the ship, noticing the deck was vacant for the moment. Having no one to hail, he skipped over the rail onto the deck, proceeding straight to the superstructure. As he climbed the steps, he paused on the outer wing of the bridge, and peered through the window. He knocked on the glass and caught the attention of a seaman snoozing in the captain's chair. He abruptly woke up, slipped out of the chair, and went to open the door.

"Do you need something?"

"I need to speak with Samantha Atkins," McDermott declared, holding out his identification. "Is she onboard?"

"Aye, give me a minute, I'll fetch her." Picking up the intercom, he signaled the engine room.

"Aye, Billy, what is it?" came the reply.

"There's an inspector wanting you on the bridge," the seaman said casually.

"I'll see him on the working deck," she said.

In the heated confined space of the engine room, the announcement of the police being aboard still caused Samantha Atkins's body to shiver. She placed her tools on the bench and grabbed a clean rag to wipe her hands before heading topside.

Overhearing the exchange, McDermott proceeded down the ladder ending on the open deck below. He glimpsed at the dock, noticing the constables in position, yet to confront anyone coming along the docks for the moment. The familiar shriek of metal-on-metal pierced the quiet deck as Samantha Atkins exited the superstructure.

"You've nae call to be stepping foot on this vessel, Inspector," she said.

"I've got a few unanswered questions for you," McDermott said, walking towards her.

"I'll mention it again so you can understand," Samantha said with confidence and purpose, "you've no reason setting foot on this ship. As senior officer, I'm asking you to leave, now."

Sergeant Giles and the other constables looked on, getting fragments of the exchange. "He was nae kidding," Giles said. "There's one big lass for you."

"I need to know where you were last Monday," McDermott said.

"I'll nae speak with you without a barrister present," she said. "Now you've got a minute to leave on your own, or I'll see you off the boat myself." She put her hands on her hips. "What's it going to be, Inspector?"

"Pack your bags, Miss Atkins, I'll be back," McDermott said. Shuffling backward, he kept his eye on the woman until he felt the rail behind him. "Let your captain know I'll be seeing him too." He stepped over the rail and onto the dock.

Facing the inspector, Sergeant Giles said, "I take it back, Inspector. I'd ask for help with her as well."

Peering at the constable, McDermott chuckled. "I'll keep it in mind when I come back to detain her. You can do the honor of putting the cuffs on her." As the engineer returned to the confines of the ship, McDermott realized he would have to act soon if he wanted to question her about Ian MacLeod's homicide.

Chapter Eighteen

While Inspector Fletcher was questioning Sheila's mother in Glasgow, Bernard McIntosh was stepping off the deck of the *Standard-Hercules*. After completing another run to the derricks, it was time to relinquish his cargo log to the freight brokers so he could collect payment for platforms he had just resupplied. Traipsing across the lane, he spotted the familiar figure of his mentor outside the office.

"Morning, Bernard," Clive said.

"Morning, Captain," Bernard said. The look he saw on the older man's face caused him to stop in his tracks. "Something I can do for you?"

"We need to have a chat," Clive Duncan said, puffing on the pipe clutched between his teeth. Looking about the parking area and the adjacent dock, he continued, "But it's better it be done in quiet."

"Let me drop the log book off, and we can go back to the *Hercules*, then," Bernard said, gesturing to the building in front of them.

"Aye, I'll be waiting," Clive said, turning away while tapping his pipe on his palm. After a lorry went by, he was soon making his way across the pavement towards the docks.

After meeting with the cargo schedulers, Bernard stepped out of the building, hustling back to his boat, not wanting to keep the older Scotsman waiting too long. He was soon standing next to Clive dockside, waving his senior officer onto his boat.

"Welcome aboard, Captain Duncan."

Passing over the deck, they entered the superstructure, ending up in the crew's galley. After closing the door behind him, Bernard pulled out two chairs from his table at the far end of the room. "Coffee?" he asked, taking a mug.

"No, I'm fine," Clive said.

"What is it you needed to talk about?" Bernard asked.

"I've just returned from making a delivery to a French vessel," he said. "It concerned a crewman you and Dillan know from your

161

service time. Both you and your crew are in a fine mess because of that last transaction Dillan and his crew undertook."

"I've heard the talk about someone having snitched on Dillan," Bernard said. "But who is this crewman you mentioned?"

Leaning back in the galley chair, Clive looked at the younger captain. "A Frenchman called Louis Clement. Does the name ring a bell?"

It was now Bernard's turn to settle back in his chair. He rubbed his hands over his eyes. "Aye. There's a name I'd nae expect to hear again," he sighed. "This fella Clement was a Legionnaire. Dillan and I drove the crafts during several of their training missions in South America," he said. "But I've nae heard from him in, say, two years' time or more. Why'd he go to you and nae come see me?"

Over the next fifteen minutes, Clive Duncan described the ongoing predicament to his younger colleague. This included his run-in with Dunbar, though he only knew him by the name of Walker. "Your Frenchman seems to think this Walker fella is nae one to muddle with alone. Clement mentioned he's a former SAS-type, with a penchant for doing dirty work without getting caught."

Captain McIntosh looked across the table at Clive, his disposition being one of serious resolve. "The name means nothing, Clive," Bernard said. "And you said there were two of Clement's fellas looking for him, too?"

Getting up from the table, Clive stepped over to the counter and poured himself a glass of water. After having a sip, he looked back at the younger captain. "This Clement fella, he's hopeful that his two associates will find this Walker on short notice," Clive said. "He likewise mentioned this fella Walker has an unpleasant habit with women. They think because of this habit, it'll make him vulnerable, something they aim to exploit." Looking at Bernard, Clive's mood took a serious turn. "And having faced this Walker, I'm glad it's the French looking for him and not me."

***

Maneuvering her car into the visitor's spot outside the Police Scotland offices, Priscilla El-Sayed and Sean Gilmore each nodded in agreement before going into the building. Marching through the front doors, the barristers came face to face with Sergeant McKee and Constable Howe staffing the reception counter. "Can we help you?" McKee asked.

Priscilla reached into her briefcase and presented a written petition. "I'm representing Mister Logan Wallace," she said, "and I'm here to request access to evidence under the Freedom Act. It's my understanding there are listings I've yet to receive from this office for evaluation."

Sergeant McKee looked at the woman and her colleague, slowly grasping what they were seeking to do. "If you don't mind, I'll need to examine your request," she said, holding out her hand. Glancing at the document, she saw the content didn't indicate a date or quantity. Reaching under the counter, she presented a form and slipped it towards the barrister. "If you'll just fill this custody form out, I'll see it's handled through the proper division." There was a hint of amusement in her tone.

Priscilla was a bit taken aback by the sergeant's request. "This memorandum is quite satisfactory," she said, holding her letter.

"Yes, ma'am, I'm sure you think it is," the sergeant said. "But we've protocols to follow, and if you want to receive anything, you'll need to fill this out." She gently slid the custody form toward Priscilla, using the tips of her fingers.

Sensing this debate would circle itself if he didn't step in, Sean picked up the form from the counter and said, "I'll see this is handled. Sergeant, could you contact your evidence custodian to assemble the files we're seeking?"

"Sir, as I mentioned, we've procedures for doing things. And part of those is having the proper documents," she said. "When you're done filling it out, then we'll proceed." She pointed to a nearby folding table and some chairs. "If you'd like, you can sit at the table along the wall while you—"

Before the constable could complete her sentence, Priscilla stormed away, fuming from the exchange. Sean thanked the sergeant and followed his colleague to the table. "They've got their nose bloodied over Wallace, so let's play their game, shall we?" He took out a pen from his briefcase.

Ambling in from the car park, Chief Inspector McDermott and Sergeant Giles returned from their encounter at the docks to see the barristers huddled together. "Is there something you need, hen?" McDermott asked, stepping behind Priscilla.

"Why yes, there is, Inspector McDermott, since you've asked," she replied. "Seems your esteemed colleague, Mister Hamilton, he's been remiss in granting us access to your evidence in the Wallace case. Mister Gilmore and I are here to make sure our client is afforded his rights to equal representation by accessing our copies."

"First, need I point out to you, I'm a Chief Inspector with Scotland Yard," McDermott said with a sneer. "Second, you've made this arrangement through the courts, am I right?"

"We'll make our notification with Mister Hamilton later today," she said. "Now if you don't mind, be a good sport and see this is registered, will you?" She handed him the letter and form her colleague had just finished.

Peering down at the documents, McDermott snickered before drawing a step closer to the woman, detecting a whiff of her jasmine perfume in the process. "I'm not your valet, Miss El-Sayed, so you'd be best served if you handed the documents to Sergeant McKee," he said, nodding toward the counter. "And if you continue to disrespect me, I'll see you have your arse scalped." He turned and headed for his office.

As he ambled down the central corridor, the inspector made a detour, stopping in the forensics lab. Here, McDermott caught Chief Inspector McIntyre fixing his coffee. "Graham, you've got a minute?"

"Aye, what is it, Inspector?"

"Have you finished sorting out the recordings Inspector Fletcher dropped off the other day?"

"Yes, the crew from the second shift got them done last night," he said, picking up a notebook from his desk. "I must say, the two of you've got a gold mine to employ against the sergeant. We came across dozens of calls between him and those boat captains alone."

"Can you have the lads put together a list affecting the Sutherland boy?"

"Aye, it shouldn't take long," Graham said. "But why the rush now?"

"The sergeant's barristers are here, wanting their take of the evidence," McDermott said. "But I'm not prepared to hand over the lot, at least not yet. Inspector Fletcher and I have a few suspects from those calls we still need to question."

"All right, then, we'll start breaking up the files," the technician said. "Should take about an hour, maybe two. I'll call you when we're done."

"Thanks, Graham," McDermott said.

When he reached his office, he tossed his jacket over the chair and snatched the phone. Dialing the office number for George Hamilton, he caught the barrister after the third ring.

"Hello, Aberdeen Sherriff's Office, can I help you?"

"Aye, Mister Hamilton. It's Chief Inspector McDermott, and I need your help."

"Oh? And what might that help require?" the counselor asked, clearing off a paper to take the inspector's information.

Over the next five minutes, McDermott explained needing a warrant dealing with both crews of the *Standard-Apollo* and *Nordic Supplier* to continue his questioning. He likewise told him about his run-in with Priscilla El-Sayed and Sean Gilmore at the station.

"I was wondering when they'd be asking for those," Hamilton said. "But, I can slow them down if you still need time to separate out the audio files."

"I've got them being sorted already; they'll be ready in about three hours," McDermott said. "But if you can frustrate them a spot longer, it would nae hurt."

"All right, and I'll have St. James start working on the warrants," Hamilton said. "And while he's preparing them, I'll give Lord Maxwell's office a call, letting them know we'll need his signature. Is there anything else? We'll not have another chance with the court until Monday."

"If you get the warrants, I'll have my hands full enough as it is," McDermott said. "Call me when it's ready, will you?" Their conversation ended.

Turning his attention to the names on his board, he circled Alistair Hunt's name twice. "Now to include the captains to the fray," he said, jotting down McIntosh's and Duncan's names below Hunt's. "I'm wagering Sutherland was your go-between, wasn't he?" he said to himself.

"Chief Inspector McDermott?" a squeaky adolescent voice said, coming from his door.

McDermott turned around and saw Kyle from the forensics lab holding a folder in his hands. "Aye lad, what've you got?"

"Mister McIntyre said you needed these files," he said, handing him the folder. "There's a dozen specific examples noted, just like you asked for, Inspector."

"Thank you, Kyle. Nicely done," he said, grasping the packet.

Changing his attention back to the board, McDermott continued working out relations between Hunt and the vessel captains, including Sutherland's name being added to the mix. "Where did your mate fit in, though?" he asked himself. Putting Ian MacLeod on the board but to the side, he included a question mark beside it. "Were you an innocent victim or a pawn being sacrificed for the common good?"

Back in the foyer, Priscilla kept looking at her watch. "I'm done waiting, Sean," she asserted. She marched up to the counter and slapped her hand on its surface. "I want to speak with Superintendent MacCallum right this instance!" She was speaking loud enough for people in the lobby to hear.

Constable Howe stood behind the kiosk, undaunted by the woman's action. "I'll contact the sergeant and see if he's in. Just a moment, ma'am," he said, picking up the phone. "Yes, this is Constable Howe, I have a citizen wanting to meet with Chief MacCallum. What . . .? Yes, I'll let her know." He hung up the phone.

"Well?" Priscilla asked.

"Ma'am, the superintendent is in a meeting," Howe said, "but he should be available in the next five to ten minutes. He appreciates your patience and apologies for any inconvenience."

Fuming at the excuse, Priscilla glared at the young officer who barely flinched under her withering gaze. "I've been waiting for over two and a half hours, young man, and if your department wishes to avert an unseemly incident, your super better show his face, or I'll—"

"Or you'll do what, Miss El Sayed?" the senior officer asked from behind her. "Rest easy, Constable Howe."

"Yes, sir," the young officer said, stepping back from the counter.

Standing toe to toe with MacCallum, looking into his steel-grey eyes, Priscilla said, "I came to retrieve copies of evidence, but your inhospitable staff seems to be lacking enthusiasm for undertaking their duties."

"Is that so?" MacCallum asked. He turned towards the corridor and saw Chief Inspector McDermott walking out of his office with a folder. "Oh, Inspector McDermott, a minute of your time, please," waving him over to where he was standing. "Is this the information you developed for the court?"

"Yes, it is, Mister MacCallum," McDermott said, smirking. "I was just preparing it for—"

"Give me that," Priscilla said, reaching for the packet, her acrylic nails snapping the air as the folder was drawn from her grasp.

Bringing the file against his chest, McDermott continued: "As I was mentioning, sir. I was preparing it for Mister Hamilton . . ." He looked toward the building's entrance. ". . . Whose timing is impeccable." He greeted the barrister as he approached the group. "Thank you for coming, Mister Hamilton, you should find everything in order," McDermott said, turning the folder over to him.

"Thank you, Chief Inspector McDermott," Hamilton replied. "And here are the documents you requested earlier." He handed the inspector the summons. "I'm sure you'll find those written to encompass all particulars of your activities."

"Are the two of you finished?" Priscilla asked, her patience strained by the men's exchange.

"Yes," they replied in unison.

"Then could you please give me the files so my colleague and I can get on with our business?" she asked, her foot tapping impatiently on the floor.

Holding the folder, George Hamilton slid it under his arm while opening his briefcase. "In due course, Counselor," he said. "There's a slight matter of liability to perform before you have access to these." He drew out the court's custody form for evidence. "If you'll be gracious enough to fill this out, endorsing the bottom, I'll be happy to surrender the files into your custody."

"I'll take that," Sean said, grabbing the form.

Priscilla looked at McDermott. "Those files better be complete, or I'll have your arse, Inspector McDermott."

"Sorry, Counselor, my arse is spoken for already," McDermott replied with a sneer. "Now, if you'll excuse me, I've got more police work to do." Turning to the senior officer, he added, "Superintendent MacCallum, please dispatch Sergeant Giles and three constables to Regent's Quay."

Nodding to Constable Howe, MacCallum relayed McDermott's request. "You don't need more than those four?" he asked.

"Not for this go-round," McDermott answered. He then turned toward George Hamilton. "Is Mister St. James available?"

167

"Yes, he'll be waiting for your call," Hamilton said. "He's ready with all the paperwork if you need it."

"Thanks," he said. "If you'll excuse me," he said, throwing a mock salute.

Stepping up to the barrister, Sean handed over the custody form. "Here you are, Mister Hamilton. We will need a photocopy for our files."

George read it over and handed it back to Sean. "It requires a signature," he said, pointing to the bottom block.

Priscilla, after grasping the form from Hamilton and the pen from Sean, signed her name to the bottom with a flourish, practically breaking the pen tip in the process. "There, satisfied?" she said, passing it back.

"You wrote it in Arabic," Hamilton said.

"It's valid," she said. "Verify your court docket. I endorse all my papers with my proper name in my native writing."

Slipping the document back into his briefcase, Hamilton concluded his business with Sean and Priscilla. "Have a delightful weekend, and I'll see you on Monday morning," he said. "Good afternoon, Mister MacCallum," calmly walking away.

Chapter Nineteen

Dunbar sat in silent concentration, cleaning his gun for the third time this morning. In his mind, he replayed the call from last night and regarded his choices against the Frenchman. *I'm willing to wager he's not alone*, he thought, piecing his weapon together. "Where can I have the superiority? Here in the hotel is no good, too many individuals to avoid," he said to himself. I'm nae familiar enough with the roads and alleys, so they're out of the question too.

Leaning back in his chair, he closed his eyes, imagining where he could be the hunter and not the prey. "Aye, the docks," Dunbar said to the empty room. "And I've got the proper host in the captain." He slipped a full magazine into the pistol grip.

He went to the closet and drew out his gun case, along with the service cover-all he wore the previous day. Changing into the workman's clothes, he packed a pair of clean shirts and slacks in a duffle bag to wear on the ship. Lifting the gun case and the duffel, he headed out the door and grabbed the lift to the garage level. In minutes, he was back in the stolen panel van heading towards the harbor and his encounter with Captain Duncan onboard the *Nordic Supplier*.

In his haste, Dunbar didn't see the Frenchman, Pasqual Sequin walking towards the hotel entrance. Each man passed the other. Pasqual made his way inside heading for the lifts.

Stepping off on the fourth floor, Pasqual glanced at the room numbers and went on to the one vacated by Angus. Finding Room 415, Pasqual stepped to the one next door, listening for any noise.

Utilizing a master key, the same one he removed from the café server last night, he unlocked the door while drawing a dagger from under his coat. Before closing the door behind him, he stuck the DO NOT DISTURB badge on the doorknob.

Stepping carefully into the uninhabited room, he moved to the door, which joined Angus's room. Within a minute, he had picked the lock, turning the handle, and easing the door free, listening for any unusual movement. With the door open a mere fraction, Pasqual peered inside, seeing the bed half made, but not hearing any movement.

"He's left," he murmured.

Across the roadway, Hector sat listening on his end of the surveillance equipment. He heard his partner go in the rooms and now learned their proposed victim was no longer present. "Do a cursory check and see if he packed," he said. "But touch nothing."

"Very amusing," Pasqual said, opening the closet. "His business suit is still in the closet." He stepped next to the bed and hoisted off the covers in order to peer beneath the frame. "And there's a pair of dress shoes under the bed."

Hector considered his next action. "Ok, go ahead and plant the package like we discussed, but use the pressure switch and not the timer."

Pasqual reached into his jacket and pulled out a modest improvised explosive, placing it under the edge of the bed. Next, he slipped the trigger, a basic doorbell switch, under the covers before placing the blankets back in place. "Finished," he said. "I'm on my way out."

Peering back into the room, he made certain everything was just as Dunbar had left it. With this carried out, all they could do now was wait for him to return.

***

After parking the stolen van in a vacant area near the docks, Dunbar took his bags and walked to the Commercial Quay berths. After about a hundred meters, he showed up alongside the *Nordic Supplier* as it was being loaded with equipment. Strolling up to the boat, he placed his bags down before he cried out to one of the deck hands, "Is your captain on board?"

"No, just the second officer, Mister Collins," the crewmember said, pointing to the bridge wing overlooking the dock. Squinting up, Dunbar noticed a youthful man watching the movements on the working deck and holding a clipboard and a mug. Waving upward, he called out to the officer, "Mister Collins, I need to have a talk with your captain."

"Give me a minute," the seaman said, disappearing inside. A moment later, he was on the lower deck walking towards the rail and Angus. "Can I help you?"

"Yes, my name is Mister Walker, and I'm an advisor for the rig you're going to service. I was hoping to review your schedule with

Captain Duncan," he said. "When do you expect him to come back?"

"Right now," the officer said, pointing down the dock towards Clive Duncan.

As he rounded the corner of the docks towards his ship, Clive spied the worker talking with his second officer. As he grew closer, he could make out the details, recognizing it was the same armed man he talked with at the park the day before yesterday. Striding up to his ship, Clive joined the conversation.

"What can I do for you, Mister Walker?"

"As I was just telling Mister Collins, I'd like to discuss your schedule," Dunbar said. "There's been an unforeseen development in the crew that we need to take into consideration before departing. To date, it won't disturb your team, but it's best to make certain, don't you think?"

"Collins, I'll see to Mister Walker; you can go about finish loading the supplies," Clive said, dismissing the officer. After Collins left, Clive returned his focus on Angus. "What do you need from me?" Clive asked.

"I'm in need of a more secure environment, at least for the next few days," Dunbar said. "It turns out there are two gentlemen in town looking for me, and I don't want them to have any advantages when we meet."

"And you hoped staying onboard my boat would be safer?" Clive asked. "What happens to my crew and me if they show up looking for you here? Are you going to defend us? I read the paper and found out about the young fella at the courthouse," he said. "It's not in my nature to attract trouble, Mister Walker, but whenever I run across it, I have it settled."

Dunbar beamed at the conviction Captain Duncan displayed in front of his men. "It's my intention to prove no violence happens to you," he said. "As long as you and I can agree to cooperate. Moreover, you do as I direct when the time arrives. Now, can you offer me a cabin, so I can put my bags away?"

Eighty meters away, Chief Inspector McDermott and Sergeant Giles were talking on the opposite side of the harbor as the hitman and ship's captain spoke. Searching down the dock, they came upon the *Standard-Hercules*; her crew was busy conducting a scrub-down of the working deck.

"Now remember, I'll go aboard to meet Captain McIntosh first, and have the engineer brought to me," McDermott instructed to the constables grouped around him. "Constable Ames, once we have the engineer in custody, you'll handle her well-being."

"Aye, no worries, Inspector," she said.

Bernard McIntosh saw Chief Inspector McDermott from the bridge as he and the constables walked towards his craft. Picking up the ship's intercom, he signaled the engine room. "Officer Atkins, to the bridge, if you please." Hearing the captain, Samantha Atkins put down her clipboard and began making her way topside. Just as Samantha was entering the bridge, McDermott reached the railing and signaled one of the deck crew over. "I need to see your captain," he said.

Glancing up at the aft windows of the bridge, McDermott saw Captain McIntosh and his engineer in a conversation. "And what might you be conveying to the lass, Captain?" he murmured. Seeing the Scotland Yard inspector waiting, Captain McIntosh once again clutched the intercom, diverting to the external speakers. "Stand by, Inspector," he said. "I'll be there in a minute."

Facing a crewmember on the bridge, Bernard said, "Make an entry in the ship's journal; Mister Young takes the con until I state otherwise."

"Aye, captain," the crewmember answered, making the notation.

With his order issued, he next turned to Samantha. "C'mon, let's find out what the police have in store for us, shall we?" After leading her down the stairs to the working deck, they both exited into the sunlight reflecting off the wet deck.

Constable Ames took one glimpse at the ship's engineer and said, noticing the woman's size, "Marcus, I'm nae expected to restrain that beast, am I? She's two of me, for God's sake."

"Aye, you'll be fine," the sergeant responded, chuckling to himself. "Chief Inspector McDermott will back you if there's any trouble."

Facing the inspector with Scotland Yard at the rail, Captain McIntosh spoke first. "You've come to have another conversation, have you?" he asked. "Everything you want to ask will take place with a barrister present. And I happen to have one." The captain waved his hand above his head. In moments, Robert Burns moved into view, exiting the lower hatch and sauntering up to the captain.

"I've got a warrant to chat with Captain Bernard McIntosh and Second Engineer Samantha Atkins," McDermott said. "If you'll just be so cordial and follow the constables," he said, gesturing to the officers behind him, "I'll try to make this as brief as I can."

Burns walked up to the rail. "Do you mind if I examine your warrant?" he asked, holding out his hand. McDermott handed the letter to the barrister and watched him read it. Burns turned his back to the police and said to Captain McIntosh; "They've called out your engineer here about a homicide and you for sheltering."

At hearing the statement Burns just said, Bernard's relaxed disposition was visibly tested. "We've nothing to withhold. We'll be finished with this in a few minutes," he said. "Sam and I will go, but I need to let Captain Duncan of the *Nordic Supplier* know about this."

Turning, he spotted Blake Young, his first officer, stepping to the rail joining them. "You've got the ship for now, Blake; I've made an entry in the log," he said.

"Aye, Cap'n," the seaman replied.

"Come along, Atkins, we can't let these fine officers be seen spoiling the good taxpayers' cash," he said with an overt jovial expression. "You too, Mister Burns."

McDermott stood back as the captain, engineer, and barrister stepped onto the dock. "Right this way," Sergeant Giles said, gesturing to the police vans parked nearby. Constable Ames stepped up near Samantha Atkins, demonstrating a sense of courage, even though her eyes revealed more dread and uneasiness.

Staring across the harbor, Bernard McIntosh could make out his colleague, Clive Duncan, conversing with someone on the deck of his boat. As the police vans sped away, he pondered if he had made the right decision in giving in to the police's wish to question Atkins and himself.

***

While McDermott and the constables were detaining Captain McIntosh and his second engineer at the Regent's Quay, the express train from Glasgow groaned to a stop as it entered the Aberdeen station. Standing by for an elderly couple to exit, Inspector Andrew Fletcher took his briefcase and jacket from his seat. As he stepped off the train, he was promptly embraced by his companion, Inspector Sheila Gordon, standing near the message stand.

"Hello, stranger," she said, embracing him.

"Hello back," Fletcher said. "How come I didn't get this greeting when I came back from Marseille in June?"

"We were merely on our second date, back then," she giggled, taking his hand. "Do you need to go to the station first? Or is Conor going to give you a few extra hours with me?" she asked, giving him a mischievous pout.

"He's not requiring me back until . . ." Fletcher paused, seeing the familiar face of Clyde Smith near the long-term lockers. "What's he doing back in Aberdeen?"

"Who is that, Andrew?"

"It's one of the hired gunmen Conor and I apprehended with Sutherland last month." He started walking towards the lockers. "Go find a patrolman," he said, passing his briefcase to her. "And keep clear of the lockers." He had no idea if Smith was armed or not.

Sheila headed to where she had last seen the foot patrol constables and spoke to the first one she saw. "I'm in need of your help, officer," she said, pulling out her credentials.

"How can I help you, Inspector Gordon?" the constable asked after reading her ID.

"Inspector Fletcher from Scotland Yard has sighted a known felon near the long-term lockers," she said, pointing in the general direction. "He'll need you as a backup if matters get serious."

"Aye, ma'am, we'll take it from here," the patrol officer said, nudging his associate. Both officers advanced towards the section that Fletcher was at, breaking up to encompass the most area. As they closed the distance, they spied Fletcher, gun drawn, going around the corner. Observing this, each man drew his service pistol, advancing towards the lockers.

Stepping up to the row of cabinets, Clyde slid the key and unlocked the door, pulling the gun case from inside the locker. Angling away from the direction Fletcher was approaching, he continued towards the taxi stand.

"Mister Smith, I want you to stop right there," Fletcher said, walking up from behind, his pistol drawn. "Put down the case and take two steps to your left," he instructed.

The felon stopped and set the case down as instructed, turning to see who'd been able to sneak up on him. "You're the one who pinched the young fellow at the docks, aren't you?" Clyde asked. "I read he's not with us anymore, poor soul."

Moments after halting Smith, the two constables appeared, pistols at the ready. "Inspector Fletcher?" one policeman asked. "Can I see your ID, please, sir?"

Fletcher fished out his credentials and showed them, all the while keeping his pistol trained on Smith.

"Thank you, sir," the officer replied, assured of Fletcher's rank and position.

"What brings you back to Aberdeen?" Fletcher asked.

"Me laundry," Smith responded, nodding towards the case.

"Constable, I've reasonable suspicion that this gentleman may not be telling the whole truth," Fletcher said. "Can you contact District and arrange for transport? There are a few questions I'd like to ask him."

"Certainly, Inspector," the constable said, pulling out his radio, and contacting dispatch.

While the constables were detaining Smith, Sheila walked up next to Fletcher. "Am I going to be busy?" she asked, looking down at the case.

"I'm afraid we're both going to be busy, if my intuition is correct," Fletcher said. "That case is like the one I used when I went on deployments. They're rugged, mobile, and waterproof. Perfect for storing precious pieces from becoming broken," he continued. "Our armorers used them to keep their cleaning kits together for each squad that was embarked."

Pulling gloves from her handbag, Sheila assumed her position as a forensics technician. "Constable, I'll handle this as evidence from here on out," she said. "Inspector, be a dear and get the constables information for the record." She then rolled the case through the crowd towards the exit.

"That was rather cheeky of her," the constable said, looking at Fletcher. "Still, she looks to be a handful, if you get my meaning." He gave Fletcher a wink.

"Constable, you're speaking about an inspector with Police Scotland," Fletcher said. "You've received your instruction on how to be a professional, I assume. Which I'm sure included how to manage yourself around female officers." He produced his notebook and pen.

"Oh, aye, but she looks friendly," the constable smiled.

"And she's seeing someone," Fletcher said with a more commanding emphasis to his speech.

Picking up on the last remark, the constable realized what Fletcher was trying to tell him. "I'm very sorry, Inspector," he said, flustered. "My apologies for the way I acted. It won't happen again." He held out his identification to be copied.

"I'm certain it won't, Constable Fleming," Fletcher said, copying the officer's information.

***

The two Scots sat nervously in the hotel café, unsure of what was delaying their friend. "What in the hell is taking Clyde so long?" Reggie Brown exclaimed, looking at the time. "You gave him the right key, didn't you?"

"I only had two, and I gave one to Angus," Stuart Ross said, finishing his coffee. "Do you want to go looking for him? I'm guessing it's best to stay in one spot."

As the two men discussed their friend's absence, Pasqual Sequin walked through the vestibule and spotted Stuart Ross from the other night in the pub. Heading out of the lobby, he made his way to where his friend Hector Pichon sat in the nearby park. "Our guest from the pub is meeting in the hotel café with another fellow," Pasqual said, standing in front of the bench.

"Oh, really?" Hector said. "I wonder if he has any idea where we can meet with Angus?"

"Is it possible this gentleman Stuart is with now is the one we're looking for?"

"I don't think so," Hector replied. "Stuart was noticeably shaken the other night. He almost fears this Dunbar and what he might do to him. Still, it wouldn't hurt to have another conversation with him." He got up from the bench. "I'll go in first, you follow to the right and keep an eye on the other guy."

Sauntering into the lobby, Hector spied Stuart Ross and Reggie Brown having their discourse at a small table. Hovering behind the Glasgow criminal, he quickly captured the attention of Reggie.

"Can we help you, fella?" Reggie asked.

"Bon jour," Hector said, lifting his open hands up for Brown to see. "It's good to see you again, Stuart." He patted the criminal's shoulder. "You're looking much more refreshed, I might add, than the other night."

Stuart was dismayed to meet the Frenchman again so soon. He nervously gulped down the rest of his coffee. "What do you want, Hector?"

"I was hoping you and I could discuss our mutual friend and where I might find him," Hector said. "We chatted last night, but he's no longer returning my calls."

"I don't know where he is," Stuart replied. "And if I did, I don't want to be nearby when you two meet each other." He now saw Pasqual walking near the corner of the room. "You've got the number; I suggest you keep calling him until he responds. Plus, we're waiting for a colleague to meet with us, if you don't mind."

"Then at least provide me the name of the individual your young companion was meeting with last month," Hector said politely.

"He met with a crewman from one of the boats," Stuart said. "All I know is the last name, Atkins. I don't know the boat or a first name. But the meet was down on the Commercial Quay side of the harbor," he said.

"Then I recommend we try to find this individual," Hector said.

"What do you mean we?" Stuart asked. "And if Angus is there, then what?"

"Pasqual and I will handle Angus, and you can see your young associate's death was not wasted."

Stuart stood gawking at Reggie. "Want to give it a go? We can leave a note for Clyde to meet us at the docks."

"Aye, we'll go," Reggie answered. "Beats waiting here for Clyde. But I don't like being empty-handed on these wee excursions, either."

Chapter Twenty

Sitting together in the hotel café, the barristers for Sergeant Wallace were both engrossed in the transcript evidence provided by Chief Inspector McDermott and Police Scotland. Leafing back and forth between pages, Priscilla spoke first. "Sean, if any of these are true, we've got a tough uphill battle on our hands. I've got three separate instances where Wallace is speaking with one of those boat captains about a patrol, or a constable's assignments."

Sean looked up from his sheath of papers, a worried look furrowing his brow. "It turns out the sergeant wasn't especially careful in how he discussed matters. If we take these at face value, how do we turn it into him following orders to bring down this Frenchman?"

"I'm not sure we can," Priscilla said. "First off, he's mentioned the young bloke's name who was just murdered. And, in two of these write-ups, he's mentioning a fella named Campbell who the police have in custody on the assault charge." Turning another page, she continued. "This one from May eleventh has him talking with a captain named McIntosh, and it's not police business, mind you."

Sean took a drink from his water bottle, trying to digest it all. "We need to have a face-to-face with our client," he said. "Then I'll need to discuss things with a barrister named Burns before it gets too far out of hand."

"And what of your employer, Sean?" she asked. "Do you think he cares enough to allow us to cut this poor soul a deal with the prosecution?" She couldn't help sounding defeated. "I mean, there's no way we can write this story any other way, is there?"

"I'm positive Mister Higgins won't suffer himself to allow any merciful solution to this," Sean said. "Specifically, if it means allowing Sergeant Wallace to speak about whom he had dealings or discussions with, or when those talks took place. Our only hope is these are the only recordings the police have."

"And if they have others?" she asked.

"I'd like to not think of those circumstances at the moment," Sean said. "Now then, when was the last call on your sheet? I think it's time we prepared our defense strategies, wouldn't you agree?"

"The last transcript is dated May fourteenth," Priscilla said. "It shows the sergeant's talking with Captain Duncan; the *Nordic Supplier* is being dispatched, based on a separate call." Reading down a few lines, she stopped. "It says he'd be contacted by a representative of an Irishman from Belfast." She looked up at her colleague.

Sean fought hard to keep the color in his face but felt it to be a lost cause. "Does it name the party in question?"

"It says Callaghan and Higgins is the business name. Isn't this the same as your employer, Sean?"

***

While lawyers for Sergeant Wallace discussed their next step, the counselor working for Alistair Hunt, Robert Burns, paced the small interrogation room inside police headquarters listening to Captain McIntosh describe things he might be asked to justify. "Is there any chance the police or this inspector will find something illegal on your boat?"

"Nothing, Burns, I swear," the captain said. Looking about the room, he felt nervous discussing the boat's illegal activities, fearing his every word was being recorded. "Is it really safe to discuss things? Dillan and I have a lot invested in our boats, and I for one don't want to muck it up, you know."

"I understand what you're saying, Bernard. But you need to trust me to do my job, if you want to see yourself free of this mess," the barrister said. "As for your friend Dillan, I've not spoken to him, so, for now, he's best kept out of the conversation, you understand?"

"Aye, I'll do my best," Bernard said. "On the boat, you said the summons for Sam was for murder? I'd say the police are fishing for something because I've had her on the boat the last four days getting things ready to sail."

Burns looked at the captain. "And you've known her whereabouts the entire time? The police will push hard if they suspect her of killing someone, and she must sing the same tune you do."

"I've got a standing rule that when we're getting ready, I've got at least one of the engineer's onboard at all times. My chief, Mister

Fischer, was taking care of personal business in Dundee, so Sam was left to prepare the engine room."

"Then I must get Mister Fischer's accounts in line," Burns said. "Hopefully, he can find someone that'll voucher for his time away from the boat." He walked to the door and knocked on it, alerting the constable standing guard. "I'll be back in a moment; I want to talk with Miss Atkins," he said. "And remember; don't utter a word unless I'm in here, okay?"

"Aye, I'll be quiet," Bernard said remaining seated.

After the constable let him exit, Burns was shown to the next interrogation room, where Samantha Atkins sat at the table dozing. At the sound of the door opening, she brought her head up, spying the barrister as he walked into the room. "About time, Mister Burns," she said.

"Your captain and I were just setting a few ground rules," Burns said. "Now, how about you and I have a wee chat about the police charges, shall we?"

"What's there to talk about? That inspector came to the boat the other day wanting to know where I was the Monday evening before," she said. "I told him I was onboard getting things ready."

"Captain McIntosh said he always requires that you or the chief engineer stay onboard; is that true?"

"Aye, one of us is always getting the mechanicals ready before we head out," she said. "Mister Fischer had to go to Dundee on business, so I was left in charge. It's helping me get ready for my engineer's exam in November."

"The summons the police have on you is for murder. Can you think of any reason they would file something like this on you?" he asked. "Think back, any altercation or arguments with anyone come to mind?"

"I've nae had a fight with anyone since I signed on," she said. "My last go-round was in Inverness with a fella who grabbed me arse in a pub. I was cited for assault and battery and paid five hundred pounds for his medical bill to fix his nose."

Burns felt himself smiling, imagining the engineer defending herself against the poor chap in the pub. Collecting his thoughts, he continued. "Other than this one time, you've not had any other run-ins with other crewmen, the lads on the docks, nothing?"

"I've nae had a reason to worry. Word gets out amongst the lads after something like that," she said. "They accept me for who I am."

Sitting forward in the chair, Sam buried her head in her hands. "Is it possible someone is trying to frame me? You know, like on the telly?"

"To be honest, I'm not sure. But, based on what you and your captain have told me, I don't think so," Burns said. "Let me ask you one question, nevertheless. Did you ever deal with Ewan Sutherland?"

Sam was glad to have her head down, knowing her expression of hearing the name would have told everything to the barrister. She knew who Ewan was; she was the first person the informant from the police department directed him to for his meeting with the Frenchman.

"Aye, I met him once," Samantha said with a sigh. "He was asking about a safe place to have a discussion with a few of the fellas. I told him his best bet was along the fence on Sinclair Road near the pallet company."

Robert Burns sat in silence, wondering how he could keep this young woman from falling victim to the same fate as Ewan. *If the shooter could find about Ewan, could he likewise find out about Samantha and the boat captain as well?* he asked himself. "The most important thing to remember Miss Atkins," he said, breaking the momentary silence, "is the captain keeping you onboard. If the police are asking about a specific time and day, and you've both agreed to the same thing, you'll be fine."

***

As the barrister for Alistair Hunt was discussing the allegations with his clients, Chief Inspector McDermott was reviewing the case file on Ian McLeod with Robert St. James. Relaxing, while the barrister looked over the forensics report, McDermott kept looking at his list of names on the whiteboard.

"Looks like the coroner and your forensic chief concur on the manner of death," St. James said. "What makes you think this woman could have done it, though?"

"We've got the discussion from Willie Jones, remember?" McDermott said. "And did you see the size of the lass? She'd handle most fellas with ease. We've still reason to believe this captain and his crew is the second third of the drug trafficking triangle."

"How so?"

"The recorded transcripts we gave to Hamilton this morning was just a snippet," the inspector said. "We've others that include

181

this captain and the sergeant; they're just not cataloged and reviewed in evidence yet."

Closing the file on Ian McLeod, St. James stood. "Well then, shall we get on with this one? I've got a handful of notices to review before Monday, and I don't want to work tomorrow or Sunday."

Getting to his feet, McDermott opened the door. "This way, then, Mister St. James," he said, motioning down the hallway. Passing forensics, he saw his partner Andrew Fletcher talking with Inspector Gordon. "Fancy a wee chat, do we?"

"We're completing an evidence entry," Fletcher said. "It seems one of the two fellas from Glasgow came back for an article at the train station." He pointed to the gun case on the counter. "The inspector and I were just annotating it as a locked parcel of a suspicious origin."

"What makes it suspicious, Inspector Fletcher?" St. James asked his curiosity now piqued.

"The individual in question was cited for carrying a firearm within the city limits without a license," Fletcher replied. "We believe he was dispatched by an associate of our drug trafficker, Ewan Sutherland. Knowing this makes me curious enough to have a look inside the case, how about you?"

"Fair enough," St. James said. "When I'm done with Chief Inspector McDermott's suspects, I'll see your report is pushed forward since it's tied to the shooting victim." He turned his attention back to McDermott. "Can we get to the room now, Inspector?"

"Aye, we can," McDermott said. "Andrew, be a good lad and wait till we're done before you do anything with that thing."

In moments, McDermott and St. James were sitting opposite Samantha Atkins and Robert Burns in the department's interrogation room. McDermott opened the file and slid a photo of Ian towards the engineer and barrister. "Have you ever met this young man?"

Samantha picked up the photograph and studied it. "No, can't say I have," she said, passing it to Burns.

"He's a known acquaintance of a young man you might have met in the past," McDermott said. "Last Monday evening, he was found in a bind, you might say." He now took out a photo from the crime scene and pushed it in front of her.

"Does nae look like he was a willing party, now, does he?" the woman said. "If you think I'm shocked by blood and flesh, you are wrong, Inspector. I'm not. There have been fellas smashing their hands between pipes on the rigs or losing a finger when hatches close in a storm. Mind you, this looks unfortunate, but I'm nae sick by it."

St. James pulled the folder towards him and flipped to the page that contained the list of physical evidence from the crime scene. He took particular note of the exterior items before speaking. He then got to his feet. "Inspector, can I have a word in private?"

McDermott looked at the barrister, his mind seething at the interruption. He snatched up the two photos and pushed them back into the folder. He then rapped on the door to exit. After stepping out, the two men stood in the hallway a pace or two away from the door. "You've got something on your mind, now?"

"She's not your suspect," St. James said. "She doesn't fit the profile. If we are to believe the killer or killers entered through the back door . . ." He took the folder from McDermott and turned to the evidence page. "See? The casting taken from the back door suggests the boot print was no larger than a size nine. This young woman is wearing a man's boot which is size ten or larger right now."

McDermott looked at the barrister, grasping for what he was saying to him. "You're trying to say her boot size is getting her a free pass?"

"If the report of the evidence was submitted for trial, I'd be laughed off the docket," St. James said. "But that doesn't dismiss her or her captain of involvement in the drug trafficking if your transcripts are genuine."

McDermott was never one to admit being bested, but the barrister's argument appeared valid. "If this is the case, then maybe we put a fright into them and they'll do something wrong the next time. Let's have a chat with her captain and see what he has to say before we do anything rash."

"Agreed."

Walking into the interrogation room, McDermott said, "Mister Burns, we'll be needing you. Mister St. James and I want to discuss events with your other client." He motioned for him to leave the room.

"I'll be back soon," Burns said to Samantha.

As they strolled down the hall, they entered the room where Bernard McIntosh sat, feet propped on the table, waiting for their arrival.

Choosing a seat opposite the captain, McDermott opened the file and slid the first photo of Ian in front of him. "Do you know this lad? He's frequented the docks from time to time in the past," he said.

Peering at the picture, Bernard shook his head. "No, can't say I've come across him."

"What about seeing him in this position?" He slid the crime scene photo next to the first.

"No," the captain said, staring at McDermott.

"Can you offer documentation showing the whereabouts of your engineer on Monday?" McDermott asked.

"I've my ship's log. Every order I give onboard the boat, the watch writes it down," Bernard said. "It'll show my chief engineer Mister Fischer was granted four days' shore leave; he needed to attend to matters in Dundee. This in turn shows Miss Atkins being placed in charge of our pre-sail operations."

"I look forward to reading the entries, then," McDermott said. "And it'll show you keep a tight hold of everything on your boat. Does that include your communications log?" He stared intently at the captain.

"Yes, it does, Inspector," Bernard said. "It's a requirement by the Maritime Agency, why do you ask?"

"It may be a matter of procedure to make sure your directions are being followed, that's all," the inspector said. "Where is your chief engineer at the moment?"

"What are you getting at, Inspector?" Burns interrupted.

"The captain has said his engine room is always manned, either by the chief or his second," McDermott said. "If the captain and the second engineer are here, who's minding the store right now?"

"I've relinquished command to my first officer," Bernard said. "And you heard me because you were standing on the dock when I gave the order."

"Aye, I was," McDermott answered. "But did the order include the chief being identified as the second in command? I know I was fifth in line onboard the HMS *Edinburgh* during my Navy days. So, who's next for your boat if we detain the first officer?"

"These questions are absurd," Burns protested. "We're not having a trial here." Glaring at St. James, he continued: "What's the basis for my client's detention, Counselor? This officer is treading a fine line of accusing the captain of something he's no knowledge of."

St. James looked at McDermott and back to Burns before speaking. "The captain of the *Standard-Hercules* is being detained for questioning on suspicion of harboring a felon. The second engineer is cited as a possible suspect in the murder of Ian McLeod."

"And yet none of the questions I've heard pertain to those citations," Burns said. "My clients will exercise their rights to withhold any further comments unless asked a specific question based on the summons."

McDermott was listening to the barrister, but he never let his eyes stray from Bernard McIntosh. I've got you, mister, and you know it, he thought. You've not a chance of squeezing out from your involvement in the drug trafficking. However, can you give me the Irishman?

Realizing the room had gone silent, he noticed both barristers looking at him.

"Do you have anything else to ask, Inspector McDermott?" St. James asked.

"No, but, Mister Burns, I'd tell your client to remain available," McDermott said. He faced the captain. "We'll be seeing each other again." He placed the pictures back in the folder and exited the room.

Walking out of the interrogation room, McDermott motioned St. James aside. "Can you find an extra minute? I'd like you to be in the room with the fella Andrew has for questioning."

St. James looked at his watch. "Fine," he said. "I'll give you five more minutes, then I'm back to my office."

McDermott walked to the constables' station. "Where is Inspector Fletcher questioning his suspect?"

"He's in room five, Inspector," the officer said.

Heading down the hall, they soon came to the designated room where Inspector Fletcher was preparing to question Clyde Smith. With a gentle knock on the door, McDermott poked his head in. "Mind a few extras, lad?"

"Not at all," Fletcher said with a note of disgust in his voice. "I was just about to start; please join us."

McDermott and St. James entered as Fletcher offered an introduction. "I believe you recall Chief Inspector McDermott and Mister St. James from the trial with Ewan Sutherland?"

Clyde Smith sat and nodded to each of them.

"This morning you were seen caring suspicious luggage at the train station," Fletcher said. "Mind telling us what is in the case, Mister Smith?"

"I've nothing to say until my barrister is present," Clyde answered.

Before Fletcher could ask another question, there was a knock at the door. As the constable opened it, Robert Burns stepped in past him. "This is getting to be a busy day, isn't it?" He took a seat next to Clyde.

"And you are?" Fletcher asked.

"Burns, Robert Burns. I'll be representing Mister Smith as his counselor. Anything you wish to ask him will take place in my presence. And if you don't mind, I wish to study the summons used to detain my client."

Fletcher turned to glance at McDermott, his face flush with embarrassment. "A word with you, Chief Inspector," he stammered, motioning to the door.

Stepping outside, McDermott's expression told Fletcher everything he wanted to hear from his partner. "What have you got to say for yourself? You've nae summons, have you?"

"No," Fletcher answered. "But when I met him at the station, and he's carrying the case, I knew something wasn't right," fiddling with his notebook. "I've seen you do the same, and it always turned out in our favor."

"Aye, lad," McDermott said. "And I've been lucky because I've likewise made mistakes, which I learned from. Tell me what you were thinking and be quick; Mister St. James won't stay for long."

Fletcher spent the next few minutes telling McDermott his thoughts about the case containing weapons. Moreover, in his opinion, the rifle used to kill Ewan Sutherland. "That's why I had to take a chance. You understand, don't you?"

Placing his hand on the young man's shoulder, McDermott replied, "Aye Andrew I do. Let's see if we can make this right." He led him back into the room.

"Inspectors," Burns said, "if you can't produce a warrant or summons, I'll have to—"

"Referring to the recent events here in Aberdeen, we've probable cause to question your client, Mister Burns," Fletcher said. "To that effect, we're requesting permission from your client to inspect the contents of the case he retrieved at the train station."

Clyde looked at Burns and back at Fletcher. "It's nae mine. I was picking it up for a friend; I've no means of opening it."

"Your client understands, due to his earlier citation on possessing a weapon without a permit, we've probable cause to inspect the case?" It was St. James's turn to begin asking the questions now.

Burns turned to Clyde. "They've got a reason to search the case, you know, don't you? Is there anything you want to say before they open it and find something you can't explain?"

Glancing at each of the men in the room, Clyde folded. "It's the property of a Mister Ross from Glasgow. He sent me to retrieve it. I've nae idea what is in it, I was just asked to pick it up, I swear."

McDermott looked at Fletcher and St. James before speaking. "Mister Burns, Scotland Yard, and Police Scotland Aberdeen have no warrant on your client. Nevertheless, if the contents of the case in question has anything illegal or can be attributed to a crime, he'll be charged. Do you understand?"

"Aye, I do," Burns said, disgusted. Looking at Clyde, he added, "You swear you've no knowledge of the contents? And whatever it is, you've no knowledge what it was used for?"

"I swear, Mister Burns, I've no clue what's inside the case," he said.

"I will ask the constable to stay with you, Mister Smith, while we review the contents. Mister Burns, do you wish to join us?" Fletcher asked, getting up.

"Yes," the barrister said, "on behalf of my client, I'll witness your search."

The four men left the room and made their way to the evidence locker. Following the constable, Fletcher signed the custody log for the case and placed it on the table outside the secured space. Tearing the seal, McDermott handed him a pair of bolt cutters, allowing Fletcher the honor of cutting off the lock.

"Shall we look at what Santa has brought?" McDermott asked, swinging the lid open.

Inside, each man knew the various pieces of a rifle, each piece placed in the foam cut-outs surrounding the interior, along with two boxes of bullets. "Shows your instincts were right, Andrew," McDermott said. "Mister St. James, we'll be needing a proper summons prepared against Mister Burns' client."

"Of course," St. James said. "And how shall I address the summons?"

Looking at Robert Burns, McDermott replied, "For possession of an illegal firearm and for the murder of Ewan Sutherland."

"You can't be serious, Inspector McDermott," Burns said. "Just because my client was carrying a case doesn't imply he was the shooter. Where's your evidence to support the charge?"

"As the saying goes, possession is nine-tenths of the law. If you're so sure that Mister Smith is innocent, what're a few moments to check the other evidence?" Turning to the constable, McDermott asked, "Can you give Chief Inspector McIntyre in Forensics a call to join us, and have him bring his kit?"

"Aye, Inspector," the officer replied, picking up the phone.

In moments, the chief technician walked into the evidence room joining the four men. "What have we got here, McDermott?"

"Seems Inspector Fletcher might have found our possible murder weapon in the Sutherland case," McDermott said. "I was hoping you could give it a quick swab to discover if it was fired recently."

Opening his bag, Chief McIntyre pulled on a pair of gloves before lifting the rifle barrel from the case. "It shows to be well maintained," he said. Placing the end of the barrel to his nose, he sniffed at it several times. "It's been fired," he said, wrinkling his nose, "but some time ago." Pulling a tube from his kit, he took a swab and swirled it inside the barrel several times before removing it and showing the tip. "There's virtually no residue, Inspector."

"I'd have to assemble the weapon in the lab for a more thorough check," McIntyre said. "But in my opinion, the weapon hasn't been fired in, oh, I'd say the past few weeks." He pulled two boxes containing bullets from the case and opened them up. "And all the munitions are accounted for too."

"Thank you, Graham. I'll see that Inspector Fletcher brings the case to the lab in a moment," McDermott said. "Mister St. James, if you don't mind, please prepare the summons as discussed earlier, but with the understanding it may be amended in a day."

"I'll have it taken care," St. James said. "Gentlemen, have a pleasant afternoon," taking his leave of their company.

Turning to Burns, McDermott added, "We'll see that your client is looked after for the time being. And unless you've got a question for me or Inspector Fletcher, I'd say we're through."

"I'll be back in the morning," Burns said, storming out of the room.

"Well, Andrew, what are we left with?" McDermott asked.

"Besides me making a cock-up of the whole affair?"

"I'm nae upset with everything now," McDermott said. "You've found an important piece in the investigation, so what would be your next step?"

Fletcher closed his eyes for the moment before answering. "I'd say we try to find this Mister Ross that the suspect mentioned."

"Good thinking, lad," he said, leading him out of the evidence locker. "But more important for us is asking why do we have Mister Burns stepping in? And not just with Smith, but likewise the ship captain and his engineer," McDermott said. "Seems queer to have the same barrister working on something separate, doesn't it?"

Fletcher smacked his hand down on the gun case. "Sutherland," he exclaimed. "Each one has a tie to our dead drug runner."

"Well done, Andrew," McDermott said. "And our next step will be . . ."

"Find out who Mister Burns is working for and what he knows," Fletcher replied. "Can we get the super to assign a few constables to shadow him?"

"I'm nae sure, but along the way, we need to find out if he's linked to Miss El-Sayed and Mister Gilmore."

189

Chapter Twenty-One

Robert Burns scurried out of police headquarters and hailed a passing taxi. "City Centre hotel," he told the driver. *How in the hell can I tell Alistair that one of Stuart's men was pinched with a sniper rifle?* he thought.

"Here you are," the driver announced outside the hotel. "That'll be four quid."

After settling with the driver, Burns stepped out of the cab and into the lobby. He headed straight for the lift and went up to his room.

He entered to find Gordon Wallace finishing his lunch at the table. "It's 'bout time you got back; I was thinking you hightailed it back to Glasgow."

"If only I could be so lucky," Burns said. "Did your cousin ever discuss the two fellas watching over Ewan with you?"

"Like I told you and Gilmore, it was just he was pinched with the drugs, nothing more. Why are you asking again?"

"One of those men was arrested at the train station with a sniper rifle, that's why," Burns said. "And I'm guessing the fellow who asked to look after Ewan knows the reason." He pulled out his cell phone and called Stuart Ross's number.

Stuart Ross was meandering toward the pub along the Commercial Quay when he felt his cell phone vibrating and answered it.

"Ross, it's Burns. Where are you?"

"Reggie and I went for a wee walk," Stuart said, blatantly lying. "We're just getting a quick bite to eat, why?"

Hector Pichon looked at the Scotsman, hearing only half the conversation he was receiving.

"Your friend Smith was pinched at the train station," Burns said. "And he was taken with a gun case. The police think he's Ewan's killer. The worst part is he declared you as the gun's owner."

"Damn him!" Stuart shouted. "Where are you?"

"I'm back in the hotel, but we need to get together and somehow wrap our hands about this before the police find you."

Looking at Hector, Stuart contemplated his next step. "Give me half an hour and I'll meet you there in the lobby." He immediately hung up.

"What was this all about?" Hector asked.

Looking at the Frenchman, and then Reggie, he said, "Clyde was pinched at the station with the other case. The police think he's the assassin of the young fella the other day."

"And who was telling you this?" Reggie Brown asked.

"Burns did," Stuart replied.

"Who is this 'Burns' gentleman?" Hector asked, stepping closer to Stuart.

"He's an associate of mine from Glasgow," Stuart answered. "He's a lawyer looking into the events of the young fellow who met with several parties here in Aberdeen. If he's worried, then I'm worried."

"Do you trust this fellow?" Pasqual asked.

"Yes, I do. We've got the same employer, and he's been able to help me and a few associates like Reggie out of some tight places," Stuart said. "If you want to keep looking for Angus, you're welcome to stay, but I need to go and see Burns." He began walking towards the end of the docks.

"I'm nae staying, so wait and I'll join you," Reggie said, following Stuart.

Pasqual looked at Hector. "We've looked around and seen no proof of the Scotsman. I choose to return to the hotel and find out what this counselor is saying." He watched as the two men from Glasgow walked away.

"You're right, we've looked around long enough," Hector conceded. "But tomorrow morning, we're back here looking for Angus, with or without them, agreed?"

"Oui, mon Ami," Pasqual replied as they hurried to catch up with Stuart and Reggie.

Several hundred meters away, tied to the dock, the *Nordic Supplier* gently swayed with the tide and passing vessels. Resting in the small cabin onboard the vessel, Dunbar spread the small cloth across the desk and placed his pistol on it. Breaking it down, he began to clean it, all the while considering his options. *It's obvious the French don't have the means to follow me*, he thought. He squirted lubricant on the barrel, and then wiped it clean. *Nevertheless, how did they find me in the first place?* he asked himself. A knock on the door interrupted him. He quickly tossed a towel over his weapon.

"Come in."

A seaman entered. "Excuse me, Mister Walker, the captain wanted to make sure you knew about breakfast being served."

"Thank you, I'll be out in a minute," Dunbar said. Once he was alone again, he lifted the towel and continued working on his weapon. After concluding the task of cleaning, he soon had the Glock 41 pistol reassembled and placed in its holster located in the small of his back. Picking up the cleaning kit, he was soon walking down the passageway, his nose leading the way to the galley and breakfast.

"Good morning, Mister Walker," Captain Clive Duncan said, seeing his guest enter. "Grab some coffee, I'd like a chat."

Picking up a cup, Dunbar proceeded to fix himself some coffee before heading to the table where Captain Duncan sat. As he took a seat across from the captain, Dunbar felt uneasy, as if he was about to receive a lecture in school. "So, what is it we need to discuss?" he asked.

"I had several deckhands talking about past activities last night. Seems there were several men wondering about Sutherland, and who was taking his place," Clive said. "Turns out the young lad had started something people want finishing." He paused to slurp his coffee. "And, I found out another good friend of mine is now in police custody. I've made plans for departing the harbor to avoid being detained as the next suspect."

"I'm not done with my business, though," Dunbar said. "You've agreed to help, or did you forget?"

"I didn't forget," Clive said, "but our agreement was made before I learned of these new police actions. Moreover, I'll not subject myself or my crew to rot in some cell if I can avoid it. There are a few friends who'll look after me if I need to avoid being pinched." He looked about the galley at his crew and felt sorry for allowing himself to be drawn into the criminal activities of Alistair Hunt and the Irishman, Higgins.

"After Monday, you'll be free to operate your business as usual," Dunbar said. "I should be able to tie up the loose ends by then." He drank the rest of his coffee and stood. "If you don't mind, I'm going to eat," he said, striding to the food line.

A crewmember approached the captain. "You've got a message, sir." He passed a handwritten note to Clive. It read CALL ME, MOST URGENT WE TALK. MISTER GILMORE. Crumbling the paper in his hand, he rose and left the crew and Dunbar in the galley and headed to the bridge.

Upon entering, he was greeted by the first rays of the sunrise, the glistening light reflecting off the glass of several other boats tied fast to the docks.

Picking up his pipe, he stepped outside, pulled out his cell phone, and dialed the barrister's number. After the fourth ring, a tired voice answered. "Hello?"

"Morning, Mister Gilmore. Captain Duncan returning your call." He lit the briarwood bowl of tobacco.

"Ah yes, thanks for getting back so promptly, Captain," Sean said. "I need to let you know the police may further come to you because of recent developments. It seems they might have come across evidence on several of your illegal activities undertaken for Mister Higgins."

Drawing on his pipe, the tobacco sizzling as he did, Clive asked, "And how did you find out about this?" Wisps of smoke curled from his lips.

"Yesterday, I was given some evidence on Sergeant Wallace, and part of it included you," Sean said. "It seems the police got recordings of shore-to-ship calls from the Coast Guard. And they're using it to cite conspiracy to traffic illegal drugs against Captains McIntosh and McKenzie."

"Have you reviewed all the recordings?"

"Yes, all those provided by the police, why do you ask?"

"I suspect they've more than what has been handed over, Counselor," Clive said. "You best push for everything they have, or you and your colleague will lose the case by the end of Monday." He took another drag on his pipe.

"What are you going to do?"

"I've got a passenger to see to first," Clive said. "After I rid myself of him, then I'll be taking my leave for a wee bit." He looked out and observed the crew begin its morning routine on the deck below. "Mind yourself, Mister Gilmore. I've got a feeling some events will get ugly soon."

"Thank you, Captain," Sean said. "I'll do my best."

Hanging up, Clive Duncan banged his pipe on the rail, sending the remnants of tobacco into the water below. Scrolling through his listings, he came across the legionnaire, Louis Clement, and selected the number. His call was answered by the Frenchman before the second ring.

"Bon jour, Captain," Louis said.

"Contact your friends in Aberdeen," Clive said, speaking in a firm and telling tone. "Angus is on board my boat for the next twenty-four hours."

"Understood, Captain," the Frenchman said. "And thank you."

Sitting on the edge of his bed, Sean felt defeated at what the captain of the *Nordic Supplier* had told him. *If the police have recordings from calls the sergeant made to the ships*, he asked himself, *is it possible they have other calls?* Scrolling through his phone he saw at least a half-dozen times he phoned the Coast Guard and Maritime offices to contact Captain Duncan.

The ringing of the hotel phone broke through the fog of uncertainty he was experiencing. Answering it on the third ring, he heard the familiar voice of Priscilla El-Sayed.

"Are you coming down soon?" she asked. "We've got a nine-thirty audience with Sergeant Wallace."

"Yes, I'm sorry," Sean said. "I'll be down in five minutes." He put on a clean shirt, got dressed, grabbed his notes, and shoved them into his satchel bag. He got into the lift just as a family from Inverness was stepping off and was soon exiting the lobby meeting his colleague.

"Sorry for keeping you," he said. "I was taking a call from another potential client."

"For both of us?" she asked, sliding behind the wheel of her car.

"No, this is a separate affair," Sean replied, closing his door. Looking out the car window, he contemplated letting Priscilla know about his discussion with Captain Duncan. *Best she not know,* he realized. If I need help, I might have to call her to defend me. "What are the possibilities the police have more recordings?" he asked.

"They'd be treading a very dangerous line then, I'd think," Priscilla answered. "If they have more associated with this case and haven't divulged them to us, we can cite them for tampering. Are you assuming they've kept something from us, Sean?"

"There's always the possibility they've not finished going through all of them, isn't there?" he asked.

"I mean, if we have transcripts for calls Wallace made up to the fourteenth, but they cite something afterward, then we've got them by the balls," she said.

She drove them into the car park and pulled into an empty stall at the jail facility for the sheriff's office.

"How would you find out?" he asked, then considering his next suggestion. "We've just as much a right to the originals as they do, correct?"

"Are you saying we go to the maritime office ourselves and ask for the recordings?"

"Why not? If nothing else, we can learn what the originals are like," Sean said. "If they have something different in court, like you say, we've got them by the balls," he said.

"First off, we talk with Wallace," Priscilla said, opening her door. "Afterwards, we'll pay a visit to the Coast Guard and see how cooperative they are." She stepped out of the car and strode towards the entrance to the jail.

Clutching his satchel, Sean followed behind her, still worried about his own involvement. *Funny, I haven't heard from Mister Higgins in the last week, either*, he reflected while standing behind Priscilla.

"Yes, Constable, I'm Miss El-Sayed, counselor for Logan Wallace," she said. "I understand we were granted access to our client for nine-thirty session this morning."

Looking over his schedule, the officer replied, "Yes ma'am. If you'll just sign in, I'll arrange a meeting room."

As the constable called for the former sergeant to be brought from his cell, Priscilla continued her conversation with Sean.

"Have you heard from your man, Sean? I've not checked my accounts, but I'd like to think we're due our checks yesterday, wouldn't you say?"

"Funny you mentioned it, I was wondering just the same thing," he replied. "When we're done, I'll give the office a call and see what's being done about it." *It'll give me a chance to ask Erin if Mister Higgins is back from his holiday or not*, Sean thought.

In moments, the constable reappeared at the window, "I'm sorry to inform you, but your client's been taking to the infirmary. If you need any more information, you'll be needing to ask the watch officer."

Priscilla turned and looked at Sean. "What do you make of that?"

"I'm not sure," Sean said. "If we want answers, we need to find this watch officer, though." He stepped up to the window to speak to the constable sitting behind the desk. "Excuse me, where can we find the watch officer?"

"That'll be Sergeant Williams," the officer said, glancing at the clock. "He's at breakfast now, but he should be back in fifteen minutes or so."

Soon an announcement came blaring over the intercom. "Constable Owen, prepare to receive medical staff at the entrance."

"Please stand aside," the constable said, getting to his feet while rushing to the entrance. In short order, an ambulance's siren could be heard getting louder as the vehicle drew nearer.

Moments later, the medical staff of the jail was wheeling a patient to the entrance where the ambulance had parked. Priscilla and Sean both glanced at the body held on the gurney, realizing it was their client under the oxygen mask. Straddling the sergeant, a nurse was attempting to conduct CPR, sweat pouring down her face as she performed chest compressions on the patient.

Priscilla sought to step closer, but Sean pulled her back. "Let them be; we'll know soon enough." Standing to the side, they observed the sergeant being loaded into the ambulance which soon pulled away. "Which hospital is he be taken to?" Sean asked the constable.

"BMI-Albyn, if they get there in time," the officer said, making the sign of the cross as he spoke. "He was nae in a good way when the walking patrol found him this morning."

"What do you mean?" Priscilla asked.

"It seems your client had had enough. He tried hanging himself in his cell," the constable said. "The watch said he was blue as the River Dee when they cut him down."

Priscilla saw a blank stare on Sean's face. He showed no emotion at the potential suicide of his client but likewise showed little concern for the outcome and its ramifications to their trial.

"Sean, what do we do now?"

"I'm not sure," he said. "We can try to contact Mister Jenkins and see if there's any precedence to this we could follow." He slumped into the chair outside the constable's office. "Going to the hospital might not be the best step; it seems somewhat morbid if he passes away."

"Well, the police will have a guard near him, so we won't have much chance talking with him," Priscilla said. "But you're right. We need to contact the courthouse and prepare for the next step." She sauntered out the door where the ambulance had just been.

Sean stood and looked about the jail facility, wondering if he'd just been given a free pass. *If the sergeant dies, the trial will be over*, he thought. Which meant sealing any evidence and setting it aside, its submission would void in any future trial. He advanced through the doors in time to see Priscilla finishing a call on her cell phone while waiting for him.

"Who were you talking to?" he asked as he joined her in the car.

"I was just listening to a message left on the phone, that's all," she lied. *I can't let him know I needed to talk to my father about the circumstances I've got pulled into,* she told herself. "Let's get to the courthouse and see what Mister Jenkins has in order because of this new twist, shall we?"

She left the lot and joined the city traffic, making her way to the Crown's Office. Here, they hoped to find the court clerk and with any luck, the prosecutor George Hamilton. As Priscilla drove around the building trying to find parking, Sean's mind raced, trying to figure a way to distance himself from the evidence. He knew there was a possibility the police had recordings with him speaking to the captains.

"Sean, come on," Priscilla said, nudging his arm as she exited the car.

Staring out the window, he noticed she'd found a spot behind the office building and was making her way to the entrance. "Let's see if Saint Patrick can keep me in good graces with the Lord," he muttered, stepping onto the sidewalk, following his colleague.

Chapter Twenty-Two

The hotel lobby was chaotic as businessmen and families on holiday alike were checking out. Hector Pichon and Pasqual Sequin stood off to the side waiting for Stuart Ross and Reggie Brown to make their way down from their respective rooms.

"We'll wait just a few more minutes," Hector said, looking at his watch. "If they're not here, we'll head out on our own." Glancing through the crowd, he quickly spied the two men exiting the lift, meandering their way towards him.

"Whatever happened to your man Burns?" Hector asked Stuart Ross. "I thought he was meeting us."

"He's got his hands full with a few issues of his own," Stuart said. "We'll be seeing him again, I'm sure. Any chance for a quick bite? I'm knackered at the moment."

"Aye, so am I," Reggie Brown stated, joining the conversation.

"Get something to go, I don't want to waste any more time than I need to," Hector said impatiently. "And then meet us outside near the valet." He headed towards the exit, and Pasqual followed him.

"Come on, Reg, a biscuit and coffee, then," Stuart said, nudging his partner.

Hector and Pasqual concealed their departure by accompanying a family of six leaving the hotel. As the husband and wife attempted to herd their four children outside, Hector and Pasqual stood off to one side near the valet station.

"Do you think they'll handle themselves if Angus begins a fight?" Pasqual asked.

"I'm not sure," Hector said. "Stuart's friend looks capable, and it sounded like he could protect himself. But Stuart has shown he's grown soft in the last few years." Peering back at the entrance, he noticed the two men making their way out, hands full with their food and drink.

Traipsing to the valet attendant, Stuart motioned to have a taxi called forward. "Mind yourself when we get to the docks, Reggie," he told his friend confidentially. "I've got a feeling our two Frenchmen will be more apt to save their own skins before ours."

As the four men slid into the taxi, Stuart gave the driver directions to take them to the Commercial Quay. The two Frenchmen sat looking relaxed as if they were going to a football match. As the taxi turned a corner, Reggie spilled some of his coffee onto his shoes, just missing Pasqual's feet. "Sorry 'bout that," he said.

"Just for that, you can pay the fare," Stuart said.

As the taxi turned the corner, they could see the masts of the service vessels over the warehouses lining the docks. "This is fine, pull over," Hector told the driver. "Pasqual and I will walk the rest of the way. You and your friend can meet us near the cruise ship offices." He started getting out of the cab.

"We'll nae wait long for you," Stuart said. He instructed the driver to continue to the docks.

"What do you think they're up to now?" Reggie asked.

"I'm nae sure, but they're on their own, as far as I'm concerned," He motioned for Reggie to exit the cab, which had now stopped at the cruise line offices.

"That'll be five quid-fifty, gentlemen," the driver announced.

Reggie pulled his billfold out and handed the driver seven for the fare. Closing the door, he turned and followed his friend to the gates leading to the waterfront and the service vessels.

"Any idea where we should start?" he asked after reaching his friend's side.

"We'll ask the first few blokes we come across. I'm sure we'll find someone chatting about a fella who does nae belong here," Stuart said as he meandered down the roadway.

"You mean, like us?" Reggie asked. "We're no more welcome here than this Angus you keep talking about."

Trailing a few paces behind the two Scots, the Frenchmen were exchanging their own thoughts on what might happen shortly. "What are you thinking, Hector?" Pasqual asked.

"These two—Ross and Brown—they're no match for Angus," he said. "At best, they could serve as a distraction for us when we meet him." Walking closer to the docks, they could make out the various vessels swaying with the motion of the incoming tide. As the Frenchmen turned the corner near the cruise ship offices,

Hector's cell phone buzzed. Sliding it open, he noticed the number of his associate in Marseille. "Bon jour, Louis."

"I was just told our friend is on the *Nordic Supplier* for the next day," the former Legionnaire said. "The captain will make sure he remains onboard, but you must subdue him before they sail, do you understand?"

"Oui, we'll finish the task before the end of the day," Hector replied. "I'll call you when we are on our way to Manchester."

"Don't forget, you still need to call your brother. Tell him you lost a bet and need the bottle of cognac," Louis said.

"I recommend we change the bet; I'm not sure he will part with it, even if you traded the cigars for it," Hector laughed. "If anything happens outside of our control, I'll contact you at the hotel." He ended the call.

"Is it good news?" Pasqual asked.

"Yes, we're to find a boat named the *Nordic Supplier* by the end of the day," Hector said. "It looks like Angus has taken refuge on it in the hopes that he can control the scene." Peering over his companion's shoulder, he saw Stuart Ross and Reggie Brown walking along the docks towards the cruise offices.

"Do you see a way to set up for a shot?" Hector asked, looking at the various sizes of buildings surrounding them.

"The tower across the way looks to have the best vantage point," Pasqual said. "If we can draw Dunbar into the open, I'm sure I could place a round on him at close to seven hundred meters. Give me a few moments to get to the top and I'll let you know for sure. What was the name of boat our target supposed to be hiding on again?"

"Louis said it was the *Nordic Supplier*, but he didn't mention where it was docked."

"Okay, I'll be back," Pasqual said. "Find the container and get our bags ready; I won't be long." He headed toward the multi-storied complex across the street.

Hector waved his friend off as he made his way towards a stack of shipping containers awaiting movement to the various boats. Pulling out his phone, he located the photo from Louis with an image of a container and its number where a cache of smuggled weapons was hidden. Exploring the many multi-colored metal boxes, he quickly found the one he needed. Getting out his keys, he unlocked it and pulled out two black backpacks.

As Hector retrieved their weapons, Pasqual made his way to the rooftop of the building, scanning the harbor for the vessel Dunbar was taking refuge on. In minutes, he spotted the orange and cream-colored service boat tied along the pier, just over three hundred meters from his vantage point.

***

Chief Inspector McDermott left his partner Inspector Fletcher to search for connections between the lawyer Burns, and the two lawyers representing Logan Wallace. Entering the constable's office, McDermott caught Sergeant Giles reviewing the paperwork on their earlier detainment of Captain McIntosh and Samantha Atkins.

"You ready for another go?"

"You're kidding, right? I've just spent the last hour on the two from earlier, and I've nae had my tea," the sergeant said. "Why didn't we do a clean sweep of the docks the other day if you had more than the captain and the lass to question, anyway?"

"Trust me, your tea will keep," McDermott said. "As for nabbing everyone, I don't want them talking too much amongst themselves. Now come on, I want to strike while the iron's hot. Our next guest might not be as willing to join us as the last two."

"I'll meet you at the car, then," Sergeant Giles said. "I need to let the lads know we're nae done yet," He made his way to the squad room where his fellow officers were preparing for their patrol shifts.

Leaving through the front lobby, Chief Inspector McDermott wrote a hasty note for Fletcher to join him when he was finished with the evidence from Clyde Smith. Exiting the building, he noticed the sergeant waiting in the car for him. "Where to this time?"

"Aye, the Commercial Quay side of the harbor," McDermott said. "We'll be looking for the *Nordic Supplier* berth. And with any luck, she'll nae be sailing soon, either."

As they pulled out of the police station, two other patrol cars took up station following them as they headed to the harbor. In less than five minutes, all three cars were parked across from the ship, followed by two more patrol cars.

"Same as before, lads," Sergeant Giles said, lifting the boot for his kit.

While the officers put on their gear, Chief Inspector McDermott walked to the gangway leading to the working deck and boarded the vessel. Signaling to one deckhand and flashing his ID, he said, "I'm here for your captain, can you go fetch him for me?"

In under a minute, Captain Duncan walked out of the superstructure towards the inspector. "What is it you want now?" he asked McDermott.

"I've got a summons for you," McDermott said, handing him the subpoena.

Unfolding the paperwork, Clive read over it, his demeanor was unchanged, even when he read that he was being charged with conspiracy and drug trafficking. He gave the paper back to McDermott. "I've noticed the charge, but where's your evidence?"

"You or your counsel will have a chance to look over the evidence at the district office," McDermott said. "I suggest you put your first officer in charge, for the time being; this might take a few hours."

"I've nae got a first onboard at the moment," Clive said. "Mister Spiers is in Inverness preparing for his captain's exam. Mister Collins has been acting in his absence, but he's not licensed to sail the boat outside the markers without myself being present."

"Well then, I'd say the *Nordic Supplier* is going to be a fixture in the harbor for a while."

As the exchange between the captain and inspector was taking place, Dunbar stood on the bridge, away from the windows, watching. Turning to the second officer Joseph Collins, he asked, "What happens to the boat if the police take the captain away?"

"We sit until he returns," the young man from Dornoch said.

"You're not able to set sail?" Dunbar asked.

"Oh, aye, I can sail the boat, all right, but I'm nae licensed," Joseph said. "If the captain was onboard, I'd be fine, because ultimately he's the one responsible when we're underway." Peering down on the working deck, he noticed his captain waving at him. "I'll be back," he told Seaman Carr, who was the bridge watch.

He clamored down the outer stairway and was soon standing next to Captain Duncan and Chief Inspector McDermott.

"Mister Collins, hand me your radio," Clive said. "Who's on the bridge right now?"

"Seaman Carr and that fella Mister Walker," Collins said, giving the two-way radio to his captain and taking a step back from him.

"I see," Clive said. Holding the radio up to his mouth, he spoke. "Seaman Carr, it's Captain Duncan."

"Aye, sir," the young woman responded, looking down on to the open deck.

"Make an entry in the log; Mister Collins has the con until I return," the ship's master said. "Under no circumstances does the *Nordic Supplier* get underway without my presence. Do you understand?" He gave his second officer a look.

"Aye, sir," Collins said, nodding his understanding.

"Aye, sir. Mister Collins is in charge, and we're secured until your return," the seaman replied, making the entry.

As he heard the exchange on the radio, Dunbar felt trapped onboard the vessel. *If the Frenchman comes for me*, he thought, *I've nowhere to go.* He moved away from windows and sat down, contemplating how he could gain control of the vessel to suit his needs. The movement of Seaman Carr caught his eye, and he realized he was in control as long as he placed the police in an unwinnable position.

Captain Duncan handed the radio back to Collins before speaking. "Inspector, I'd like a private moment with my officer, if you don't mind?"

"Aye, I'll give you a minute," McDermott said.

Together they stepped towards the wet-side of the boat. With his back to McDermott and Sergeant Giles, Captain Duncan spoke to his second officer in a matter-of-fact tone. "Listen carefully, Joseph. Under no circumstances do you leave Mister Walker alone in any space, do you understand?"

"Aye Captain," Collins replied. "Can we nae trust him? I'm nae keen having him onboard, to begin with, just so you know."

"I appreciate your honesty, Joseph," Clive said. "When you can, pass the word to the crew to mind their backs and keep him in sight as best you can. I'll see that I get back aboard as quick as possible."

Turning away from his second officer, Clive walked up to Chief Inspector McDermott. "Let's get this fiasco over and done with, shall we?" He stepped over the ship's rail onto the dock.

As his captain was escorted away by the police, Collins glanced at the bridge, wondering how he'd handle their guest. He grabbed the radio, changed the channel, and called the engineer. "Aye, Donnie, can you come up to the working deck? We need to have a chat."

As he stood near the dockworker's office, Hector was watching three police cars leave the berthing space of the *Nordic Supplier* as they headed back to the station. In one car, he noticed an older gentleman, wearing a fisherman's hat, sitting in the back seat.

"I found the boat," Pasqual said, brushing the dirt from his pants. "It's on the other side of the warehouse. If we can bring our target onto the deck, I'll have an easy shot at him."

"It turns out the police took one of the crew or the ship's captain in for questioning," Hector said. "Which means someone is in charge who might not be so stern. Our friend might not present us with an opportunity as he goes about roaming the deck. Could you make the shot if he's on the bridge?" the older Frenchman asked.

"Shooting from the rooftop means I'll already be taking the shot at an oblique angle. The glass on the aft sections is all angled downward," Pasqual said. "I'm not sure the strike would be clean once the bullet hit the glass. It would cause an offline ricochet and strike something or someone else. We're better off getting him in the open; it's the only way of succeeding."

Scanning the surrounding dock space, Hector considered the alternatives of drawing the sniper into the open. "This is where we put our two Scotsmen to good use," he said. "Let's see if we can persuade them to take part, shall we?"

As the two Frenchmen walked over to where the men from Glasgow stood, Reggie Brown was first to notice they carried black backpacks, which they didn't have earlier. "Where did you get the bags?"

"A friend of ours left them behind," Pasqual said.

"I need both of you to listen for five minutes," Hector said. "I've got a notion for drawing Angus out, so we can go about our business, okay?" Each man nodded as the French Legionnaire outlined the plan to take down the SAS sniper.

"You want us to dae what?" Reggie exclaimed after hearing Hector's idea.

"You're not serious about this, are you Hector?" Stuart asked. "For all we know Angus is making notes as we stand here in the open." He glanced nervously over his shoulder.

"Listen, all I'm asking for you to do is persuade a crewman to get Angus in the open," Hector said. "Pasqual and I will do the rest."

"And if he refuses, then what do we do?" Stuart asked. "He'll have his guard up for sure, then we're stuck waiting him out. Not to mention, I'm nae armed for taking him on, are you, Reg?"

"I'm no fool, Stu; of course, I've got a means to fend off someone," he said pulling his pant leg up, exposing the grip of his pistol to his friend. "And if we do anything, you need to be first up. Angus knows me by sight."

Hector and Pasqual shared a glance as the two Scotsmen discussed the plight.

"Are the two of you done arguing?" Hector asked. "We might only have one chance to neutralize this gentleman, so I'm open to any ideas you may have. If our target feels threatened in any way, he might take one or more of the crew hostage."

Each man looked at the other before Stuart spoke. "How much time do you need to be ready for a shot? And what is the plan for escape? We've no motor at our disposal."

"I need a few minutes," Pasqual said. "As for escaping the police, we'll leave that up to you to arrange. In fact, you mentioned your friend Ross getting you out of jams; have him get a car for us."

"He's a good point, Stu," Reggie said. "Call him and have him get us a motor ready."

Stuart pulled out his cell and dialed up the counselor for Alistair Hunt. The call went directly to his voice mail. Stuart left him a brief message. "Until he calls back, we're on our own," he said.

Whoop, whoop, whoop echoed across the water as an emergency signal sounded from the berth of the *Nordic Supplier*.

"What the hell was that?" Reggie said after he collected himself.

"It was a collision warning," Pasqual said, looking at his partner. "Something has happened on the bridge; they don't sound off on their own."

"Go get yourself ready," Hector said. "Stuart and Reggie, follow me." He began heading towards the ship.

In moments, the three men stood in the shadows of a warehouse, looking up at the bridge of the ship. "I don't see anything, do you?" Reggie asked.

"There's at least one person moving about," Hector said as his phone chirped with a text. He read the message aloud. "It's Pasqual; he can see into the bridge. There's a man with a gun and a person tied to a chair."

"Now we've no chance to get him in the open," Reggie said.

"We've got company," Stuart said, pointing to several dockworkers making their way towards the boat.

"If they create a scene," Hector said, "they might do the work for us of drawing out Angus." As he peered over to the building where Pasqual was preparing his position, he saw the telltale sign of his partner's silenced weapon at the ready.

Chapter Twenty-Three

After escorting Captain Duncan to interrogation, Chief Inspector McDermott went to his office to call the lawyer's Hamilton and St. James. Between the second and third ring, the lawyer answered. "Hello, this is George Hamilton, can I help you?"

"Aye, you can," McDermott said. "I've got the boat captain in for questioning and was wondering if you'd like to join me?"

Looking at the wall clock, Hamilton said, "Give me five minutes, and I'll be there."

As McDermott placed the phone down, Sergeant McKee stuck her head in the door. "Inspector, we've just taken a call about a disturbance at the docks," she said. "The Coast Guard received a distress signal from the boat you and Sergeant Giles just came from."

"Where's Inspector Fletcher?" he asked, pulling his pistol from the desk drawer.

"I'm nae sure," she said.

"Find him and tell him to get his arse in gear and meet me at the docks," McDermott said rushing passed her. On his way to the door, he noticed that Sergeant Giles and Constable Howe were next to the car, waiting with the doors open.

"Let's go," McDermott said, jumping in the passenger seat.

The people milling around the docks could hear the wail of sirens emerging from the city streets as every available officer responded. Two cars were parked at the entrance to the dock areas at the Commercial and Regent Quay's, while three more sped along the docks, led by Sergeant Giles.

The officers got out of their cars and donned their gear and assumed positions on the docks facing the vessel.

Sergeant Giles handed over a bullhorn to Chief Inspector McDermott. "You may need this to get your point across," he said. "Dispatch says they took a call from someone requiring the Captain Duncan being returned. And the caller mentioned having several hostages too."

"I'll wager whoever made the call considers himself having the upper hand," McDermott said. "Tell the lads to keep their eyes open and get a couple to clear the dockside of anyone not in uniform." He tapped the sergeant's shoulder boards. "Constable Howe, you stay with me."

"Aye, be back in a minute," the sergeant said, trotting off in a low crouch towards the officers along the dock. Glancing at the first group, he instructed two of them to clear the civilians off the dock. "Pass the word, lads; if someone's not part of Police Scotland, they did nae belong here," Giles said before returning to McDermott's side.

"Nae time like the present," McDermott said, picking up the bullhorn. "Ahoy, on the bridge! This is Chief Inspector McDermott of Scotland Yard. You've no chance at escaping what you've started, so come out onto the bridge wing and we'll have a chat."

A screech and crackle emanated from the speaker above the bridge windows before a voice spoke. "I'm in need of Captain Duncan's return, Inspector McDermott. You've got thirty minutes or I've got a fair, young lass and an able-bodied seaman who'll pay for your stupidity."

"Well, for the sake of being civil, how should I address you?" McDermott asked.

"For the moment, it's Walker," the voice blared over the speaker.

McDermott glanced at the sergeant. "Contact Inspector Fletcher and have him bring the captain here in a panel van," he said. "I'll see if we can stall this loon a wee bit." Turning to the younger officer, he asked, "Who's the best shooter in the ranks, Constable Howe?"

"That'd be Trevor, the armory tech," he said. "He's taken a few quid from most of the sergeants and all of us constables. He's a magician with his rifle—nearly catatonic, hypnotic-like. You think he can take this fella down?"

"Someone will," McDermott said, spying dockworkers across the harbor lining the rail of the *Standard-Apollo*. He extended his hand toward the young officer. "Give me your two-way, will ya?"

The constable handed over the radio when he heard the inspector give out instructions.

"I need several of you constables near Regent's Quay to get those deckhands off the boat, does anyone copy?"

"Aye, I copy you, Inspector," came the voice of Sergeant McKee.

Peering across the water, McDermott followed the bodies of the female officer and two others as they made their way to the boat to rustle the men away from the rail.

The minutes passed in short order. "Your time is nearly up, Inspector. Where's the captain?" said the voice from the bridge loudspeaker. "I don't believe Scotland Yard or Police Scotland Aberdeen want the death of innocent people on their conscience, do you?"

"It nae be the first for either, I'm sure," McDermott replied. "Since we had the captain as our guest, you can imagine the process to check him out. So, in good faith, how about you give me an extra fifteen minutes?"

On the ship's bridge, Dunbar sat and shook his head. "This fella is a piece of work wouldn't you say so?" He gestured with his pistol at the restrained figures of Seaman Carr and Second Officer Collins. He got back on the radio. "It's only ten from the district office," he replied. "But I like your spirit, Inspector, so I'll give you five more minutes."

McDermott glanced at his watch. "What the hell is keeping Andrew?" he asked no one in particular just as the police van pulled into the parking space for the cruise ship office employees. Inspector Fletcher got out the back and walked towards McDermott and Constable Howe's position on the docks.

"Afternoon, Inspector," Constable Howe said, greeting Fletcher.

"Constable," he replied, nodding towards the young officer. "A fine day to be at the harbor, don't you think?"

Before Howe could reply, McDermott interrupted their pleasantries. "I've nae time for the chit-chat. Did you bring the skipper back?"

"Yes," Fletcher said, "and your guest says he wants to talk with you."

"Keep an eye on the bridge, then," McDermott said, handing over the bullhorn before trotting to the van. He opened the back doors and saw Captain Duncan sitting, facing him with his back against the cab. "Mind telling me who this Walker fella is you have onboard your boat?"

"I met him the other day," Clive said. "He mentioned that if I knew what was important, I shouldn't cross him." He pulled off his

209

cap and pushing his greying hair back with his hand. "I got the impression he's one of those 'soldier-of-fortune' types. But I've nae seen him before until he caught me in the park."

"A mercenary-type, you say," McDermott said. "How'd he come about picking you out of the crowd? You have something in common maybe, like running drugs for a bloke in Glasgow, heh?"

Clive Duncan picked his head up and stared at McDermott before speaking. "There are no drugs on my boat. And you're free to scour it once you get that lunatic off my bridge," he said. "I've never laid eyes on him until we met in the park. I'll swear before God and country, even on my mother's gravestone, Inspector."

McDermott could understand the determination and resolute behavior in the seaman's eyes. "Aye, I believe you, Captain. But mark my words, when we're done, you'll be answering my questions in another manner."

Before Captain Duncan could respond to McDermott's statement, the voice boomed over the speaker from the Nordic Supplier again. "Inspector, you've two minutes left." McDermott looked at the captain, then to the constable outside the van. "Get me an extra vest and be quick about it."

Going to the front of the van, the constable returned with the bullet-resistant garment. McDermott took the vest and tossed it to the captain. "Put this on under your shirt."

"You plan on using me as bait, is that it?" Clive asked, donning the vest.

"Aye, you're a big fish and this bloke wants tae put a hook in you, so I'm going to accommodate him."

Sergeant Giles stepped up to McDermott as he was preparing Captain Duncan's exit. "I understand you called for a wee help."

"Aye, I did," McDermott replied.

"Well, Trevor and his partner have themselves in position," the sergeant said. "He's just waiting for your permission, Inspector. But he said it's nae a clean shot, with the tilted glass and all."

"Dammit, I forgot about the windows," McDermott said, looking at the vessel's captain.

"You're planning on shooting through ballistic glass, are you?" Clive asked.

"Aye, with the rubber bullets," McDermott said with a sneer. "It's nae my first go about with a lunatic on a boat." He turned back to the constable. "Is the first shooter ready, Sergeant?"

"Aye, Trevor and his partner have it all set," the sergeant said. "I've never seen a shooter use a metronome to sequence a shot before today. They've said they plan on playing it at 120 beats a minute."

"Next thing you'll hear them using is a rendition of the drum line from the tattoo," McDermott said. "Keep our guest company; I'll let you know when he can make his grand entrance."

Across the water, crouching behind the top of the roofline, a lone gunman prepared to take his shot. Putting the rifle scope to his eye, Pasqual could make out the silhouetted figures of three people on the bridge. Two he saw were restrained back-to-back in the center of the bridge, while the third shuffled about on his knees below the window sills. "What do you want me to do?" he said over the phone.

Hector turned away from Stuart and Reggie before speaking. "Be ready at a moment's notice," he said. "The police look to have something planned which we can take advantage of it if it all works out in our favor."

"I'm only good for another ten minutes, you know," Pasqual said, alluding to the unwritten rule shooters use about eye strain when using a rifle scope.

"I suspect something will happen soon, and if it doesn't, I want you to take your break as usual," Hector instructed. "If the police act ahead of you, we'll handle it when it happens." Turning his attention back to Stuart and Reggie, Hector told them of his plan.

"I need the two of you to get with several of the dockworkers and start a ruckus," he said. "Just enough to get the police looking in separate directions. We need to get the police moving about to make Angus nervous enough to show himself."

"You're daft," Reggie said. "One wee dust-up and they'll cuff me again."

"Are you saying your partner can't take a shot from his position?" Stuart asked.

"There are two individuals on the bridge along with Angus. And he has them tied up," Hector said. "It's best to draw his attention away from them before Pasqual can fire at him. Our only chance is to get him onto the bridge wing, or at least to the doorway allowing Pasqual to have a clear sight for his shot."

211

"We've nae weapons, Reggie, we'll play it up like a rugby scrum," Stuart said. "Get the crowd chanting." He began tugging his friend's arm.

"You keep this, then," Reggie told Hector, pulling the snub-nosed revolver from his boot. "It may not be much, but it's better than a butter knife." Chasing after Stuart, they were soon mixing up with several of the dockworkers, and their voices grew louder.

Hector saw the melee the two Scots were creating and its desired effects on the police as a handful of officers moved in on the crowd. Glancing back to the Nordic Supplier he noticed a figure moving about the bridge. On the other side of the water, he saw several officers and the captain he noticed from earlier, beginning to move, making their way closer to the vessel.

***

"Sergeant, we've got movement near the doorway," came the voice over Giles's radio. Through the reflection of the water on the bridge windows, constables could see Dunbar pacing behind the console.

"Aye, we see it too," he responded, looking at Chief Inspector McDermott. "It's a matter of timing, you know. If we show the captain too soon, Trevor can't make the shot soon enough; too late and this Walker fella could possibly get off his shot."

"Let's hope Trevor and his partner are paying attention, then," McDermott said. Staring at the captain of the Nordic Supplier, he said, "You'll nae do anything foolish now, will you?"

"Not at your expense," Clive Duncan said, squatting behind the patrol car.

Picking up the bullhorn, McDermott said, "All right, Mister Walker. This is McDermott, again. We've got Captain Duncan nearby. As a gesture of good intentions, why don't you let the crewmen on the bridge get some fresh air, like a good lad?"

Dunbar listened to the Scotland Yard inspector and chuckled to himself. He looked at Seaman Carr and the second officer, Collins. He was hard-pressed to give in to the police's demand and lose his advantage. Picking up the microphone, he provided McDermott with an alternative.

"I'll consider an officer-for-an-officer exchange," he said. "One of your constables for the second officer. Come now, what do you think, Inspector?"

"I'm keener on seeing you release the young lass first," McDermott replied.

"I'm sure you would prefer that, but I'm a bit of a ladies' man inspector, so she'll stay and keep me company," Dunbar said, glancing at Fiona.

McDermott looked at Giles before he spoke. "I'm nae keen placing any of your constables at risk, but we need to get something to leverage this lunatic with, to keep him off balance." Peering at the end of the docks, he noticed the crowd becoming increasingly vocal. "Looks like the dockworkers are getting restless, too. We've not much time to end this."

"I'll go," Fletcher said, chiming in. "Best to have the troops at the ready." Peeking at the boat, he continued. "Plus, I've always wanted to play the part of Cornwall at Yorktown." He looked at the sergeant standing next to him. "Mind the suit jacket, will you?" He stripped off his coat and began putting the bullet-resistant vest over his head. As he passed his pistol over to McDermott, he added, "No sense causing a scene with this."

"Remember, for Trevor and his mate to get a clean shot, you need to draw him out to the bridge wing," McDermott said. "We've but one good chance, so let's not muck it up, okay?"

"Talley-ho, then," Fletcher said, stepping out from the car and walking towards the vessel as the crowd cheered him on. "Sounds a bit like I'm entering a lion's den in ancient Rome," he said into his microphone as he stepped over the rail.

Standing away from the glass, the gun-for-hire took note of Inspector Fletcher making his way onboard the vessel. "That's good. Right there, young man. What's your name?" Dunbar asked over the loudspeaker.

"Inspector Fletcher of Scotland Yard," Fletcher tried shouting above the din.

"Lose the vest; you won't be needing it up here. After you toss it on the dock, you can make your way up the outer stairway."

McDermott and Giles heard the exchange, and both looked at each other before McDermott spoke. "If he has him go up the stairwell, that'll put Andrew on the port side of the boat. Will Trevor have a shot?"

Giles grabbed his radio and posed the question to his sniper. The answer was not what they wanted to hear. Looking back at the boat, the officers saw Fletcher complying with Dunbar's instructions.

Fletcher pulled off the vest and tossed it over the rail onto the dock, his ears ringing from the crowd's shouts of encouragement. Having stepped onboard the boat, it wasn't long before he soon felt the onset of nausea, being susceptible to getting seasick at the slightest sway of the vessel.

Watching the inspector's uneasy ascent up the outer steps of the superstructure, Dunbar pulled the second officer to his feet, shoving him to the port side door. "Don't get fancy on me, Mister Collins, or you'll take a wee bath," he said. "Now, open the door gradually," he said, turning the handle for his hostage.

Collins nudged the door open with his knee, just as Fletcher reached the top step to the bridge wing. Fear was etched on the face of the young seaman; the uncertainty of what was to happen next was weighing heavily on his mind.

"You can stand right there, Inspector," Dunbar said as he shoved the barrel of his gun between the arm and body of the second officer. "Pull your shirt up and turn about," he said, motioning the gun at him.

Fletcher followed the instructions, followed by shouts of "Take it all off" coming from the crowd on the docks. Facing the seaman, Fletcher looked past him and into the eyes of Dunbar.

"You're in a bit of a jam, I'd say," Fletcher said. "We've enough officers waiting for their chance at you." He nodded towards the docks. "And if the constables don't get their chance, I'm sure the dockworkers or seamen will see to you," he added, trying to buy McDermott time to find a solution. "I'd say it'd be best if you hand over your weapon and walk away from all this instead of being carried."

The SAS sergeant looked Fletcher in the eye, never wavering his focus. "I've been in worse positions," Dunbar said. "This is a bit of a lark, you know. I've got you to fend off the police and her," glancing at Fiona tied to the chair, "for entertainment, you understand. For later on." Easing the ship's officer further out the door, Dunbar leveled his weapon at Fletcher. "No quick moves, Inspector, but I want you to switch places with Mister Collins now."

Inspector Fletcher kept his gaze on the gunman as he spoke. "It's all right," he said. "Do as you're told and you'll be just fine. Your name is Collins, is it?" He gathered himself on the step.

The second officer responded with a nod of his head.

"What's wrong with you?" Dunbar asked, noticing Fletcher's pale look.

"I'm prone to seasickness, that's all," Fletcher said.

"Good thing you've never served in the RN, then," the gunman said, inching further outside the bridge.

"The RN wasn't manly enough for me." Fletcher said proudly. "I'm a Royal Marine."

From across the harbor, Pasqual saw his chance as Dunbar edged the second officer further out the door. Focusing through the rifle's scope, he narrowed as his breathing until it became shallow and rhythmic. Exhaling, his heart rate edging slower, he pulled the trigger. A clang of the rifle's action cycling could be heard, as the round was released, spiraling through the chamber and passed the silencer.

In just one fleeting moment, before the Dunbar could respond to Fletcher's comment, the assassin's head exploded across the bridge console. The bullet tore thru his right eye, mushrooming as it impacted bone and tore through the soft flesh. Blood, bone fragments, and remnants of brain matter spewed throughout the interior of the ship's bridge.

Seaman Carr's screaming could be heard echoing across the docks as the remnants of Dunbar's skull spewed onto the ship's controls.

Falling back, Fletcher grabbed the second officer and pulled him free of the door, covering him from possibly being hit by another bullet.

Dunbar's body tumbled backwards into the bridge, collapsing where he once stood, blood oozing from the gaping wound and surrounding the body.

The scene caught the constables on the docks by surprise. "What the hell just happened?!" Sergeant Giles exclaimed, seeing Dunbar drop from sight. "Trevor, what happened? Did you take the shot?" calling over the radio.

"It was nae me," the armorer said. "It must have come from the south side of Blaikie's Quay." Swinging his scope around, the constable began to scan the rooftops for another shooter.

As the constables were talking, McDermott was racing towards the vessel and up the stairwell to his partner. Forcing his way past Collins, who was retching as he stumbled down the steps, he reached the top as Fletcher was lifting Fiona Carr over the prone figure of Dunbar. "Conor, help her down the stairs," he said, handing her to the inspector.

Clive Duncan stood behind the police van, relieved knowing that his crewmembers were safe. *What arrangement can I make with the police?* he thought, knowing he wasn't clear of the job.

Amongst the crowd, Stuart Ross and Reggie Brown witnessed the shooting along with the fifty or so others gathered on the dock. "Come on, time for a wee stroll," Stuart said, nudging his partner. "Let the French fend for themselves," he said, climbing into one of the taxis parked across the street.

"You not staying for the fireworks?" the driver asked.

"No, take us to the Holiday Inn," Stuart said without looking back.

Wandering away towards the weather station, Hector Pichon dropped his backpack into the water as he passed the cruise line offices. Angling away, he saw his partner Pasqual Sequin walking across the boulevard towards the bus stop. Acknowledging him, they stood to wait for the local line that would take them to the train station.

Chapter Twenty-Four

As they stood on the exposed bridge wing, the crisp salt air swirling in from the North Sea kept the stench of the slaying from abusing their senses. "We'll never figure out who set him up to all this," McDermott said. "We'd one chance and someone else took it from us." He looked over the water towards the weather office.

Screening his eyes, he could see the occasional constable walking behind the façade of the rooftop. "Just like the shooter who killed the Sutherland lad," he muttered. "Did you pick up anything when it happened?" he asked Fletcher.

"Nothing. Not a whisper," the young inspector said. "Suggests I've turned into the grim reaper, what with this bloke and Sutherland. Everyone I'm dealing with has taken a bullet."

"I'm nae dead, am I?" McDermott asked. "You're just fortunate to be close by." He looked over the bridge console. "Seems Graham and the lads will be busy cleaning this place up. Either that, or they'll leave it to the crew."

"What a mess," Constable Howe said as he reached the bridge doorway. "Inspector, Sergeant Giles wants to know what you want done with the captain."

"Aye, the captain," McDermott said. "He'll be our guest at District for the next few days while we scour the boat. See tae getting him settled, will you Howe? I'll be there in a wee bit, once Chief Inspector McIntyre arrives."

Hollering down at six constables moving towards the boat, McDermott said, "Work through the boat and find the other crew members. Mind yourselves and watch for possible traps and such. No need to get anyone else killed." Hearing the inspector's orders, the constables paired up and entered the superstructure below the bridge.

Leaning against the rail, McDermott's head was awash with bits and pieces yet to be fitted in the puzzle he was trying to solve. "Andrew, we know the captain had spoken with this Irishman, right?"

"Yes, at least once," Fletcher said. "Plus, we've got the sergeant making one call to the boat. What are you thinking? That the Irishman is protecting the captain?"

"Aye, he's at the center of it all," McDermott said. "But what if it was the Frenchman, this Remesy fella doing the protecting? Or, let's say he's removing people who could identify him, where does that leave us? And more significant is how this Frenchman might have found out about all this going on here in Aberdeen."

"You suggesting we might have another snitch?" Fletcher suggested.

"I'm nae sure," McDermott said.

Glancing at the dock, they both saw Constable Howe escorting Captain Duncan away and place him into a waiting police car. The captain looked at the boat and the two inspectors, nodding in their direction as a look of relief became clearer on his face.

"Aye, I'd wager he's pleased with himself for the moment," McDermott said.

"You don't think it's because he knows his crew is safe from this fella," Fletcher said, pointing to the body of Angus Dunbar. "He had two of the crew at gunpoint here, and at least eight others locked up below deck. If I was in his boots, I'd be pleased as punch knowing they were safe."

Soon Chief Inspector McIntyre was seen on the dock along with his technicians, Devin and Kyle. The two young men took to unloading the forensics gear, moving it to the deck of the service boat. Graham made his way to where McDermott and Fletcher were standing until he reached the top of the outer stairway and noticed the legs sticking out of the door.

"You two are making a habit of helping me earn my pay these days," the forensics chief said. "Another gunshot victim, I see." Glancing at Fletcher, he asked, "Did you do this, Inspector?"

"No, we believe the shooter was on the rooftop of the meteorological building at Blaikie's Quay," Fletcher said, pointing to the seven-story structure to the north. "I was standing here against the bulkhead. And our victim was standing behind a hostage in the doorway, there." He gestured to where the body lay. "Sounds odd to call him a victim, though; he was threatening to kill me."

"Well, this poor fella didn't choose to die here, so he is a victim," Graham said. He began pulling on his white overalls and gloves. "I'll expect a copy of your version of the events on my desk before you leave tonight." He peered down at the lifeless body. "Now, what version of the story are you going to tell me, heh?"

Stepping over the body and into the bridge, CI McIntyre took a closer look at Dunbar's face. The forensic chief soon found himself in a triage tent outside Tuzla in Bosnia-Herzegovina. "I know this fella," he said, looking at McDermott. "I mean, I've treated him when I was a medic in the Black Watch serving in Bosnia. He's an SAS-type, with the Twenty-Second Regiment. Or at least he was at one time."

"Are you sure, Graham?" McDermott asked, wanting to believe what he was hearing.

"Aye, I'm sure," the forensic chief said. "He came into the medical tents one night with a broken nose and several knife wounds. When we reported him to the Sergeant Major, he told the command staff he got pissed about losing a bet with one of his mates. It ended with them fighting. About a week later, they shipped him back to Stirling Lines. We didn't find out anything after that."

Grabbing his scissors, the forensics chief cut open the victim's shirt. Moving an arm aside, he pointed to several scars on the torso. "See? Here and here—this is where I had to close up his wounds."

"Do you recall his name? His real name, Graham?"

"What? Ah, no. I don't recall it. I'm sorry," CI McIntyre answered, his thoughts drifting back to his younger days serving in Her Majesty's Scottish Regiment.

***

As Chief Inspector McIntosh and his technicians processed the murder scene with the coroner, having removed the body of Angus Dunbar, the two inspectors from Scotland Yard returned to their office.

"Is my crew safe?" Captain Duncan asked, sitting in the interrogation room.

"Yes, they're quite safe," Chief Inspector McDermott said. He opened a folder and placed a photo of Louis Remesy on the table in front of the captain. "What can you tell me about this fella?"

"Before you and I have any further discussion, you'll need to allow my lawyer to be present. Without him, I'll be exercising my right of silence."

McDermott turned to the glass window and nodded to the constables behind it. In moments, the door swung open and Sean Gilmore entered. Having a seat next to the captain, he pulled out a notepad and pen from his satchel. "May I see your summons, Inspector?"

"Like I told your lady friend, it's Chief Inspector McDermott, Counselor. Don't make me remind you again," McDermott said as he passed the summons to the lawyer.

Sean nodded as he opened the document and read through it. "If you'll be so kind and give me a few minutes with my client to discuss these charges, Chief Inspector McDermott," he said, stressing McDermott's rank.

McDermott turned and made a cutthroat motion to the glass before pulling the photo back and placing it in the folder. He then left the room, leaving the captain and lawyer alone to confer on the summons.

"What am I looking at?" Clive asked.

"They've filed several charges against you," Sean said. "The first is for participation in drug trafficking. Of course, they'll have to offer evidence to this effect to make the charge valid. The other is the obstruction in a police investigation. This one will be a bit more muddled, I'm afraid."

"Why's that one more of an issue?"

"If this goes to trial, all the police have to show is your reluctance to answer questions or give access to conduct a search," Sean said. "Of course, they have to show just cause for conducting any search before serving this summons, mind you. So, anything they've done before this is on shaky ground."

"And what about you?" Clive asked the counselor. "How's your stature in all this?"

Staring down at his scuffed and dirtied shoes, Sean spoke. "You know who I work for, and you know what he has asked both of us to be involved in. It suggests I'm somewhat in a pickle, as it were." He stood and leaned against the glass window, looking at the ship's captain. "Just so you know I've already made my decision to make this my last effort for Mister Higgins. But, I'll stand in for you, because I believe, just like myself, you and I were played as pawns in a bigger game."

"I was well aware of what I was getting asked to do," Clive said. "I'm nae ready to retire to some accommodation for the affirmed, mind you. I'm prepared to see to myself after I'm done sailing, but that's a few more years from now."

"How do you want to press on, then?" Sean asked.

"Let the police file the drug trafficking charge, they'll nae find any evidence on my boat," he said. "And I'm confident you and I can beat the obstruction charges, too."

"All right, then," Sean said. "But, if I'm going to defend you before the magistrate, I must tell Miss El-Sayed she's on her own with the constable. I'm not sure how she'll take the news. But, I'm willing to give your summons my all," He turned to face the glass and rapped his knuckles against it.

McDermott reentered the interrogation room, taking his seat across from the two men. "You've decided, have you?" he asked.

Sean cleared his throat before beginning. "Chief Inspector McDermott, my client, Captain Clive Duncan, denies having any knowledge of or taking part in any action as it relates to these charges. To this effect, we will contest these accusations in court."

"Well, then," McDermott said. "Before we had the pleasure of Mister Gilmore's company, I asked you a question, which I'll ask again. Captain Clive Duncan, do you know this fella?" He slid the photo of the Frenchman back in front of the seaman.

Snatching it up, Clive studied it before setting it down. "I've never seen nor met this gentleman before you showing me the photo."

"And what about this gentleman?" McDermott asked, sliding the photo of Ian Campbell across the table.

"Aye, he's one of the workers on another boat. He's been about when we've docked in the past. But he's nae set one wet boot on my vessel before."

Getting the photo back, he then slid two others in front of the captain. "And these two gentlemen?" He then moved the crime scene photos of Jimmie Keller and Alvin Doyle at the signal house in front of both men. McDermott noticed the color drain from the lawyer's face as he looked at the pictures, each one depicting the dock workers with a bullet wound to the forehead.

"Aye, this fella was a super with the dockworkers," Clive said, tapping his finger on the picture of Doyle. "He'd sign my log on several occasions, confirming my loads leaving Aberdeen."

Standing behind the glass, Fletcher turned to Robert St. James, who was watching the responses rather intently. "Do you think we can put him away?" he asked. "He's identified the dead workers, acknowledging the fact he worked with them in the past."

"It's possible," St. James said. "But if they can prove Doyle was the supervisor on the docks, it won't hold much water in court. I'm curious about Gilmore, though. He's been sitting second on the Wallace trial with Miss El-Sayed, and now he's stepping into this fray for the captain. Which makes me wonder why he's placing the captain's affairs ahead of the sergeant."

"Is it indeed an uncommon occurrence?"

"I'd normally say no. But the sergeant's trial is a bit of a big opportunity," the lawyer said, half-listening to the conversations between Chief Inspector McDermott and Captain Duncan. "With Gilmore's quick arrival, it leads me to believe they've had prior contact."

Fletcher stood in silence, knowing they had recordings of the captain and the Irish lawyer sitting in the evidence room. "Speaking of Sergeant Wallace, have you learned how he's doing?"

"From what we're being told, he's still in a coma," St. James said. "I believe Mister Hamilton will ask Lord Maxwell to pass judgment on the sergeant in absentia because of the circumstances."

"Is something like this fair to the defendant or his family?"

"There have been several cases, most dealing with families fighting over trusts and estates when there's a member suffering from dementia. It comes about when the originator can't be expected to answer for themselves, but none involving an attempted suicide. I'll have to crack a few of the statutes open to see if this will set a precedent for the courts." Turning his attention back to the room, he said, "Looks like your inspector is done."

McDermott walked back into the control room. "They've decided they can go before a magistrate and let a jury decide their fates." He handed the folder to Fletcher. "But I'm nae sure this Gilmore fella knows he's next in line, though."

***

The gentle rocking of the speeding train was nearly hypnotic to its passengers. One, however, was busy recalling the day's events to his associate. "If there are no delays, we should be in Manchester before nine o'clock," Hector said, watching his drink swirl with the trains swaying. "The rooms are available at the Marriott. Then tomorrow, it's a short flight to Paris, then the TGV to Marseille."

"It'll be good to get back home," Pasqual said. "I've hated traveling on the run like we've been doing the last three days." After having the last bite of his sandwich, Pasqual finished off his beer. "Was it worth it?" he asked, wiping his mouth with a napkin.

"Are you talking about protecting the captain?" Hector asked. "Of course, if you wish to keep the police away from our business interests, it's always worth the effort. Besides, you've heard the stories about the Scotsman and what he's done in the past. Someone like him shouldn't be allowed to prey on the innocent at will."

"So, you believe what Louis told you about him?"

"Tickets, gentlemen," the conductor asked, interrupting their conversation.

Each of them produced their rail vouchers, which the conductor noted and returned to them. "Thank you very much," he said as he continued making his rounds.

"As I was saying. Louis was adamant we would be justified in our actions," Hector said. "The downside to ending it the way we did was not having time to question this gentleman on the whereabouts of the Irishman."

"I take it Gregory and Louis are still mad at how we were duped into passing over the last container?"

"You've been on deployments with Gregory before, haven't you?" Hector asked. "When he learns of being tricked or mislead, he becomes a mongoose hunting a cobra, quiet but determined. Wouldn't you if it meant losing three hundred thousand euros?" Hector asked. "The ships don't sail on promises; we are trying to conduct legitimate trade, aren't we?"

"I've never tried to think that deep when it comes to the business side of the organization," Pasqual said, getting up to buy another beer. "Another one?" he asked, nodding to his companion's empty glass.

"If you're paying, then yes," Hector said. Sitting back, he looked out at the darkening landscape as it went flashing by the window. Green rolling hills dotted with occasional homes, livestock roaming the fields. "Ah, to have such a simple life," he said to his reflection. Hector's thoughts were soon interrupted as Pasqual placed the scotch in front of him.

"What of the rumor I heard about François?" he asked. "Is it true he was killed in Algiers?"

"It's what Gregory was telling Louis and me," Hector answered. "Seems after he fled France, Franco was found out in Tunis by an associate of Nazim. When the cruise ship he was sailing on docked in Sicily, members of the Mafioso disguised as police abducted him. Gregory believes it was by someone Nazim was associated with, and they had him killed in a jail cell in Algiers," Hector added. "I know Gregory and Nazim were not happy with Francois trying to peddle his own products, so maybe it was for the best."

"I was just beginning to like him," Pasqual said. "I mean, he wasn't one of us, but he was showing some signs of holding his own. Do you think he could have survived the camp on Corsa?"

"I'd be surprised if he could survive the four months on the Farm," Hector said with a chuckle. "I recall being there in December through March, and my balls felt like two icebergs the entire time. We had four international recruits: a Spaniard, an Afrikaner, and two from Ireland. They bitched the entire time. And their French was horrendous." He chuckled at the memory of his basic training.

"I remember we had twelve, but only seven survived till the end," Pasqual said with a smile. "I guess I was lucky to train in the spring, we didn't have to worry about freezing. But I hated the Marche Kepi Blanc; those were the worst two-and-a-half days."

"But you were proud to wear the Kepi Blanc in the end, weren't you?"

"Of course; to Honor and Fidelity, mon Ami." He raised his bottle to Hector.

"Honor and Fidelity," Hector replied. "They made the best of times, didn't they?"

"The Legion made us who we've become today," Pasqual said. "Getting back to the issue of the Irishman, do you think Gregory and Louis will continue to pursue him?"

"I do," Hector said. "It's always better to be the hunter rather than the prey. In time, this Irishman will either make a mistake, or we'll be fortunate enough to meet another one of his associates." Looking back out the window, past his reflection, Hector continued, "In reality, it doesn't matter much. Men like him always miss one detail in their planning which becomes their undoing in the end."

Chapter Twenty-Five

The table in the evidence room was cluttered with items seized from the search of the Nordic Supplier from the previous day. Clothing from Dunbar's duffle bag was situated on one side, while a satchel containing the broken-down sniper rifle and cleaning kit was on the other.

Inspector Gordon walked up to Chief Inspector McIntyre, holding an evidence bag with the gunman's personal effects. "Here's everything the coroner pulled from the corpse," he said, setting the bag down in the middle of the table.

"Let's have a look at Mister Dunbar's life, shall we?" Chief McIntyre said.

He slit open the bag and began pulling out its contents. He held up a key card for the City Centre hotel. "We'll need to pass some of this off to the constables," he said. "I'm sure they'll want to take a look at what was left behind in his room." Next, the forensics chief pulled out Angus's billfold and a small notebook.

"Inspector Gordon, you and Devin inventory this for the record," he said, handing Sheila the man's wallet.

As he held the well-worn notebook, Chief Inspector McIntyre opened it to see entries of names, dates, and locations. The depth of the killer's exploits was soon obvious as he turned to the first page and noticed the first date. "My God, he's been at this for the past sixteen years," McIntyre mumbled to himself.

"What was that, sir?"

"Do we have anything that gives us his age?" McIntyre asked.

Inspector Gordon looked over the wallet for anything that would offer a glimpse into the killer's age. She opened his passport and checked the birthdate. "His passport shows him to be thirty-six this past March."

"Based on this notebook, this Dunbar fella has been involved in some form of killing since he turned twenty," the senior officer said.

225

"Well, it seems someone is paying to do the work," Sheila said. "Sir, this fella had nearly ten thousand pounds in his wallet." She laid the cash out on the table.

"What was that?" Chief McIntyre didn't hear the comment. His thoughts were back in a snow-covered field in Bosnia. *This man was killing before I treated him*, McIntyre told himself. *Is it possible he killed his commander and sergeant-major like everyone thought?* he wondered, recalling the incident from his days in the military.

"I said, the killer was flush with money," she said. "He's got nearly ten thousand in small bills." She held up the stack of cash. "And not one credit card or bank card to his name."

"Just make sure it's properly accounted for, Inspector," the forensics chief said. "And Devin, give Superintendent MacCallum a call. Ask him to join us as soon as he can; he's going to want to see this." He held up the notebook.

In less than five minutes, the superintendent of the Aberdeen police was sitting across from his forensics chief, reviewing the pages of Dunbar's notebook. As he carefully turned the pages, he saw the same trail of murder that Chief McIntyre had seen.

"There are nearly fifty names listed here," MacCallum said. "Am I correct in my count?"

"Yes, sir. Seems this fella had a rough life and took to focusing his anger at the expense of others," the forensics chief said. "And look at the date on the first page. He started in his teens, I'd guess."

"I'll need to share this with the Commandant in Edinburgh," the senior officer said. "See that we carefully catalog the names and dates," MacCallum said. "We'll want to review our cold-case files to see if there are any connections." He handed back the notebook before shedding his gloves. "Do McDermott and Fletcher know about this?"

"No, sir, we've just being given the items from the medical examiner's office," McIntyre said.

Before McIntyre could continue, his private line rang, interrupting him. "This is Chief McIntyre."

"Yes, sir, could you please inform Superintendent MacCallum that he's needed in dispatch at once," the constable on the other end of the line said.

"Yes, of course, I can. Is there anything else?"

"What is it?" MacCallum asked.

"It seems they need you in dispatch at once, sir."

Robert St. James sat quietly, his hands folded on the table while waiting for Sean Gilmore and Captain Clive Duncan to enter the conference room. Chief Inspector McDermott stood off to the side, a new leather-bound notebook in his hands, a pencil at the ready. In moments, the door would open, allowing the constables escorting the lawyer and his client to enter the room.

"We have thirty minutes before Lord Livingston expects us both in court, so we need this conversation to be quick," St. James said. "The message said you've important information to pass, so I'm listening.

"My client wishes to exercise his right to offer Police Scotland with evidence of a crime," Sean Gilmore said, "in exchange for leniency regarding the two charges being brought before the court this morning."

McDermott nodded to St. James to proceed. "Go on, then; we're listening."

"Before we begin," Sean said. "In exchange for information, my client requests a suspended sentence and probation for a period not to exceed five years," Sean said. "Captain Duncan is likewise willing to have his captain's license suspended for one hundred eighty days. Are we in agreement?"

St. James looked at McDermott, who gave a heavy sigh before answering. "Scotland Yard agrees to the terms, in principle, depending on the information provided, though." He looked directly at the captain.

Gilmore turned to Captain Duncan. "Go ahead, you've the floor."

For the next twenty minutes, Captain Clive Duncan recalled the events from the last six months. From his contacts with Sergeant Wallace about patrols on the Aberdeen waterfront to participating in moving a container requested by the head of a Glasgow crime syndicate. "This concludes what I'll be saying as my testimony to his Lordship," Clive said, dropping his head onto his chest.

"Mister St. James, I'd further include myself in this declaration," Sean said.

"It does nae absolve you of any crimes," McDermott said, hearing the lawyer speak.

"I was never made aware of any crimes to be committed," Sean said. "But about eight months ago, an anonymous client approached me with a business proposition. This person came soliciting me to make specific phone calls for this gentleman in question," the lawyer said. "But, I was never privy to any face-to-face conversations with this man. This client was willing to pay me to request contact information and to set up meetings here in Aberdeen, and in Glasgow, and Edinburgh."

"So, you're saying you've known about this all along?" McDermott asked. "Were you told this Mister Higgins had a paid assassin roaming the streets of Aberdeen? Or killing a young lad in the prime of his life because he mucked up a meeting?"

Sean looked down at the table. "I did not realize what was to take place with the young boy, I swear before God."

St. James glanced at the clock before speaking. "You'll be expected to make a full disclosure in front of his Lordship, you understand?" He stared at both men in front of him before turning to face McDermott, "Have you heard enough?"

"I want their names and the places where meetings took place," McDermott said. "Then I'll be satisfied."

"You'll get them when I'm telling the court. Do you agree to my request?" Clive asked, looking McDermott in the eye.

"Aye, I agree," the inspector said. Opening the door, he summoned the constable, directing him to escort Captain Duncan to the courtroom. "Gentlemen, let's get this over and done with, shall we?" He motioned the lawyers out of the room.

As the three men left the room, Sean spied his colleague Priscilla El-Sayed in a discussion with George Hamilton outside the courtroom. He went over and interrupted their conversation. "Excuse me, Counselor, but I'd like a word with Miss El-Sayed."

"What is it, Sean?" she asked.

"Regardless of what happens today," he said, "I want you to know I'm proud of how you handled things." Looking into her eyes, he stammered. "I'll be disbarred by the end of the day, but I'll always enjoy our time in court together." He kissed her cheek and gave her a brief hug. She didn't notice the note he had secretly slipped into her pocket. "Goodbye, Priscilla."

Sean went into the courtroom through the door McDermott was holding and was soon out of sight.

"Miss El-Sayed," George Hamilton said, "may we continue our conversation?"

"Yes," she said. "I'm sorry about the interruption. You said that Lord Maxwell was dismissing the case due to Sergeant Wallace passing away."

"Yes, he was willing to dismiss the charges against the sergeant. But he's allowing the investigation to continue against others associated with him," Hamilton said. "I need to learn who you'll be representing in future trials as we continue."

"I'll be representing Mister Gilmore," she said with a smile.

As the lawyers discussed their pending trial, CI McDermott and Inspector Fletcher sat in the courtroom, listening as Captain Duncan and Sean Gilmore entered their pleas and testimony to Lord Livingston.

"Mister St. James, do you accept this account?"

"The prosecution accepts the accounts in principle," the lawyer said. "But, we are requesting full disclosure by the individuals as discussed outside of chambers. There was an agreement to include the identity of specific individuals and locations of prearranged meetings."

"Your Lordship, if I may be permitted to address the court," Sean said. "My client is prepared to declare himself the sole instigator in this matter."

"Your client may do so," the judge declared.

Clearing his throat, Clive Duncan looked at the judge. "Your Lordship. I was contacted by the principal shareholder of Highland Stag Investments, and his name is Alistair Hunt of Glasgow. It was at his request I aided in setting up a means of transferring drugs from offshore vessels to the docks of Aberdeen."

Clive Duncan spent the next five minutes recounting the events which lead to his involvement, from securing a shipping container to making the at sea transfer from a nondescript freighter to arranging a lorry to move it to Glasgow.

"And, Mister Gilmore," the judge asked. "Do you have anything to add?"

"Your Lordship, I was contacted to help in insuring meetings took place between the captain and the longshoremen, who are now deceased, I'm afraid," bowing his head. "I also arranged for one of the deceased to meet a Frenchman, Louis Remesy, as part of the transaction."

"Mister St. James, is this true?"

St. James looked back at McDermott and Fletcher, who both nodded back. "Yes, your Lordship," St. James said. "But I must add that Mister Gilmore is not considered a suspect in those events, since he was deemed to be present in court when the killings took place."

"I see in your amended summons, Mister St. James, you're accepting the testimony for a reduction in sentencing," the judge said. "Are you satisfied they've met the agreement from earlier?"

"Yes, your Lordship, the prosecution is."

"Well, then," Lord Livingston said. "As agreed upon, the court suspends the sentence of Captain Clive Duncan based on his testimony." He signed the order for the clerk. "In addition, Mister Clive Duncan will serve his sixty-months' probation within the Aberdeen shire jurisdiction, reporting monthly to Police Scotland officers." Looking at the veteran seaman, Lord Livingston continued. "This order includes surrendering of his captain's license to the Coast Guard and Maritime Agency for the same period."

"Your Lordship," St. James said. "The Crown wishes to add a provision to reduce the period of probation based on good conduct by the pannel." He glanced at both Sean and Clive Duncan.

"Amendment to the order is accepted," the judge said. "Now, Mister Gilmore . . ."

"Yes, your Lordship," Sean said, standing before him.

"You agree to surrender your license to practice law within the confines of the United Kingdom and her Commonwealths for your role in these actions?"

"I do, your Lordship," he said.

"So be it," Lord Livingston said, signing the court order. "This session is concluded," bringing his gavel to bear upon his desk.

Chapter Twenty-Six

The conference room table was crowded with packets of information laid across its surface. Printed documents lay neatly in front of each folder as the secretary created a group for each client's signature. Just as the last page was slipping out of the printer, the phone rang.

"Highland Stag Investments, how can I help you?" a female secretary answered.

"This is Mister Burns; I need to speak with Alistair."

"Just a moment, please." Janice Gordon pressed the intercom key, announcing the call to her boss.

"Mister Hunt, you've got a call on line two; it's Mister Burns."

"Thank you, Janice," he said, picking up the phone. "Hello, Robert, this is Hunt."

"Good day, Mister Hunt," the lawyer said. "I've just found out an acquaintance of yours has been booked in Aberdeen. Does the name Clive Duncan sound familiar?"

"Yes, he's done work for me in the past, but just once, mind you," Alistair said, sipping his tea. "Do you know what the charges are being brought against him?"

"Aye, a charge of drug trafficking and one for obstructing an investigation," Burns said. "The captain was due in court today, but I've nae heard anything else since this morning."

"I see. And how goes the work with the other captains and their crews?"

"It's a mess," Burns said. "The police have transcripts from several of the vessels to the constable who hung himself. My understanding is the judge will dismiss the charges against the sergeant, so his widow can collect his pension."

As Alistair Hunt was discussing issues with his counselor in Aberdeen, several police cars pulled up to the front of the building. Two officers stood at the front entrance while two others made their way to the back.

Straightening his field coat, the inspector from Scotland Yard pulled out his credentials, slinging them around his neck. "Shall we?" Chief Inspector McDermott asked, looking at his partner Fletcher and Chief Superintendent Cameron, along with her two constables.

As each officer entered the building, they took notice of where the offices of Highland Stag were located and entered the lift, moving to the third floor.

After getting off, they came to the office entrance and entered, catching Janice Gordon fixing her makeup. "Inspector Fletcher, Chief Super. What can I do for you?" she said, recognizing Fletcher and Grace Cameron.

"We're here for your boss," McDermott spoke, striding to the outer door of Alistair Hunt. Opening it, he surprised the crime leader, who was still speaking with his counselor.

"Who the hell are you?" he asked, holding the phone out from his ear.

"My name is Chief Inspector Conor McDermott of Scotland Yard," he announced. "And you, Alistair Hunt, are under arrest for the distribution of illicit drugs, money laundering, and conspiracy to commit murder."

He was immediately joined by Fletcher.

Janice had stood at the door with tears rolling down her cheeks as McDermott spoke of the charges. "I'm sorry, Mister Hunt. I'm so very sorry," she sobbed, leaning against the door frame. Turning away, she went to her desk and sat under the watchful eye of Constable Weir.

"You've nothing on me, Inspector," Alistair said defiantly.

"We've noticed your dealings with Captain Clive Duncan, vessel master of the *Nordic Supplier* in Aberdeen," Fletcher said. "The good skipper provided testimony to the effect you requested a container be obtained from a French freighter sailing between Marseille, France and Hamburg, Germany."

"The man's daft. Why would I want a shipping container, I negotiate in securities and bonds for several well-respected clients here in Glasgow," Alistair said. "I don't even have an affiliation office in Aberdeen."

"No, you don't, do you?" McDermott said, taking control the conversation. "What you had was a once-promising footballer from St. Mirren, who's dead now because of you. And if we find any evidence, even a wee shred of possibility, I'll nail you with Ian McLeod's murder, as well."

"Who's Ian McLeod?" Alistair said. "I've never heard of him."

"You'll come to appreciate him soon enough," McDermott said. "And we've got your friend Gordon Wallace tied in this as well. It so happens he's been rather helpful in filling in a few wee tidbits we've nae had."

"Gordon wouldn't do anything of the sort," Alistair said.

"You'd be surprised what a lengthy term in a Grampian cellblock would do to one's conscience," Fletcher said, chiming in with his partner. "With his brother on trial, he's ready to save his own skin."

Alistair laughed at Fletcher's statement. "The sergeant's nae a worry, you realize."

"What do you mean?" Fletcher asked.

"You've nae heard? He's dead. Gone and took the cowards way out he did," Hunt said. "Hung himself with a bedsheet."

"And how did you learn about him?" McDermott asked.

"It's been on the telly, the newspaper," Hunt said.

"Funny, I don't recall reading about it in the Herald," Superintendent Cameron said. "I recall the official police notifications, though, and they're nae made public. So, Mister Hunt, how did you learn about Sergeant Wallace?"

Looking at each officer, Hunt realized his mistake. "I'll make you a deal; I've valuable information about a transaction." They could hear his voice cracking as he pleaded with the officers.

"I'm more interested in how you know about Sergeant Wallace's medical condition," McDermott said. "Not some maybe arrangement you've made with a ghost."

"My counselor has been following the trial; he told me."

"And how did he get this information?" Fletcher asked, writing down what Alistair was saying.

"He's got a young fella who he's coaching; he's been watching the trial for him. He's in the know on a number of the comings and goings in the sheriff's office in Aberdeen."

McDermott grabbed the phone. "Call your man, get the name of the young whelp he's got working with him." He said, offering the phone to Alistair. "And put him on speaker. Nae tricks, now."

Moments before the call went to voice mail, Robert Burns answered the call. "Burns here."

"Burns, it's Alistair again. Who's the young lad helping you? I want to see he gets proper compensation for his efforts. I'm having Janice prepare a few things, and I want to include him."

After a few awkward moments Burns spoke. "His names Forbes. Gavin Forbes. But he's not available anymore; he's being put on a case defending a third-year student from the university for peddling marijuana."

"I'll still see he's taken care of. Thank you, Robert," Hunt said and hung up.

"Get up," McDermott said. "Alistair Hunt, you're under arrest for drug trafficking, conspiracy to distribute illicit drugs, bribery of an officer, and accessory to murder." He got behind Hunt and placed the handcuffs on him. "Andrew, make a note to have Sergeant Giles detain this Mister Burns as a coconspirator as well."

"But I can give you the Irishman," Hunt pleaded.

"When and where did the two of you meet?" McDermott asked. "What does this fella look like, heh?"

"We've never met. My contact with him was always over the phone," Hunt said. "But he's prone to calling whenever something goes wrong. I'm certain to get a call soon."

"I'm nae worried about you giving me anything on him," McDermott said, leading him out of the office. "Someone's already done me that favor."

"But we had another arrangement," Hunt said. "I can tell you what I know about it."

"Inspector, I'd like to see what he has to say," Superintendent Cameron said, interrupting the conversation.

The inspector pushed the criminal back into his desk chair. "Go on, then, tell us about this arrangement," McDermott said. "Andrew, take this down, if you please."

"About a month ago, I got a call from the Irishman, Mr. Higgins," Alistair Hunt began. "He asked if I could arrange a few fellas to act as security. Like for a meeting, you know." He glanced around at the three officers staring at him. "Higgins said I'd need about twenty or so, and the men would need to be able to travel to Northern Ireland by the first week of September."

"Did he mention what it was for?" Superintendent Cameron asked.

"Aye, he said they would be guarding another shipment," Hunt said, his shoulders slumped in defeat.

"More drugs?" McDermott asked.

"He did nae say. Just that the men would be doing the work in Northern Ireland."

Leaning on the credenza, McDermott looked the criminal over, wondering if he was providing him with information worth pursuing.

"And where were you going to get twenty or so fellas to do this work?" he asked. "Were you going to put out an advert for them? Or do you already have someone helping you?"

"Of course, I had already . . ." Hunt began saying before he caught himself. I can't implicate Gordon, he thought. He may be my only hope in getting out of this mess, "Of course, you realize I'm not in a position to say anything else without my barrister being present," the crime boss said, ending the conversation.

"Are you satisfied with what he said?" McDermott asked the senior officer as he pulled Hunt to his feet and pushed him to the outer office.

"Seems rather thin," she said as she turned to walk out of the office. "But it's more than what we had yesterday."

"I can likewise give you Ewan Sutherland's killer."

Stopping at the office entrance, McDermott pulled Hunt aside. "Go on, then."

"His name's Angus Dunbar; he's known for not getting caught doing anything illegal because he's good at keeping in the shadows," Hunt stammered. "He's a former SAS-type, a sniper from what I was told by a former client, you see. He was drummed out of the service for raping a girl instead of patrolling with his unit in Northern Ireland."

"It seems you're a bit late with that information; we already know who he is," Fletcher said. "This Dunbar fella you speak of was shot dead the day before yesterday." He noticed the color drain from Alistair's face.

***

Michael Connelly paced his office like a caged animal. It had been several days since he'd last spoken with his counselor, Sean Gilmore. The only news he'd seen regarding the trial of the sergeant, Logan Wallace, was when his hired gun, Angus Dunbar, killed the informant for Alistair Hunt.

The buzz of his office intercom broke the silence.

"Yes, Erin?"

"Sorry for the intrusion, Mister Higgins," Erin said, "but there's a call from a Mister Taggert on line three."

"Thank you," Michael replied, picking up the handset. "Hello, this is Mister Higgins."

"Thank you for taking my call, sir," the voice on the other end began. "I've recently been made aware of a relative passing away. I believe you knew of him," the man continued. "His name was Angus Dunbar."

Michael sat down in his chair. "And what makes you believe I'm an acquaintance with this person?" his mind racing at the callers' intent.

Blayne Taggert cleared his throat before continuing. "I was contacted by a member of the Armed Services. Seems there was a series of documents left that provided instructions for the family after his passing."

"I see. And part of those instructions included contacting me?"

"There were separate instructions leading to an account in a bank located in Cardiff, Wales. Once I showed proper documentation I was given access to its contents," Blayne said. "It was a series of ledgers and a letter with your information."

The color drained from Michael's face.

How did Dunbar set this up? he asked himself, and why?

Collecting himself, Michael sat upright in his chair. "Since you've made the effort to contact me, what is it that I can do for you?"

"There's to be a service for Angus tonight at five o'clock in Dundee," Blayne said. "It's being held at Birkhill Cemetery. I'd like you to be there, so we can meet," he added. "I believe it's important for your well-being and mine."

"This evening? I'm not sure I can get there on such short notice," Michael said.

"Mister Higgins, I wouldn't have called unless I felt it was of grave importance," the young man said. "I'll be the one wearing the fedora so you'll know who to meet," Blayne said. "Have a safe flight." He hung up on the Irishman.

Connelly stepped out of his office to find his secretary and driver in animated conversation. "Erin, arrange for a pair seats on the next flight to Glasgow," he said. "Geoff, please make arrangements for a rental while we are there." He then returned to his office and closed the door behind him.

***

Just four hours removed from his office, Michael Connelly and his driver were standing in the cemetery outside of Dundee. The trees behind the cemetery began casting long shadows as the sun sank behind them. The echoes of a lone bagpiper could be heard as the vicar stood comforting the few members of Angus Dunbar's family who were there to attend his burial.

"I'm still not sure why we were asked to attend this," Michael Connelly said, turning to Geoff.

Watching the family members making their way towards their cars, one man stood out, hovering near the edge of the others. As the crowd dispersed, he walked up to the casket and after removing his hat, placed his hand upon the polished wooden surface.

Noticing the Irishman and his driver, the lone member stepped away from the coffin, allowing the members of the cemetery to lower it into its final resting place. Donning his fedora, the gentleman walked towards the two visitors.

"Thank you for agreeing to come," the man said, reaching out to shake Michael Connelly's hand. "I'm Blayne Taggert by the way." He politely tipped his hat. "If you don't mind," he said to Geoff, "I'd like a private word with your employer."

As the two men strolled between the tombstones and monuments, Geoff kept his distance but also kept a watchful eye on both of them. The two came to a halt in front of a grave marker, a bouquet of flowers set in a holder. The name chiseled in the stone read PATRICIA DUNBAR.

"This is where the mother of the Dunbar boys lies, gone too soon from our lives," Blayne said, brushing grass clippings from the rose-colored stone.

"I'm sorry to learn of that, I suppose," Michael replied, perplexed by the statement.

"Michael . . . or should I call you 'Mister Higgins'?" Blayne Taggert asked, facing the Irishman.

"And what gives you the notion to address me by that surname?"

"Angus was meticulous with his manners and habits, leaving information to the family he felt was important. And because Angus was my twin brother," he said. "You see, our mother was too young to raise us, so we were given to the church for adoption. I was sent

237

south to a family in Kilmarnock, while Angus was passed on to an aunt here in Dundee."

Michael looked closely at the man before him. His hair was styled differently, and the beard masked some of his facial features. However, it was the eyes. Yes, the eyes appeared to be the same as those of the former sergeant turned criminal.

"What is it you want from me?"

"In simple terms," Blayne said. "To be given the chance to avenge my brother's death."

Michael Connelly stepped aside, looking out across the rows of markers laid upon the ground. "You may want to let the grave diggers know they should begin preparing a spot for yourself," he said, looking back at Blayne.

Blayne reached into his jacket and pulled out an envelope. He gave it to the Irishman. "This is all but two items Dunbar had in the bank vault," he said. "It's a series of communications between you and him over the last five years. It's how I found out where to contact you."

Michael leafed through the documents, noticing dates, times, and locations he had Dunbar conduct a murder to further his criminal ambitions on behalf of the drug company. "And the other two items?" he asked.

"They're in a safe place."

"And what makes you capable of avenging your brother's death?" Michael asked. "Angus had a unique skill, not something you can learn from a book, you know. His work for me included conducting, shall we say personal interviews with stubborn clients," glancing towards his driver.

As quickly as the Irishman had blinked, Blayne had drawn his knife and brought the tip to Michael's throat. "We had a lot in common Mr. Connelly," his nostrils flaring in the face of his prey. "Where Angus might have used his skill as a marksman, I'm nae afraid to look my mark in the eye's up close," returning the knife to its scabbard. Releasing his grip of the jacket, Blayne took a step back.

Geoff saw the motion but failed to act before the Scotsman was holding the dagger against his employer's throat.

"We had similar ambitions as boys, with similar paths," Blayne said. "Where Angus chose the Army, I decided upon the Royal

Marines. And I can assure you, I've no 'quirks,' as it were, like Angus."

Michael stood, feeling a slight chill overcome him. *Was it the freshening wind off the glen? he wondered. On the other hand, was it the souls of the departed trying to warn him of something else?* Pulling his billfold from his jacket, he handed a business card to the Scotsman.

"That number is the only one I'll take a call on from you," Connelly said. "If you attempt to contact me any other way, all you'll hear is a ring tone. Call me on Monday between three o'clock and four-thirty, and I'll have my decision for you," waving towards Geoff.

"Yes, Mister Higgins?"

"Fetch the car; we're leaving."

*** THE END ***

Discover other titles by Anthony J. Harrison:

The Irishman's Deception – A Conor McDermott Novel

Suspicious by Design – A Geneviève Benoit Novel

Obscure Intentions – Geneviève Benoit Novel

Thank you for reading my book. If you enjoyed it, won't you please take a moment to leave me a review at your favorite retailer? Thanks!

Anthony

Acknowledgements

First and foremost, I'd like to thank my wife, Mary, for letting me scratch this itch called writing and for supporting me with her comments and encouragement, even after I locked myself away for hours at a time. Also, a big thank you to my daughter's Rebekah and Jennifer for letting 'Dad' to his thing without the need to keep asking "why'd you write that?"

Next, to my good friend and co-worker, Doretta Burgess, for providing the first level of sanity checks, grammar checks and being that punctuation pundit on all my many pages of random thoughts. Also, to the members of the Ventura Fiction Writer's Group for helping me understand the difference between 'showing' and 'telling' in my writing.

To my friend and fellow motorcyclist, Rob for taking my ideas and descriptions for the cover and getting it right.

About the Author

Anthony is a first generation American and native Californian, the son of Scottish immigrants, and who's fraternal grandparents hailed from Ireland. A product of a mixed education (part parochial and part public schools), he developed a thirst for reading early in his childhood and took to writing fiction as an escape from his work as an Instructional Systems Designer. When not working on improving his writing, Anthony can be found on the local golf course, honing his game invented by his ancestors.

Provide your comments or feedback at;

mailto:fairwayscribe@gmail.com

www.ingramcontent.com/pod-product-compliance
Lightning Source LLC
Chambersburg PA
CBHW071521110726
47908CB00003B/910